Praise for

Tristan's Gap

"*Tristan's Gap* is simply wonderful. This elegant story reads like a page-turning mystery while providing readers a superb drama of revelation and redemption. Nancy Rue entertained me, inspired me, and challenged me with this amazing novel. I couldn't put it down."

—KATHRYN MACKEL, author of *The Hidden*

"In her new book, Nancy Rue takes us to the place of hard questions: Why does God allow bad things to happen, and where is He in the midst of our pain? For answers that go beyond the clichés and for writing that is at once beautiful, gutsy, and humorous, read *Tristan's Gap*."

—ANN TATLOCK, award-winning author
of *Things We Once Held Dear*

"Gripping… Nancy drags you headfirst into the depths of the darkness, fears, and loneliness shrouding certain life-changing decisions. Those who have lived through a 'winter place' in their life will instantly recognize the unspoken hurts and secrets that frame that bitter coldness, melted only by God's mercy."

—PAMELA PALUMBO, founder of Maryland Coalition
of Medical Pregnancy Clinics

Tristan's Gap

Tristan's

a novel Gap

Nancy Rue

WATERBROOK
PRESS

TRISTAN'S GAP
PUBLISHED BY WATERBROOK PRESS
12265 Oracle Boulevard, Suite 200
Colorado Springs, Colorado 80921
A division of Random House, Inc.

ISBN 1-4000-7034-1

Published in association with the literary agency of Alive Communications Inc., 7680
Goddard Street, Suite 200, Colorado Springs, CO 80920, www.alivecommunications
.com.

Library of Congress Cataloging-in-Publication Data
Rue, Nancy N.
  Tristan's gap / Nancy Rue.— 1st ed.
    p. cm.
  ISBN 1-4000-7034-1
  1. Mothers and daughters—Fiction. 2. Runaway children—Fiction. 3. Psychological
fiction. I. Title.
  PS3568.U3595T75 2006
  813'.54—dc22
                                        2006001030

Printed in the United States of America
2006—First Edition

10 9 8 7 6 5 4 3 2 1

For Sonia Beck,
who taught me how to learn from the gaps

Chapter One

Well-trained golden retriever versus scrappy miniature dachshund. That was the difference between my two daughters, and it was never more obvious than when we were talking about their father.

That August night as I drove Tristan to work with both of them in the car, it would have sounded to anybody else like we were discussing Tristan's hair. But when we got right down to it, everything always came back to Nick.

"Did you ask Daddy if I could cut it?" Tristan said.

"I did," I said.

"He said no, right?"

"He said he'd think about it."

"That means no," Max said from the backseat. "You're done, Tristan."

I glanced in the rearview mirror at my ten-year-old's dark paintbrush-like tails, sticking out from her head while the rest of her hair straggled down to her shoulders. We hadn't even begun to discuss *that* do.

"I really wish I could cut it," Tristan said. "All I ever do is put it up in a ponytail anyway."

The tendril of wistfulness in her voice was as close to arguing as Tristan ever came.

I pulled up to a stop sign and looked at her. Brush handle in her mouth, she secured a thick, deep-brown bundle of hair with one hand and snapped what we Soltani girls called a pony holder into place with the other. She executed the whole thing the way she did every task: neatly and with graceful resignation. I had to agree I'd seen her do it for at least ten of her sixteen years.

She pulled the tail tight and let it splash against her cheek as she leaned over to return the brush to its precise place in her purse.

"I'd miss your ponytail," I said. "It's you." I grinned into the rear-view. "Now, Max, honey, we need to talk about yours."

Max pointed to the intersection where we were still idling. "Mom, there's, like, nobody coming."

"I knew that," I said.

She cocked one eyebrow, a trick she'd learned recently.

"I *did* know," I said.

Tristan wound her arms around her lithe, long legs as she perched her feet on the edge of the seat.

"He said he'd think about it, baby girl," I said. "And that doesn't *always* mean no. He had to think about it before he let you get a job, and that turned out to be a yes."

"There's a *way* big difference between working on the boardwalk and getting a haircut," Max said.

There's nobody like a ten-year-old to reduce everything to the lowest common denominator. Must be something about the recent introduction to fractions in the fourth grade.

"Daddy's afraid you might regret it if you cut it," I said to Tristan. "They like it long for dance, right?"

"Yeah," Max said, "you gotta do that tight-bun thing that makes your eyes go all slanty." I didn't have to look at her to know she was demonstrating.

The pizza places and hoagy shops on Garfield Parkway, which led to the boardwalk, were revving up for suppertime, but I was lucky enough to snag a parking space.

"We'll talk to Daddy about it when he gets home tonight," I said. "We'll have plenty of time since you're only working a couple of hours to fill in for Sondra." I brushed my fingers against her cheek. "Maybe we'll soften him up with some ice cream."

"Chocolate chip cookie dough," Max said. "Aunt Pete's gonna want pistachio, but that stuff is foul."

I expected Tristan to answer "butter pecan" or at least wrinkle her nose at Max. But Tristan gazed through the windshield as if she were gathering up Bethany Beach details, the snippets of sunburned faces and beach toys in shop windows. Her dark chocolate eyes hinted at tears.

I felt myself melt. "I didn't know it was that important to you, honey," I said. "Okay, we'll definitely talk to Daddy."

"That's gonna mean whipped cream, sprinkles—the works," Max said.

"It's okay," Tristan said. "We can just forget about it."

"You sure?"

She nodded and swept up her purse.

"Daddy'll be here to pick you up at nine," I said. "Maybe Max and I will still buy some ice cream after my meeting—in case you change your mind."

Tristan paused, fingers on the door handle, and said, "I don't think I will."

She climbed out, and I leaned across the seat before she could close the door. "I love you, baby girl," I said.

As I watched her thread her way through the crowd, green purse with its blue *T* swaying from her shoulder, her grace erased the image of lanky adolescence I swore I'd seen in her just yesterday. It was one of those mom moments when I realized there was nothing left of my baby except my view of her. It left me momentarily sad.

Max hoisted herself over the seat and buckled into Tristan's spot. Her sleeveless pink hoodie shouted ANGEL IN DISGUISE in bright green letters across her chest. No bra was in my ten-year-old's immediate future. She was still an unselfconscious girl-child.

But there were moments, like now, when she was thoroughly Nick, sizing up the situation like a little computer. High speed, of course. Her small, dark eyes crinkled from beneath puffy lids, like his, and her mouth went straight across, curving up at the corners. Only there was no predicting what was going to come out of Max's mouth.

"I don't get it," she said.

"What don't you get?"

"Why Dad even cares about how we wear our hair." She gave the familiar husky grunt. "Why should we take beauty tips from him when he hardly even *has* any hair? It's like this short."

I felt the corners of my mouth already twitching a warning. It was a sure sign that Max was about to take me somewhere I could never resist going.

I put the Blazer in gear and backed out. "It's not really about the hair."

"What's it about?"

"It's about Daddy not wanting Tristan to make a decision she's going to regret."

"It's just hair. It'll grow back."

"Okay," I said. "How 'bout we get you a buzz cut, then?"

"Seriously?"

"Right." I tugged at one of her rakish tails. "There isn't enough ice cream in the world that would make that okay."

"Men are just weird."

I couldn't hold back the deep laugh Nick always said sounded devious. I never planned it. It sneaked up on me like an imp. The laugh never seemed to surprise Max, though. It was as if she waited for it, licking her little chops.

"Why do you think men are weird?" I said.

"Because they're not like us."

"You noticed, did you?"

"Not like they get beards, and we don't—"

"Hopefully."

"I mean, du-uh."

"Hel-lo-o."

"It's like…" I could feel her eyes sparking at me. "Give me a topic."

"Um, TV."

"Okay. Boys are all—hog the remote control. And girls are…"

"Oh, okay. Give me a second."

Max started in on the *Jeopardy!* theme.

"I have it. Girls are all—read *People* magazine."

Max cocked the practiced eyebrow.

"It's true," I said. "Boys get their information by flipping the channels, and girls go straight to the source."

"What-*ev*-er. Okay, boys are go in the kitchen and blow your nose on a paper towel during a sad movie."

"And girls are use up a whole box of Kleenex."

"Boys are point out all the things that are, like, fake in an action movie."

"I've got a great one for this: girls watch romantic movies and wish life was really like that."

"*I* don't," Max said.

My imp within couldn't pass up the chance.

"There's not some cute li'l fifth-grade boy you have a crush on?" I said.

"Well, now that you mention it," she said, "I'm totally crushing on Justin Dalberg. I'm just waiting for him to ask me out."

I jerked us to a stop inside the church parking lot. "Tell me you're kidding. You are, aren't you?"

A chuckle rumbled from Max's throat. "Got you, Mom."

"You are bad." I tugged her face into my chest by both ponytails. Max was one of the few people my imp appeared for. The imp in *her* drew it out.

Max scanned the lot with narrowed eyes while I parked. "There's Mrs. Godfried's car. I hope she didn't bring the Quantum Quartet."

"The *what*?"

"Her kids. They're, like, all scientific."

"Do you even know what *quantum* means?" I said.

Max shook her head, setting the tails in motion. "It's something nerdy that nobody understands except the kids who are so smart they're weird."

Rebecca's sons—Noah, Isaiah, Daniel, and Matthias—*were* the youngest nerds I'd ever known. Bless their hearts; they even wore little bow ties to church.

"They're just a little bit…proper," I said, reining in my imp. "That's okay."

"They're just a little bit—"

"So…have a good time playing with the kids." I hopped down out of the Blazer, wishing as I had every time in the four months I'd had it that Nick had either gotten me a step bar or let me have the little Volkswagen Beetle I wanted. My mother's old nickname for me—Squatty Body—was apt.

"It's gonna be all boys. Again. Justin sits there and plays with his Game Boy, like, the entire time. The Quantums—"

"We went there already," I said. I hugged her shoulders as we made our way to the door of the fellowship hall. "When's Ashley coming home from her vacation?"

"Not for *forever.* I don't see why Dad won't let me stay home with Aunt Pete. It's not like she's gonna try to burn the house down again."

"She didn't try to burn the house down."

"Dad said she did."

"He was just a little bit cranky that day."

Max dragged herself off to the kids' play area. Even she knew when to leave a subject alone.

"Aunt Pete tried to burn the house down, Serena?"

I turned to see Lissa Dalberg behind me, flushed face obviously amused. Everything about my best friend bounced, except her twelve-year-old son, Justin, of Game Boy fame, who appeared to be as excited about "playing with the kids" as Max was. When Lissa nudged him off in that direction, he looked as if he'd rather be shot.

"You heard that, huh?" I said.

Lissa looped her arm through mine, skin clammy in the August heat. Even with the ocean breeze, the temperature was a muggy ninety degrees.

"So *did* Nick's aunt try to burn the house down?"

"That's the way Nicky tells it," I said. "She was cooking bacon, and a little grease fire started. It wasn't her fault. She was distracted because she found her false teeth in the freezer."

"Oh, now that clears it up."

"Is this that Mentoring for Moms thing?"

I looked back to see a woman approaching us, and I felt my eyes bulge a little. I'd never seen anybody quite like her in our church parking lot.

Looking directly at me with blue eyes made startling by her leathery skin, she shook back her bangs, which were colored an impossible shade of blond. She folded her tattooed arms against her black tank top—although between the bracelets and the collection of gold neck chains she might as well have been wearing long sleeves and a turtleneck.

"So is this the group?" she said. Her voice was a cigarette alto I could have filed my nails on.

Lissa recovered first. It was one of those things they must learn in pastors' wives school.

"This is it," she said to the woman. "And this is our leader, Serena Soltani." Lissa put out a manicured hand. "And you are?"

"Name's Hazel." The woman pumped Lissa's arm, but her too-blue eyes were fixed on me. "So you're Mighty Mom?"

I choked.

"Serena's a wonderful mother. Her Tristan and Max are—"

"You have two boys?" Hazel said.

"Two girls."

"Talk about a little gender confusion."

"This is only our second meeting, and already Serena has helped us all so much—"

"That's what I need—help," Hazel said. Her voice was reminding me more and more of gravel in a clothes dryer. "So how does this work? Do you preach or just say stuff out of the Bible? I'll warn you, I don't know diddly about the Bible."

She didn't look as if she had any desire to learn. But there was something earnest in those blue eyes. I couldn't look away from her.

"Actually, it's more of a discussion format," Lissa said. She opened the door and waved an arm through for Hazel. "We each have a chance to talk about our challenges, and then Serena addresses them, sometimes from her own experience. Her children are the poster kids for—"

"Good," Hazel said and elbowed past us. "That's what I need. My kids are out of control. I need help before I kill them."

The look on Rebecca Godfried's face when Hazel crossed the room was priceless. Whenever Rebecca got even a whiff of anything "unchristian," she drew her mouth into a raisin. With multipierced ears and the biker-chick attire, Hazel must have seemed like more than a whiff to Rebecca.

Lissa carried two bags of snacks into the kitchen. As the leader, I had to stay. Besides, I had never known Rebecca Godfried to be speechless before. My imp really wanted to see what happened next.

As the rest of the moms trickled in, they all did double takes of Hazel. A couple of them slipped into the kitchen, obviously in pursuit of the lowdown on the new woman. Lissa had never had so much help putting store-bought cookies on a plate.

Christine Michaels, the advertising executive whose only child was six months old, looked baffled as she glanced from me to Hazel to the customary notepad where she wrote things down. I realized I didn't have a clue what I was going to say. My entire lesson plan had walked out when Hazel walked in.

I shouldn't have worried. As soon as Lissa herded everyone back in with refreshments, Hazel leaned forward and said, "If it's time to talk, I'll start."

"Sure," I said.

Hazel tossed her lanky hair back from her shoulders and said, "My mother gave birth to me in the front seat of an eighteen-wheeler. She was hitchhiking, and some trucker picked her up. Imagine *that* scene." Her voice dipped deeper into its gravel pit. "I mean, what kind of model for motherhood did I have?"

It went downhill from there. I couldn't look at anyone. All I could do was put my hand in front of my mouth to smother the kind of guilty giggles you get at a funeral.

Group control wasn't one of my gifts. Most of the soccer moms looked as if they were in shock, but I couldn't make a move to stop Hazel, not even when she got to the part where her mother named her for the tattoo on the trucker's arm. From there she led us through the series of cars, campers, and house trailers she'd grown up in. The entire tale was punctuated with a pair of glasses she took out of her bag but never put on. She was well into a rendition of her adolescent years before I realized the earpieces were exact replicas of Barbie-doll legs. I kind of envied her panache.

"I never lived in anything without wheels until I married my first husband," Hazel said. "We did the granola thing. Lived in a log cabin. Stopped shaving. Both of us. We were supposed to 'become one with the earth.'" She pointed with Barbie's high-heeled foot. "I should have stuck with the wheels."

Lissa darted a series of "do something" looks at me. But I merely watched with increasing fascination while Hazel enchanted my group with an autobiography that grew more outrageous by the word.

"I had my oldest in that dump," Hazel said. "Twenty hours of labor. I was really starting to hate that kid—"

Rebecca gasped out loud.

"And that midwife. About the tenth time she told me this was my finest hour, I told her to—"

"Well!" I said. "I think a lot of us can relate to getting off to a rocky start with our children, can't we?" I nodded my head like a dashboard dog. Nobody nodded back. Evidently nobody related.

Christine sat with her pen poised over the notepad, one exquisite eyebrow arched in a frozen state of I-wasn't-expecting-*this*.

"I never knew a seven-pound kid could fill so many diapers," Hazel went on. "The third time I took a load of those nasty things down to the stream to beat them on a rock, I knew I was outta there."

"You left the baby?" Rebecca asked.

Hazel laughed in a drawn-out wheeze that made me want to giggle right along with her.

"I'm not a *complete* loser," Hazel said. "I left Nature Boy and took the kid with me, but I didn't know what to do with her. I still don't, and I've had two more since."

She was only up to her first baby, which meant we probably hadn't heard half her life story yet. She looked to be at least forty. Of course considering the sun damage, maybe thirty-five. That would mean she was four years younger than I was and had somehow lived four times longer. I had to admit, I was strangely hooked.

"So, Mighty Mom," she said to me, "can you fix me?"

"Um," I said, "I don't know that *fix* is the word I'd use."

"Is there hope for me and my kids? That's what I'm asking you."

"Well," I said too cheerfully, "you're here, aren't you?"

"There's always hope in the Lord," Rebecca said.

Hazel put on the Barbie glasses and leveled her eyes at Rebecca. An outward-moving spray of lines radiated from them, the way a child draws a sun with a crayon. "Can the Lord make my kids do what I tell them?"

"He can help *you* make them do it," Rebecca said. She sat up straighter. A minisermon was imminent.

"That's true," I said. "God's our guide."

I'd been in church groups with Rebecca for six years. It was always a good idea to make her think she was right, lest she add the slicing, sideways look to the pursed lips. She was always the first one on the scene with a casserole when a family had a crisis, and she knew her Bible better than anybody in the congregation except Pastor Gary. I felt guilty every time I got a mental picture of her being baptized in vinegar.

Hazel took off the glasses and leaned toward me, bracelets clinking up and down her arms. "Okay...so...I want to be amazing at motherhood—no matter what it takes—before my kids turn out to be shoplifters or topless dancers."

"I want that too." Christine clicked her pen. "Aren't there bullet points you can give us?"

"Well," I said, "like, in this group I'm basically showing you what our Father says about parenting—in Scripture?"

I knew I wasn't speaking even as coherently as Max would have, but Christine seemed to be writing it all down. Hazel looked at me as if I was trying to sell her a time-share.

Lissa nudged me and tapped her watch. Hazel had eaten up more than an hour and a half.

"We're out of time, unfortunately," I said. "For next Thursday, why don't we continue our study of what kind of parent God is?" I rubbed my palms together, now oozing sweat from my life lines. "We'll pick up with Luke."

"We were supposed to discuss chapters five through ten tonight," Rebecca said. She sliced Hazel a look. "But we never got around to it."

"Right. That's where we'll pick up next week, okay?" I said. And then I added the obligatory, "Unless you have some verses you want to share, Rebecca."

"I might," she said. "We're totally skipping the Old Testament, and it has things I've used with my boys—"

I wimped out completely. "We'll save some time for that."

As everyone lunged for their purses, Lissa gave me a one-armed squeeze. "I should *be* the little bundle of love you are," she whispered to me. "You handled that so well."

The cell phone chirping in my purse interrupted my inner debate over whether Lissa was talking about Hazel or Rebecca. The display showed Nick's cell number, so I moved toward the room's accordion partition.

"Thank you, honey," I said, hand cupped around the phone.

"For what?"

"For saving me from the most awkward moment on the planet."

I could almost hear him grinning his straight-across grin. "You owe me, then, and I'm ready to collect."

"What flavor do you want—chocolate chip or rocky road?"

"Fudge ripple, *and* I need you to pick up Tristan." His voice tightened. It wasn't the first time that summer he'd reminded me that

I was the one who had talked *him* into letting her get a job on the boardwalk and that he still didn't think it was a good idea. That was just Nicky. "I don't want her walking home by herself."

"Honey, she knows to wait for one of us."

"Aunt Pete says Max is with you."

"You called home, then."

"I just have to check on my girls. How soon can you pick up Tristan?"

"I'm on my way," I said. "Our meeting just broke up."

"How did it go?"

I felt the irrepressible gurgling in my throat. "Interesting," I said. "Too bad it's all confidential, or I'd get you to explain it to me."

"I'll get it out of you. Okay, Tristan clocks out in ten minutes—"

"I'm gone," I said.

I closed the phone with my chin.

"Orders from hubby?"

I turned to Hazel, who was the only one left at that point. She made no attempt to cover up the fact that she'd been unashamedly listening. "That's one of the five hundred reasons I'm not married anymore," she said. "Three husbands were enough for me to figure out there isn't a man alive who doesn't want to run your life."

"Nick's just a little bit protective," I said.

"Is that what I need to be so my kids will be perfect like Jo and Hermione or whatever their names are?"

I finally let go of the laughter I'd been holding back. A slow smile broke the grip of Hazel's hard mouth, showing a nicotine-stained fence of capped teeth.

"I wasn't expecting that to come out of you," she said. "You sit there looking like a virgin petunia, and then out comes this deep... laugh thing. It sounds like it should be coming out of some 1940s movie diva. Marlene Dietrich or somebody."

"I know it sounds sort of devilish, which isn't the best—"

"Is that why you're always putting your hand in front of your mouth? So nobody will know what you're really thinking?"

I did *not* want Hazel discovering the impish Serena inside. I headed for the door, Nick's voice in my ear, Hazel on my heels.

"So maybe you *aren't* perfect," she said. "That's good to know. I'm trying to decide if this is the right place for me." She glanced ruefully at the sign over the door I was locking behind us that read: God Is Good All the Time. All the Time God Is Good. "I don't exactly fit into the church scene."

Just before she stepped out of the halo of light from the porch lamp, I saw her purse her lips and narrow her eyes into hyphens. She was a dead ringer for Rebecca. My laugh put even Marlene Dietrich to shame.

"I think you and I might get along after all," she said.

I was trying to edge toward the parking lot where Max was waiting next to the Blazer, doing the combination tap-jazz-hip-hop routine she was constantly in the midst of. But Hazel stopped me with a wave of the Barbie glasses.

"When I first saw you in this little package you present, I thought, 'Uh-oh. Supermom.' You've got the little wispy haircut. I bet you're still a natural brunette... I hate women like you. The cute little body in the boutique Capris—"

"Cute little body?" I said. "My mother always told me I was built like a fireplug."

Hazel smacked her own hefty hips. "Get over it. Anyway, I see all that, plus the churchy smile, and I'm thinking, 'What can this chick teach me? She probably says "excuse me" when she belches in an empty room.'" She peered at me. "You do belch, don't you?"

"Sure," I said, although I hoped she wasn't going to ask for a demonstration. I didn't do well under pressure.

Hazel flipped a few bleached strands off her shoulder with one of Barbie's calves. "But I was watching you while I was talking, and you weren't judging me. I can smell that kind of thing." She made another Rebecca face. "There was some of that going on with the rest of them."

I didn't bother to deny it.

"Anyway, Sarah—Savannah— What is it?"

"Serena," I said.

"Yeah, look, the Bible's not my deal, but I *am* going to study *you*. I want to dog you until I see how you do this master mother thing."

I glanced at my watch. It was later than I'd thought, and Tristan would be about to punch out. I hurried toward Max, and Hazel followed. She wasn't kidding about dogging my trail.

Beeping the Blazer's lock, I called out, "Get in, Max. We have to pick up Tristan."

"Oh, yeah. Three blocks is *way* too far for her to walk by herself."

"I really have to get going," I said to Hazel.

I half expected her to hop into her car and dog me all the way to Boardwalk Fries. But she only gave a final Barbie poke and said, "You really are a good mom. I can tell that."

"Who was *that*?" Max said when we were both in the car.

"That was a lady that wants some help with her kids," I said.

"She was scary looking." Max patted my arm. "I guess they can't all be Supermom like you, huh?"

I laughed at her. But I couldn't help thinking that, next to Hazel, I *could* be Supermom.

Chapter Two

It was a few minutes after nine, and the crowd at Bethany Beach had thinned. It was still more packed than it used to be even at peak times twenty years before when Nick had first started taking me there. Even when we'd moved into the shore house six years ago, there weren't the throngs of families that pressed the boards and the sand now.

Two blocks from the boardwalk, where I had to park, Max and I wove among people in clumps thick as beach grass. Most of them were wiped-out parents with sleeping children draped over their shoulders. Grandparents craned their necks, calling out, "Do you remember where you parked?" "Where's Mikey? Does somebody have Mikey?" I smiled at each of them for enduring the sand in diapers and coolers piled like mule packs that were involved in taking kids to the shore. *Your children will never forget this,* I wanted to assure them as I walked past. *Even if you can't wait to.*

We were five miles north of Ocean City, Maryland. Our part of the Delaware seashore still promoted Bethany Beach and Fenwick Island just to the south of us as "The Quiet Resorts." Nick growled every time he saw one of the quiet resort flags flapping along the boardwalk. His idea of a quiet beach came from his sixteen growing-up years in the Bethany shore house, before his mother died. He and his father moved to Washington, D.C., after that, and life as Nick had known it disintegrated. Now his early memories of the beach were like watercolor paintings of a sleepy shoreline where sandcastles lasted forever. Bless his heart.

A few weathered cedar cottages from those simpler times still stood, and the boardwalk retained some of its 1930s cotton-candy charm. But the stream of neon-bright beach umbrellas as far as Nick could see in both directions was more of a Picasso to him. He didn't like abstract art.

Despite the hordes of summer tourists, the town of Bethany Beach was still predominantly a residential community. Garfield Parkway, which we were now navigating like salmon swimming upstream, was the main street of surf shops and souvenir stores. But to the north and south and between the ocean and the coastal highway, the town wasn't much more than shore houses of all shapes, sizes, and decades of design nestled together in happy cohabitation. Right now the crape myrtles lining the wide green spaces down the middle of each street were in luscious, fuchsia-colored bloom, and hidden backyard gardens were ripe with tomatoes split by the sun and corn so sweet I could usually eat it without butter.

By the time I ran up the steps to the boardwalk, holding on to Max's arm, I was picturing Tristan punched out and wiping the sweat off the back of her neck with her apron before she dropped it in the laundry hopper. Still, I knew there would be no eye rolling or "Hello, I've been *waiting*" or any of the things Max would have done.

Boardwalk Fries was the first stop on the north end of the boardwalk. It was the best location on the boards, but it would have done the same killer business if it had been obscured in a second-story garret. That boardwalk offered a nose feast of wonderful, greasy smells—funnel cakes, mustard-smeared corn dogs, fried clam sandwiches—but for me, it was all about the fries. They came marvelously tangled in tubs—a small was sixteen ounces—julienned with the skins on. I always told myself that made them healthier. Dusted with a masterfully small amount of salt, they held only the merest suggestion that they had touched hot oil. To bring ketchup anywhere near them was a desecration. I couldn't get within the smell of the place without salivating, which was the reason I'd gained five pounds in the three months Tristan had worked there.

"Can we get some?" Max said.

"We have ice cream in our near future," I said. It took extreme will power.

Yuri was the only one at a counter window when I walked up, the sleeves of his blue uniform T-shirt rolled to his shoulders. He was Russian. All the kids who worked there that summer were international students except Tristan. The sign over a striped coffee can read:

Tips Are for Travel

Show Us Your Beautiful Country

I gave Max a handful of change, and she tossed it in.

"That will get you a few miles closer to someplace," I said to Yuri.

He leaned over the counter, blue eyes dancing the Drobushki. "You have come for our date?" he said.

"Hel-lo-o!" Max said.

I laughed. "I keep telling you, Yuri. I'm already taken."

"It is tragic." He reached for a tub. "You want what you get always?"

I shook my head and looked behind him. "Is Tristan ready?"

Yuri's eyebrows drew into a velvet V. "Tristan?" he said. "She did not come to work tonight."

"No, seriously," I said.

"I *am* seriously. We wonder here why."

Inga, the Swedish girl, emerged from the back wearing her Boardwalk Fries shirt two sizes too small and her shorts rolled down below her navel. There were two tiny burn marks branded on her bronzed belly.

"She never showed up, Mrs. Soltani," she said. Her English, like her skin and her cheekbones, was flawless. "We thought she might have had an emergency or something."

"But I dropped her off," I said. "You never saw her?"

They both shook their heads.

"I don't get it," Max said.

My thoughts banged into each other like orbs in a pinball machine.

Tristan wouldn't just leave without telling anyone. Tristan never did anything without telling anyone. She must have walked home.

But she wouldn't walk home. Aunt Pete hadn't told Nick she was home. She wasn't home.

Game over.

I clutched the counter and stared stupidly at my knuckles.

"You are all right?" Yuri said.

Inga patted my arm. "She probably went off with friends. I know I—"

"You don't know Tristan," I said. Unless Tristan had adopted a new personality, something was very wrong.

Chapter Three

Mom?"

I looked down at Max, who was studying me. "Where's Tristan?" she said. "How come she's not here?"

I manufactured a smile. "One of us must have gotten something mixed up. You know what, Yuri. Give us a small after all. Can Max stand right here and eat it?"

I moved to the boardwalk railing and fished out my phone. My fingers had all the dexterity of a mittened child as I fumbled to dial Nick.

"Let me guess," Nick said on the third ring. "They don't have fudge ripple."

"Tristan's not here." I barely recognized the brittle voice as my own.

"She's not where?" Nick said.

"At work."

Nick sighed. He could sigh with a martyrdom even my mother had never achieved. "How many times have I told her not to leave without one of us there?" he said. "How much clearer do we have to make it?"

"Honey, she never showed up. Nobody's seen her—"

"Whoa, whoa." His voice flattened into annoyance. "What's this now?"

"I dropped her off, but she didn't go to—"

"Okay. First of all, this is the end of her working, for the rest of the summer." There was another sigh. "All right. I'm just passing Oceanview Deli. Meet me at home. We'll sit down with her and put it to her—"

"Nicky!" I saw Max dart her eyes my way. "She's not at the house," I whispered. "I don't know where she is. *Nobody* knows where she is."

Within a split second, Nick did what he always did. He scooped up the shards of me and began to piece them back together.

"Where are you now?" he said.

"We're still on the boardwalk. I didn't want to leave in case—"

"One thing at a time. Where on the boardwalk?"

"At Boardwalk Fries. No, by the railing, right across from it."

"Okay, you stay right there. I'll meet you in ten."

"You don't think we should call the police?"

"No, hon. If she shows up before I get there, call me."

I nodded as if he could see me.

"I'm overreacting, aren't I?" I said.

"Yeah," he said. "But don't worry about it. It's in your contract." I could picture him softening his eyes at me, grinning half of his straight-line grin. "You okay?"

"I'm just a little bit freaked out," I said.

"Understandable. But just concentrate on not killing her when she shows up."

"Hurry," I said.

I closed the phone against my chest and pressed it there as if my heart's hammering could send a signal to my daughter to call me and tell me she'd stopped off somewhere between the car and the board-walk and lost track of time.

But that wasn't one of the things I could imagine just then. I was leaning more toward visions of her bound and gagged in the trunk of some psychopath's car. It was far easier to conjure up that unwelcome fantasy than to entertain the thought that my Tristan had lost track of anything. I knew as I knew every fathom of my daughter's eyes and every nuance of her face that she hadn't wandered off and forgotten to go to her job.

That realization made it impossible to stay there clinging to the railing of the boardwalk as if it might take flight and carry my mind off with it. But I couldn't face Max yet, either. While I watched her chatter away with Inga and Yuri, cheeks bulging with fries, I flipped open the phone and pulled up the number for Jessica Johnstone, Tris-tan's best friend.

"Hello?" a voice chirped in my ear.

"Jessica?" I said. "It's Mrs. Soltani. Sweetie, have you seen—"

"Hi, Mrs. Sol*tani*! How are *you*?"

Jessica always flipped her phrases up at the ends, just like she styled her hair. She was as effervescent as a soda. I could feel myself fragmenting again.

"So what's *up*?" Jessica said.

"Tristan," I said.

"Ye*ah*?"

"I mean, have you talked to her tonight?"

"No-o!" Jessica said. "She was supposed to call me when she got off work, and she *so* hasn't!" The child gasped. "She's not grounded from the phone is she? No, that's not Tristan. That's me, except not right now because my dad's out of town, and my mom doesn't care how long I talk. She's cool. Like *you*!"

I'd listened to enough of Jessica's monologues to know she had stopped only because she was out of breath. I had to cut in before she could take another run at it and before I shattered completely.

"No, she's not grounded," I said.

"O-kay…"

"I'm just looking for her," I said.

"Are you okay? You sound funny." There was another gasp. "Not in a bad way. Just not like you—"

"It's going to be fine," I said. I wasn't sure as I hung up who I was trying to reassure.

I had at least five other numbers in my cell phone for girls Tristan spent time with. Their mothers and I were a network of "Sure they can study over here" and "Sure I'll pick them up from dance rehearsal/ French club meeting/student government retreat." We charted the movements of our teenage daughters like air-traffic control. But it made no sense to call any of them. If they were with Tristan, then Jessica, the event coordinator, would have known about it.

I stared across at Boardwalk Fries, where Yuri swabbed the counter to the rhythm of a Led Zeppelin song and Inga was silhouetted at the cash register. Tristan and her ponytail were conspicuously absent from the scene. Another head was missing, which I hadn't picked up on before.

Dodging the stragglers who were making their way toward the stairs, I went back to the counter. Yuri's velvet eyebrows shot up when he saw me.

"You found Tristan, yes?"

"Not yet." I plastered on a smile. "Is Aylana still here?"

Aylana Kalidimos was a young Greek college student who usually worked Tristan's shift with her. Tristan always came home with an Aylana story. One night she reported that Aylana had pierced her belly button during break. Nick had warned Tristan not to get any ideas about putting a hole in any part of her anatomy. Another evening she said Aylana had everyone behind the counter doing a synchronized dance to a Creedence Clearwater Revival tune. I'd enjoyed imagining Tristan's kicking it to "Down on the Corner." I always loved watching her dance...

"Aylana called in sick tonight," Inga said.

Her cheekbones grew sharper, as if she doubted the credibility of said illness, but I dove for it like it was a lifeline.

"Do you have her home number?" I said. I already had the cell phone open.

Looking slightly sheepish, Yuri dug into the pocket of his T-shirt and extracted several folded slips of paper. He held an unfolded one up between his index and middle fingers.

I was poking the numbers on my phone before the paper came fully to rest on the counter.

"If my sister went off with Aylana," I heard Max tell them, "she is in *so* much trouble."

I stepped away from the counter and counted the rings, my heart sinking further with each one until a female hip-hop group spewed out something unintelligible to the tune of "If I Were a Rich Man." Aylana's throaty voice broke in, heavily accented but rolling in American teenage rhythm. "If I were a rich girl, I would have my personal secretary answering my phone, but I am a poor college student, so talk at the beep, 'kay?"

The beep was interminable, which probably meant either Aylana hadn't checked her messages in a while or she received frequent calls. I suspected the latter. According to Tristan, the girl stirred up more male interest than Janet Jackson at the Super Bowl. It was actually Max who had thought of that analogy, which had prompted an instant interrogation from Nick.

I left a message for Aylana, asking her to call me when she got in. The final beep cut me off before I could leave my number. Judging from Aylana's legendary social life, I was sure she had caller ID.

I clung hard to the phone. When Tristan told Aylana stories, she always looked as if she was having a near-death experience. She seemed to find the telling delicious, but the thought of the incidents themselves all but made her hyperventilate. Wherever Aylana was right now, I knew Tristan wasn't with her. I let go of that lifeline.

My baby was gone. She'd vanished somewhere in the crowd that had now disappeared from the boardwalk, and I wanted to scream after them, "Where is she? Which one of you has her?"

I wrapped my arms around myself to keep from ripping apart. That's when I heard Nick bark, "Serena." It was obviously the last of several attempts to get my attention. His hands on my shoulders turned me around to look into his Mediterranean-dark face, which had grown even darker.

"She's not here," he said. It wasn't a question, but I shook my head anyway.

"No," I said, "and she didn't go to Jessica's, and—"

"She's not home, either. I just called there again." Nick scanned the boardwalk with an irritated squint. He ran his hand over his dark head, a gesture I recognized as an attempt to keep the top of it from blowing off.

"Okay, now I'm ticked," he said. "What was she thinking?"

I wanted to join in the Tristan bashing, ached to assume as he obviously did that our daughter was off partying while we wrung our hands. But I couldn't.

"What if somebody grabbed her after I dropped her off?" I said.

Nick's eyes flinched. "Serena, come on—"

"You're the one who didn't want her walking home alone because something might happen to her. What if something did?"

Nick pulled me against his chest. "Okay, you have to get a grip, hon. We have a hundred other possibilities to explore before we go there."

I didn't believe it. And I could tell from the way he held on to me that he didn't, either.

But in true Nick fashion, he had Plan A formed before he let go to look at me again. He told me to take Max home and call the rest of Tristan's girlfriends and anybody else I could think of. He'd canvass the shops.

As I turned to leave, I took one last doubtful look at the boardwalk. The awning was already down on Tropicana Beachwear. Inga had her hand on the shade pull at Boardwalk Fries. Neon lights flickered out in both directions as I watched.

I wondered what Plan B was, but I didn't ask Nick. The face he turned toward the beach was a frightened gray.

It didn't occur to me until then that I hadn't looked at the waterfront. Maybe I had been too stunned. Or maybe some automatic self-protective mechanism had kicked in. But the entire time it took me to drive the three blocks to our house, with Max uncharacteristically silent beside me, was devoted to the possibilities that lay in the sand and beyond.

Every year Tristan was required to listen to the "Don't go on the beach at night" litany from Nick once a week from Memorial Day to Labor Day. She was ten when we'd moved to the shore, which meant she'd heard it no less than seventy-two times in her life. She usually did it dutifully, doe eyes practically unblinking. Max, on the other hand, recited it right along with her father.

"It's just like a city street," they said in unison. "You don't go walking down it alone after dark. There are psychos out there."

Not that anyone in the "Quiet Resorts" had ever been attacked by a psycho on the beach, Max always reminded him. It had never stopped Nick from going on to explain—again—that the jetties were especially dangerous. You couldn't see what might have washed up there and gotten caught—anything from a jellyfish to a—

"Psycho," Max had muttered during the August 1 recitation. She'd been sent to her room for that.

Because our house directly fronted the ocean, the restless roiling of the surf was such a constant for me that it was barely more than background noise unless I was actually on the beach. Now, as I drove, every crash of a wave dropping onto the shore, every hiss of it creeping back into the Atlantic was a taunt I could feel more than hear.

Tristan could be under here, you know. We could be rolling her back and forth on the ocean floor. We could be carrying her out to sea where you won't find her until she washes up one day...

I jolted the Blazer to a halt in the driveway.

"Why don't you go in and see if she's home yet?" I said to Max.

She flung herself out of the car, and I sank my head onto the steering wheel, eyes closed. The posture brought up something I hadn't thought of.

God.

I hadn't said even one prayer.

Wouldn't Rebecca Godfried have a field day with that?

"Father?" I whispered.

My image of Him came at once, soft eyed with arms wide open. It was an image that had gotten me through my mother's death at fifty, my dad's at sixty-one, thirty hours of labor, four stitches in Max's chin.

"She's okay, right? You wouldn't let anything happen to her, would You?"

I waited for the calm. The sense of being admonished with *Serena, Serena, Serena. You know that. You're faithful—*

It wasn't there, but I knew it would come. I had to have that before I could go inside to Max and Aunt Pete.

I had a maternal attachment to our house. Nick's great-grandparents had built its front section in the early twentieth century. It had hugged its boxy three-story self with a wraparound porch until the 1920s, when Nick's grandparents added a then-modern kitchen and indoor bathrooms and a dormlike sleeping room on the third floor for their famous weekend house parties. Nick's parents had given the house a face-lift and added a pool in the early sixties when Soltani Casters gained momentum.

After Nick's mother, Maxine, died in 1980, midway through Victorianizing with blue chintz and flowered wallpaper, Nick's father, Nicholas Sr., shed himself of the house and its memories, as well as Soltani Casters, in an alcoholic fog. He let Maxine's sister, Aunt Lee Anne, live in it, and he was in such a stupor that he even allowed her to try to convert it into a bed-and-breakfast, a venture that never got beyond the redecoration of each of the seven bedrooms to reflect a different rock'n'roll personality.

By the time Nicholas Sr. caved to liver disease and emphysema in 1998, my Nick had returned Soltani Casters to its former status. Two years later he finally unsnarled the legal rat's nest in which his father had entangled his legacy, relocated Aunt Lee Anne to an assisted-living facility, and moved us back to his beloved shore house.

Judging from the condition of the house, that assisted-living facility was long overdue for poor Aunt Lee Anne. Elvis, Buddy Holly, Chuck Berry, and Chubby Checker, to name only a few, writhed on the walls. Ancient food and grime plastered the kitchen.

I touched every inch of that house the first week we were there, from the painted-shut windows in the sleeping room to the Pepto-Bismol pink porch railing that nearly gave way and pitched me into the sea. I whispered as I went, promising it that we would restore its dignity and make it proud again.

It took me four years to make good on that promise. While Nick worked sixty-hour weeks, I nurtured my three children: Tristan, Max, and the shore house. All day while the girls were in school, I tenderly pulled up my house's carpets and rubbed its hardwood floors to a shine. I eased off the life-size stick-ons of Elvis and the Victorian wallpaper beneath with its roses the size of cabbages.

As twenty years of indignities were slowly washed and scraped and chiseled away, I could feel the house sigh at times. Every time I pulled into the driveway, it seemed to welcome me with its diamond-paned eyelids and open-armed porches and arched-eyebrow roofline. I was always eager to get inside and breathe with it.

But that night I couldn't even force myself to get out of the car. It came to me that I wasn't waiting for God. I was avoiding the stark absence of Tristan that waited inside.

The front door burst open, throwing light onto the porch. Max flew down the steps toward me, phone in hand. I fumbled for the door handle, but she wrenched it open from the outside. As I tried to extricate myself from behind the wheel, I discovered I still had the seat belt on.

"Is it Tristan?" I said.

Max shook her head. "Mrs. Johnstone."

I took the phone and moved, heart plummeting, toward the steps. "Jody," I said.

"Have you found Tristan?" Her voice was high and shrill.

"Not yet," I said.

"Okay, listen, Serena, I hope I wasn't out of line, but when Jessica told me you called, looking for her, I went ahead and got on the phone and called—"

She went on to list every girl Tristan had known since fifth grade and some I'd never heard of. There were even some boys' names on the roster. With each one my heart sank deeper into the crevice it was carving in my chest. Another mother was thinking what I was thinking, and it made the possibilities all too real.

"No one has seen her, Serena," Jody finished with a gasp reminiscent of Jessica. "I was hoping you'd found her already."

"We haven't looked everywhere yet," I said.

"Then you'll find her; I know you will. I hope you don't think I was overstepping—"

"No, no, I appreciate it," I said. I felt out of breath and sank into the red wicker chair near the front door.

"I will absolutely call you if I hear anything at all," Jody said. "I had to leave a message at Dahlia Carr's house, so there's always the chance she's with her—"

I looked blankly at Max, who had her cheek pressed against mine to hear. I didn't even know who Dahlia Carr was.

"She's that RMG Tristan's in student government with," Max whispered. "She doesn't even like her."

I somehow ended the call with Jody and stared numbly at Max. The only thing I could think of to say was, "What's an RMG?"

"Really mean girl," Max said. "That time you used that crimper thing on Tristan's hair? Dahlia asked her if we had any mirrors at our house." She rolled her eyes. "Tristan is *so* not gonna hang out with her."

At the moment I wouldn't have cared if Tristan were hanging out with the Hell's Angels, as long as I knew where she was and that it was not at the bottom of the Atlantic.

Max watched me, one foot propped on the opposite leg like a flamingo.

"Maxie," I said, "do you have any idea where your sister could be? Be honest. Did she mention any plans to you, anything she might have forgotten to tell me?"

Max cocked the eyebrow. "You're kidding, right?"

I might as well have been, and we both knew it. Not only would Tristan have asked permission, but she would have written it on the family calendar and checked in twice by phone to make sure it was still okay.

"I don't know why you're just sitting there, Serena." Nick's great aunt, whom we called Aunt Pete, stood in the doorway. Ever since she'd arrived in June to stay with us for the summer, her voice had reminded me of an old-time radio announcer, complete with crackling static. She folded her arms across the front of the ancient pink chenille bathrobe she slipped into every night at eight and wore until midmorning the next day. Parts of it had turned a dirty rose color, because she regularly wiped counters and dusted furniture with it during that fourteen-hour period.

The amber light of our wide foyer outlined her wiry figure and her short, untamed white hair. I didn't have to see her face to know the Soltani eyes were squinted in the same disdain I'd already heard in her voice.

"You waiting for her to come waltzing up the driveway or what?" she said.

"I'm at a loss, Aunt Pete," I said.

"Come in, at least. You're letting all the cold air out."

She pulled the door open the rest of the way, and I was about to follow her in when beams from car lights—white and red and blue—bounced against the house.

"It's Dad," Max said. "He brought the cops!"

I was barely able to grab her by the hood of her shirt before she could bound out to meet the Bethany Beach police car that rocked to a stop behind Nick's black Nissan. Aunt Pete pulled her in the rest of the way. I stood motionless and let the red lights flash in my eyes.

I tried to read Nick's body language as he got out of the car. He rubbed the back of his head as he waited for a man who seemed to be moving in slow motion. He straightened his tie and strolled toward Nick as if someone's child were not this very moment missing. The tautness in Nick's shoulders kept me from taking any comfort in the man's nonchalance.

An eon later they arrived on the porch. Nick and I exchanged looks that confirmed what we both knew. Neither of us had found a trace of her. But we would. I knew we would.

"This is Detective Ed Malone," Nick said, nodding toward the officer. Nick's voice was as tight as his shoulders. "My wife, Serena."

Ed Malone put out his hand, and I shook it absently. If I'd been asked thirty seconds later to describe him, I couldn't have. I was still searching Nick's face for reassurance that wasn't there.

"He's going to have us fill out a missing person report," Nick said. I shook my head.

"Serena, we have to do this—"

"No, we'll do it. I just can't believe this is happening."

"I know it feels surreal." Ed Malone's voice was surprisingly soft and lacked the clipped mid-Atlantic accent that made everyone in Delaware sound as if their jaws were wired shut. "It's a precaution. Most teenagers that go missing at night show up around dawn."

"You don't know our Tristan—"

Nick took my arm, palm damp against my skin, and steered me through the doorway and sharply to the right into the living room. The warm caramels and burnt oranges that usually welcomed me were suddenly jarring and inappropriate.

Max was already there, tucked into a corner of one of the couches, hugging a pillow to her chest. When Nick nodded her out, she glanced at the detective and visibly bit back a complaint. I could hear Aunt Pete calling her from the kitchen, though I was sure Aunt Pete herself would soon be stationed behind a column in the dining room, straining to hear. Part of me wanted to join her, the part that didn't want to give the detective answers that would make my Tristan officially missing.

I kept telling myself that God was there. He was at that moment taking care of everything. He *was*...

Ed Malone sat on the edge of a chair and put a folder on the coffee table, running his fingers along its sides as if to tidy the already-straight edges. "Just so you know," he said, "we already have a team cruising the teen hangouts. Somebody from Search and Rescue will be here shortly. Things are happening while you and I are handling the paperwork."

I tried to look grateful when I nodded. Nick parked me on the couch with its back to the row of windows that overlooked the ocean. He stood behind me. I groped over my shoulder for his hand, and he grabbed on.

Ed barely got the form out of his folder when Max shouted from the foyer, "There's a lady here with a dog!" She danced in backward, motioning to a young woman with a bloodhound on a leash. His ears brushed the floor as she followed him in.

This can't be happening, I thought for the hundredth time.

Ed introduced the woman as Officer Pierce. She nodded without looking at us and spoke as if she were trying to keep all emotion out of her voice. Her seriousness frightened me. "Do you have something of the victim's?" she said. "A piece of clothing she's worn recently?"

The *victim?*

"Right here!" Max pulled a sock out of her pocket. "I just got this out of the hamper. I knew you'd need something."

"Is that going to be a problem," Nick said, "since it's been mixed up with other people's clothes?"

"No," Officer Pierce said. "If you folks don't mind, Duke needs to get a sniff of each of you so he can differentiate the victim's scent from yours. The victim's will be the majority smell."

"Tristan," Nick said. "Her name is Tristan."

The officer appeared not to hear him as she commanded Duke to snuffle at Max, who giggled, and at Aunt Pete, who didn't. Nick was stoic about it, but when the sad-eyed animal with enough skin for another dog came to me, I took his face in my hands and said, "You'll find her."

Officer Pierce dropped Tristan's sock into a pillowcase with a gloved hand. "We'll take the scent article to the point last seen."

"Right at the corner of Ocean View and Garfield," Max said. Aunt Pete shushed her.

"We have a dog going out with the Coast Guard, too, although…" The officer looked at Ed.

"Thanks," Ed said. He tilted his head toward me. It was shaved—apparently in surrender to advancing baldness—and shone in the lamplight. "Do you have a picture of Tristan?"

Max was once again on the scene with a five-by-seven of Tristan's sophomore school picture and held it out at the end of a straight arm. The instant Ed Malone took it, Max made one stiff step back and then dove for the couch where she clung to me like a baby koala.

When Officer Pierce had led Duke out, Ed looked at me again.

"Does your daughter have a cell phone?"

"No," Nick said.

"What about e-mail?"

"She doesn't have her own account."

"Can you give me a verbal description? I know you gave us a picture, but you can provide details the camera misses."

I nodded and closed my eyes. I could see her. I could practically smell her.

"She has shoulder-length hair about the color of mine," I said, "and thicker. Hers is thick like her dad's. Her eyebrows are thick too. No, she just started tweezing them this summer. And her eyes are brown—we all have brown eyes—but hers are bigger than the rest of ours, and expressive, so expressive…"

The words fractured. Ed Malone nodded and scribbled and nodded some more until I could start again.

"She has an olive complexion—you know what I mean by that? And a huge smile, perfect teeth, big teeth. She's grown into them now, but it used to look like she had more than most people. It's a shy smile. She's quiet a lot, like a deer—I always think of her as my doe—"

I flattened my hands over my mouth. My shoulders drew together in the front as I closed in on myself.

"She's no more than five-five," I heard Nick say. "Probably weighs 110, something like that."

"She had her purse with her," I said. "It was green, and it had her initial on it in blue."

"What was she wearing?" Ed said.

"Her uniform. Blue T-shirt. Khaki shorts."

I'd ironed them for her just that afternoon.

"She looked so cute in it," I said. And then I choked. I had just spoken of my daughter in the past tense.

Somehow the information filtered to me that Ed would file the report and enter it into the local MPR, missing persons reports, and the NCIC, the National Crime Information Center, which covers the entire United States.

I could feel the word *crime* blanching my face.

"Again, that's a precaution," Ed Malone said. "We have no reason to suspect foul play at this point."

Nick curled his fingers around my wrist and held on. I watched Detective Malone swallow.

"Just in case we're wrong," he said, "we're covering all the bases." He stood up, and for the first time I noticed that he was taller than Nick and broader in the shoulders, even though Nick himself was six foot and squared off. It registered that I should feel heartened by that show of strength. I wasn't.

"I'll walk you out," Nick said to him.

Ed fixed his eyes again on me. "That was a great description. I'll know her anywhere."

All I could do was nod as Nick ushered him toward the front hall. Aunt Pete entered through the dining room with two steaming mugs.

"It's about time he stopped flapping his lips and went out there and started looking," she said. She cast a glare toward the porch where Nick and the detective were still talking in muted tones. "Here." She put the mugs on the table in front of me. "That coffee's strong enough to walk across the street by itself. You're going to need it."

"For what?" Max said.

"You don't think your mother's going to sit in this house all night when your sister's out who knows where." Aunt Pete pushed one hot mug of mud toward me. "Go on, drink up."

"Don't even think about it," Nick said as he strode across the room. He picked up both mugs and put one of them back in Aunt Pete's hand. He curled his fingers around the other one as he sat catty-cornered from me on the seat Ed Malone had just vacated. He was back in take-charge mode, as if the detective had passed him the baton.

"Hon," he said to me, "what I want you to do is try to stay as calm as you can and get some rest."

"Ha," Aunt Pete said.

Nick ignored her. "When we find Tristan, and we will, I can guarantee you she's going to be shaken up—whether it's from guilt or some kind of near-miss we don't know—but she's going to need you to be strong. Am I right?"

I didn't answer.

"Huh? Am I right?"

"Of course," I said.

He set the coffee mug on the table and took my face in both hands. They burned against my cheeks.

"The police are doing everything they can. I'm doing everything I can. But we also have to give it to God."

"He already has it; He has Tristan. I know that."

"Good girl." Nick pulled his hands away. "Why don't you stretch out here on the couch and keep the house phone and the cell phone next to you? Aunt Pete, you take the other couch."

"What about me?" Max said.

"You need to go to bed, short stuff," Nick said. "We've got it handled. Your sister will be here when you wake up."

Max didn't say anything. As Nick turned to me, she pressed herself into the sofa and set her jaw.

"Where are you going?" I said to Nick.

"I'm going to walk the beach some more. They can use another pair of eyes." He leaned across the arm of the couch and kissed me. "The best thing you can do is pray."

As he disappeared around the corner, I licked off the anxious, upper-lip sweat he'd left on my mouth. He was as terrified as I was—ocean-deep in the blackest of possibilities.

Chapter Four

That night was like the one I spent in labor with Tristan. Painful spasms of fear gave way to lulls of hopeful waiting. But the respites were just long enough for the sieges to gather force and attack me more brutally each time. The difference was, in the labor room I knew each contraction brought me closer to holding my Tristan in my arms.

During the frightened moments, I charged around the house searching Tristan's room without a clue to what I was looking for, combing the family calendar in the kitchen five, six, ten times, checking the answering machine in case it had somehow malfunctioned. The chop of the Coast Guard helicopters reminded me that other people were looking too. One minute I wanted to shout "Thank you!" to them. The next I wanted to tell them it was ridiculous—my daughter wasn't really missing.

When the lulls came, I went down the wooden walkway, past the pool, to the deck jutting out over the sand, and breathed to the night,

"Father, please." Until another spasm seized me and I ran to look at the bottom of the pool or tore down the steps to the cabana.

"What the devil are you doing, Serena?" Aunt Pete said when she caught me lifting the lid of the window seat in the pool house and peering at a pile of towels.

I didn't point out that it made no less sense than her leaning over the deck railing calling out Tristan's name.

"It's not like Sissy's a puppy," Max said at my elbow. "She knows her way home."

My throat thickened again. Max had announced to us six months earlier that she was no longer going to refer to Tristan as Sissy, the version of Sister she had lisped from the age of eighteen months as she toddled everywhere after Tristan. I had the feeling Max would call Tristan the Queen of the World right now if she would just walk through the front door.

Around two in the morning, Max conked out in the Papasan chair in the family room, curled into a ball. I covered her with a throw and let her sleep. Aunt Pete succumbed a little after four, sitting straight up on the wicker love seat on the side porch, nose snorting in the air, lips puffing it back out.

I went into another panic spasm, but I had no place left to search. I put a cushion behind Aunt Pete's head and headed for the beach.

The fog that chilled the air didn't make me any colder than I already was. Even though I'd long since changed into a set of Nick's sweats, I was still shivering from the inside out. Pulling my hands up into the sleeves, I picked my way down the stone steps that led between the dunes to "our" beach. I never liked calling it that. "No one can own the sand or the ocean," I always told my girls.

I sank down at the base of one of the dunes now and plucked at a feathery tuft of beach grass. I'd said it recently, maybe just the week before when someone had come along during the night and wrecked a sandcastle Max had spent an entire morning on. She was fuming.

"How come people even come down here?" Max said, hands on her negligible hips. "Don't they know this is a private beach?"

Before I could open my mouth, she rolled her eyes at me. "Go ahead and say it, Mom."

I grinned at her from under the beach umbrella. "We can't own the sand or the ocean."

Beside me on the blanket, Tristan looked at me over the tops of her sunglasses. "No, we can't," she said. "But I think sometimes it owns us."

"*What?*" Max said.

"I don't know. Never mind," Tristan said. She rolled over on her stomach, and I went to work on her back with sunscreen.

Now I squeezed my eyes shut, but the thought came anyway, and I whispered it into the fog. "I hope it doesn't own you now, Tristan. I pray it doesn't."

The panic tried to grip me again, and I dug my hands into the grass. There was no way Tristan went into that water last night. No way she had even ventured down onto the beach.

Not of her own accord.

The back of my throat constricted, and I knew I was going to throw up. I flung myself down on all fours and retched almost nothing into the sand. When I rocked back, I was holding two hands full of beach grass, roots and all.

American beach grass, it was called. Signs all along the beach asked people not to walk on the grass so it would stay protected.

"What grass?" I'd heard more than one tourist say as he dragged his folded beach chairs over it.

That was the point. American beach grass was dying in large patches from Massachusetts to Virginia, while scientists continued to search for the reason. It was vital that they find it, because the plant was an important dune stabilizer. The grass was delicate, but its root systems helped hold down the shifting sands of the dunes so they could do their job of stopping erosion. I was always careful to leave the dunes in their contemplative solitude and sometimes even prayed over the soft patches of green when I left the beach. And here I was with two fistfuls I'd pulled right out of the ground.

I pushed the plants back into the holes and tamped the sand around them. It was like tucking my girls into their beds.

The fog was lifting a little, letting a thin gray light pass under it. A gull landed near the water's edge, just ten feet from me, and stamped his feet as if he were impatient with the lack of breakfast. Another swooped to join him, and they complained together.

Farther down the beach toward the boardwalk, I could barely make out the first of the fishermen casting into the water, planting their poles in the sand, and setting their battery-operated lanterns atop their coolers to wait. How could they go about their daily rounds when a huge piece of mine was missing? There was nothing daily about this day, this Friday morning after the night my daughter hadn't come home. I turned toward the house.

I couldn't wrap my mind around what was happening. Tristan was ten, Max's age, before she would spend the night at anyone else's house. At least three times before that I had been called to pick her up at slumber parties where she'd been struck with a sudden, mysterious illness or had awakened crying from a bad dream. She always confessed to me in the car that she really just missed us and wanted to come home. As a toddler, she'd never been one to wander away from me in a store, unlike Max, who practically had to be kept on a leash even now.

I took the porch steps two at a time in another rush of must-do-something. Nick was just climbing out of the Nissan when I reached the top. In the moments before he saw me, he didn't look like my Nick.

I always thought of him as smooth. Not in the social, schmoozing sense. His person was smooth. He wore his on-the-verge-of-black hair trimmed close to his head, the hint of a black beard contouring his dark olive skin. His dark eyes, his straight nose, even his marvelous twitchy line of a mouth—none of it disturbed the seamlessness. From the moment I'd met him, I'd found him sexy in an understated way. It still made me catch my breath when he lifted just one side of his mouth and sent me a wink softer than a kiss.

The man I watched climb the steps to our house bore little resemblance to my Nick. The hair on the back of his head was flat from constantly pawing at it in angst, I knew, and even from across the driveway I could see the dark shadow of uneven stubble. His hands were jammed into the pockets of the slacks he'd been wearing for twenty-four hours. Inside the rumpled blue oxford, his square shoulders sagged, making the shirt look two sizes too big. His gaze seemed glued to the tassels on his loafers.

When I called to him, he straightened his back and turned toward me, holding out one arm. When I folded into him, I smelled dried sweat and stale coffee. Nick never smelled like that.

I didn't ask if he knew anything. He wouldn't be holding me silently if he did, unless—

I grabbed a handful of hair on his forearm where his sleeve was rolled up. "Nick, she's not—"

He pushed my face back into the front of his shirt. "No. The dog tracked her to the boardwalk parking lot near the steps, but the trail stopped there. Search and Rescue says that probably means she left in a car."

"She wouldn't just go off in a car with somebody, Nicky. You know that."

"They're doing everything they can, hon. Some of us walked the beach all night. The police hit every hangout from here to below Ocean City. Did you hear the helicopter?"

I nodded away from his chest. "Then why haven't they found her? She's not here anymore, Nicky. They've taken her—"

"Okay, stop. Just stop." Nick's voice took on an exhausted edge, and he ran his hand down his face as if to wipe it away. "We can't go there, Serena. We can't, and we won't." He cupped his hand on the back of my head. "Okay? God just wouldn't let that happen, right?"

It was a question that didn't allow for any answer other than "I know, Nicky."

"Did you get any sleep?" he said.

I shook my head. "Aunt Pete finally did."

Nick pushed the front door open, and we both sniffed.

"She's up now," he said.

The air inside the house was filled with the unmistakable smell of overdone bacon and walk-across-the-street coffee. Aunt Pete was sliding a pair of eggs onto a plate when I sat down on a stool at the snack bar. The eggs' rim was brown and curled up, Aunt Pete's miracle cure for an appetite if I'd had one.

"If you're not going to sleep, you at least have to eat," she said. "Didn't I hear Nicky drive up?"

"I'm here." Nick dropped onto the stool next to mine and slapped the morning paper on the counter. Aunt Pete whipped it open, scanned the front page in a squint, and let it fall again.

"Nothing about our girl," she said. The static in her voice was thick. "How do they expect to find her if they don't get the word out?"

"This isn't like Philadelphia, Aunt Pete," Nick said with patience I knew was forced.

"I'm calling those newspaper people myself," Aunt Pete said.

"I'm sure they know. Detective Malone requested an AMBER Alert."

An AMBER Alert. Tristan's name in larger-than-life computer letters blinking down onto the highway? Signaling to everyone that our daughter probably *wasn't* all right?

The image slammed into me so hard that I reeled toward the floor.

Nick caught me and held my ear close to his mouth. "It's just standard procedure, hon," he said. "We probably don't need it."

What I needed was the assurance I always had that my faithful little family was being taken care of. By Nicky. By a world God made safe for us. By God Himself.

Nick made me lie down on the family room couch and at least close my eyes. I fought sleep, so it only managed to capture me in gray moments. I was aware that Lissa and Pastor Gary came in—and later that the doorbell rang incessantly. Once I heard voices battering someone—

"Mrs. Soltani, do you know anybody who would have abducted your daughter?"

"Have you heard any news?"

"How worried are you, Serena?"

"Are you afraid you'll never see your daughter again?"

"I'm not Mrs. Soltani," I heard Lissa shout at them. "And no, she is not afraid of that."

Later, other voices rose just above whispers in the kitchen, saying the beachfront parking lot that bordered our property was jammed with sound trucks and vans from channel this and channel that.

Through my snatches of sleep, I heard Pastor Gary say, "I think you need to go give them a statement, Nick. I know they look like vultures, but it can only help if they get the story out."

I woke up once to see two goateed twenty-somethings with digital camcorders peering in through the french doors, followed by tattered pieces of conversation.

"Those aren't official media people—"

"Tell that cop out front—"

"Get away before I crush your little skulls!" That, of course, came from Aunt Pete, who added, "Somebody's name is gonna be Mud."

I was jolted fully awake around noon by high-pitched shouts from the pool.

"Is that Tristan?" I cried out before I could even get untangled from the blanket. "Is she home?"

But it was just the children, Lissa's and Rebecca's and mine. Only one of mine.

"Come on, Serena," Lissa said. "Let's go upstairs where it's quieter."

She coaxed me up the steps and tried to get me to crawl into bed, but it had all the appeal of a mattress of tacks. Every nerve ending screamed, *Don't lie down! You'll lose your mind!*

"I want to stay awake," I said, "in case we hear something."

"I'll wake you up *when* we hear something," Lissa said. Her eyes were honey-brown pools of concern, and they made me want to cry. Suddenly everything made me want to cry.

I plunged my face into Lissa's shoulder and sobbed. I could feel her sliding wisps of my hair between her fingers. "You're doing great, Serena. I just think you're doing great."

I wasn't rocking on the floor in an embryonic position, if that was what she meant. It was all I could do to keep grasping for the assurance I wanted to believe was there. Somewhere.

The house was a hive of activity for the rest of the day. Women doing my laundry. People telling me to let the Lord take over and to get some sleep. Voices praying. Friends clutching their own children as if they, too, were going to be snatched away.

Detective Malone gave an official police-department statement to the crowd in the parking lot, which I listened to from inside the front door. Pastor Gary stood with me, pressing down on his auburn mustache with a freckled thumb and index finger.

"I've sat with people whose kids were dying or flunking out of school or doing drugs," he said. "But this is so different, Serena. I told Nick, I'm not sure what to say to you. There are so many ifs. It's hard to find comfort in ifs."

I didn't tell him I was struggling to find comfort in anything. I was grateful that he didn't say what I would have said even twenty-four hours earlier if this had been happening to Lissa or Rebecca or any other mother: "God is good all the time. All the time God is good." I didn't know what to do with that just now. I was still waiting for the certainty that God was going to show up on the doorstep at any moment with an unscathed Tristan.

Nick was in and out all day. At one point Christine handed him a suggested statement for the press, but beyond that I had no idea what he was doing. He was out when Christine came to me in the breakfast nook where I sat with Lissa, staring out at the ocean and not drinking Aunt Pete's molasses-colored iced tea.

"Somebody named Aylana is at the door," Christine said. "She says you left her a message."

I clawed my way out of the nook, calling Aylana's name before I got to the foyer. She was standing just inside the front door with a police officer so young he still had pimples on his chin. Aylana's large, liquid gray eyes widened as a houseful of women gathered behind me. One dark eyebrow went up, lifting its tiny gold ring with it.

"She says you called her," the child officer said to me.

"Last night," Aylana said. She stepped forward to give me her customary hug and kiss on the cheek. Her skin was sun warm, her arms willowy like Tristan's. I forced myself not to hang on to her as she spoke.

"I was on my way to work," she said, "and I thought I would stop by and see if Tristan wanted to walk with me." She glanced warily at her police escort. "What is with all this?"

The small bubble of hope that had appeared at her arrival popped almost audibly. I watched her grow blurry on the other side of my tears.

Aylana pulled her eyes from me and searched the little crowd.

"Tristan's missing," Rebecca said. "This really isn't a good time—"

"Did she say anything at all to you?" I said to Aylana. I wiped under my eyes with my fingertips. "When you saw her Wednesday, did she say anything unusual?"

Aylana shook her head, mahogany ponytail and hoop earrings swinging in unison. "We talk about music, guys…" Her full lips spread into a momentary smile. "Well, *I* talk about guys. I teased her about that one who always comes to flirt with her—"

"What's this now?"

Nick was in the doorway of the family room with Ed Malone behind him, though how Nick had gotten there I had no idea. He cut past Christine, putting his face inches from Aylana's. She arched back.

"What guy?" Nick said. I could see his jaw muscles working.

"I don't know," Aylana said. "Just a guy."

"Did she know him?"

Aylana shrugged.

"Did she act like she knew him? Did she say his name?" Nick pulled a finger from his hip and stabbed the air near Aylana's ear. His voice was so hard, the tendons in his neck strained against it. "Look, this is important. You have to tell us everything—"

"I don't know anything, 'kay?" Aylana said. She backed stiffly toward the door.

"I think you do know!"

"Nick." Ed Malone stepped around me and put a hand on Nick's shoulder. "Let's take it easy."

I watched, unbelieving, as Nick stepped back from Aylana. His red rage slid back inside him.

"All right, everybody out of the pool," Aunt Pete said.

"We're not in the pool," one of the Quantums said.

"She means leave the room, moron," Max said.

Aylana was clearly close to tears by the time the foyer emptied of everyone except Ed and Nick and me. Nick stood with his hands on his hips, still boring into her with his eyes.

Ed touched Aylana lightly on the elbow. "Start at the beginning about this fella Tristan talked to at work."

Aylana kept her guarded gaze on Nick. "I am so sorry. I should say nothing because I know nothing."

Nick's knuckles went white. I looped my arm through his. It felt like a band of steel.

"How many times did he visit her?" Ed said.

"He just comes for fries," Aylana said. "He flirts with Tristan because she's cute."

"Does she know him, do you think?" Ed said.

Aylana shrugged.

"Give a guess."

"I can't," Aylana said. "Tristan and I, we aren't close."

Nick wrenched away from me.

"Can you give us a description?" Ed said.

"I didn't look at him that much," Aylana said.

That I found hard to believe.

She muttered something about his being tall and thin and tan but always wearing a ball cap, so she didn't get a good look at his face.

"What team?" Nick barked at her.

Aylana's brow twisted.

"What team was on the ball cap?"

"I don't know about teams."

Nick grunted and stalked into the living room. Aylana's face stiffened as she stared at the doorway. Ed nodded at Aylana.

"This is my card," he said. "If you think of anything or hear anything, call me."

He put the emphasis square on the *me*. Aylana gave the living room one last look before she left. Her exit was clearly an escape.

Nick reappeared, rubbing the back of his head as if he was scouring it with steel wool. "Sorry about that," he said. "I just can't believe she doesn't know more."

"Something may come to her," Ed said. "We caught her off guard." He looked over his shoulder toward the kitchen, where low voices had stopped murmuring. "Is there someplace we can talk privately?"

Nick led us into the library, just beyond the staircase. A striped chaise longue and two butter yellow recliners beckoned, but none of us sat down. Ed put one hand on an upper shelf of a bookcase and looked at the floor.

"Your kidnapping theory," he said finally. "I'm not sure it has much merit."

I stared at Nick. "What kidnapping theory?"

"Hon, we're handling it," he said. He squeezed my shoulder.

I looked from him to Ed and back again. My head was going into a frenzy. "What do you mean, kidnapping? Somebody took Tristan for money?"

Nick put his hand up and closed his eyes.

"*What?*" I said to Ed.

"Look," Nick said, "I mentioned to Detective Malone that I've had threats from some of the people in that last layoff. I didn't take it seriously at the time—"

"What kind of threats?" I said. "Did they threaten to take Tristan?"

"No, of course not."

"Then why—"

Once more Nick closed his eyes, the way he did when he was

about to end a discussion with Max. "Asked and answered," he would say to her. "We're done." An unfamiliar thread of irritation wound around my spine.

"I've been asking around," Nick said. "Apparently there was talk—guys having a couple of beers down at Huey's—one-upping each other on how they were going to take me out." He sighed at me. "I didn't want to get you even more upset. I just thought it was worth looking into, so I gave Ed some names."

"We're following up on all of them," Ed said. "So far they have firm alibis and nothing to link them to Tristan's disappearance. You haven't received a ransom note or a call, anything like that."

I snapped my face toward Nick. He shook his head.

"If you do, you'll let us know."

It wasn't a question. Nick gave him an almost imperceptible nod.

"If it's warranted, we'll bring the FBI in." Ed looked at me. The sun attempting to slant its way through the closed blinds showed tiny lines at the corners of his eyes. They were, I noticed for the first time, green and gold, almost translucent, calm and honest. I hoped he wasn't just trained to look that way.

"You don't think she was kidnapped," I said. "I mean, not like Nick's talking about."

"No, I don't." He looked quickly at Nick. "But we do want to offer you the opportunity to make a public statement for the press. We're going to look into what the Kalidimos girl said about the kid who hung around the fries shop, but you going on camera might provide us with more leads. We really don't have much right now."

"That girl's holding back," Nick said.

Of course she is, I thought. *You scared her to death.*

The thought surprised me, and I consciously banished it. We were both tied in miserable, frustrated knots, struggling to get free of the panic and the unthinkable visions. I was paralyzed. Nick was lashing out. We were now people we'd never had to be before, and we couldn't be blamed for floundering.

"The chief's ready to set up a press conference as soon as you agree."

"Yeah, okay," Nick said. "I guess I have to try everything."

Ed tilted his head at me. Even in my bewildered state, I'd figured out that mannerism meant he was about to tell me something hard.

"Not just Nick," he said. "It would really be effective if you talked too, Mrs. Soltani. Nothing long—just a few words."

"Why?" Nick said.

Ed kept his eyes on me. "Your emotional state is going to get people's attention, make them want to help. They won't be able to get you—or Tristan—out of their minds."

"I don't know." Nick put his hand on the back of my neck, the way he did when we were crossing a street or strolling down the beach and a sand crab skittered over my foot. "Hon, you're already under so much stress."

"It's up to you," Ed said. He was still looking at me. "I'll give the chief the word and let you know when. Probably do it right out there in the parking lot next to your driveway."

When Ed let himself out, Nick steered me to the chaise longue, hand still hugging the back of my neck. I sat down and pulled the yellow shawl from the chaise around my shoulders. Nick squatted in front of me and coaxed my hair off my forehead with his fingers.

"I didn't mean for you to be blindsided by the kidnapping thing," he said. "I thought you had enough to handle."

"The detective just said he doesn't think it *is* a kidnapping. Unless you're holding out on me, we don't have the kind of money kidnappers ask for." I tried to smile.

Nick ran a knuckle down my cheek. "You have firsthand knowledge on the going rate for ransoms?"

"I saw that Mel Gibson movie," I said.

We exchanged weak grins, and for a moment things were just as they'd been twenty-four hours before. But the effort was exhausting. I sagged against the back of the chaise longue and drew the shawl around me. Nick brushed his lips across mine before he stood up and rubbed his palms on the sides of his slacks, leaving damp smudges on the khaki.

"I know what Ed said, but I still think we need to keep constant watch over Max. Not leave her alone for a minute. We'll make a bed for her in our room tonight."

"But if Tristan wasn't kidnapped—"

"Just let me deal with this, Serena." Nick's face darkened as if he were holding back frustration with a leash. His phone went off like an alarm, and he snarled a hello.

I sat with shawl fringe entrapped in my fingers and watched him close his eyes and murmur "uh-huh" until the snarl and the darkness retreated and left him gray. He put a hand over the phone and whispered to me, "I'm sorry, hon. We'll talk, okay?"

We squeezed hands, and he left the library, phone pressed to his ear. His footsteps faded upward on the stairs. I felt another rush of doubt that set me once again pacing in my cage.

Ed called as the Mentoring Moms were packing up to leave. The press conference was set for the next morning at nine.

"You want me here?" Lissa said to me. She put her hand on my arm. "I could at least help you pick out something to wear." She cringed. "That sounded so shallow, Serena. I'm sorry. I just have no idea what you need to hear, you know?"

"As soon as I figure it out, I'll tell you," I said. I gave her the last smile I had. She left looking almost transparent, the tears and the pity and the fear shivering just beneath the surface. She put her arm around Justin and buried her fingers in the wet spikes of his red hair as they headed for the door.

Every other mother who had heard our story that day was, I knew, watching her children, devouring the little world around them with her eyes and seeing them as fragile eggs. There would be cuddling in front of the television that night. Quiet talks at bedtime about the dangers of strangers. Tiptoed walks into bedrooms in the wee hours to make sure their precious ones were warm and peaceful and still there.

I wished I were one of those mothers.

It was another almost sleepless night. Nick insisted that we go to bed and at least rest. I lay there listening to Max breathe the deep, even sleep that only a ten-year-old can achieve. She was curled up on the love seat in our reading nook, and Nick lay on the side of our bed closest to her, taut as an unspent spring. He dozed off, but his sleep was so light and fitful, I tried to stay perfectly still and not disturb him.

Before she left that day, Rebecca told me the congregation would be holding an all-night vigil at the church. Several times during the bleakest hours of predawn morning I considered joining them.

The candles would be spreading their light like little Christs. The familiar beeswax smell, the warm hands of friends in a circle, the God-trusting voices—they would all offer comfort. It was the same kind of comfort I had provided for other people. Lissa when her grandmother had died. Rebecca when Isaiah was diagnosed with asthma. Tristan when she wasn't chosen to play Clara in *The Nutcracker* ballet. Those were the times I'd considered my prayer life and my commitment to God to be the most ripe and whole, as if it had to be enough for all of us.

But it seemed to be shriveling up. Over and over that night I turned to God and saw only a tsunami of terror coming for me. I whispered, "Father, please…" and got no further. All I heard were my own desperate thoughts screaming their what-ifs at me.

It was hard to hope that the prayers being lifted for us that very moment would bring Tristan home. Hope itself was too dangerous to pray for, and as I faced the dark predawn, I realized one of the reasons why.

For the first time, I was afraid God would say no.

Chapter Five

I was standing in my walk-in closet the next morning, staring blindly at my wardrobe, when Nick took me by the elbow and steered me back to bed and made me lie down.

"There isn't going to be a press conference," he said.

"I don't understand," I said.

He put an arm up on the bedpost. "All the press is after is a story. I don't want you up there being stared at like a zoo animal. Lissa told me the kind of stuff they were asking yesterday when they thought she was you, and I don't think that's going to bring Tristan home."

I lay stiff, looking up at him. A guttural sound I'd never heard myself make before escaped from my throat.

"Come on, hon," he said. "Cry, scream, whatever you have to do. It's just us here now."

I couldn't. Anxiety surged through me and left me wilted. I wanted Nick to hold me so it couldn't come back, and I put my arms up.

"I don't think a big press conference is a good idea," he said into my hair. "Malone thinks he knows what he's doing, but he doesn't know you." He put his hands on the sides of my head and tilted it toward him, searching my face as if I, too, were about to disappear. "Your job right now is to stay as calm as you can, for Max. She needs her mom strong. If she sees you coming apart, what's going to hold her together? Look—"

There was a light tap on the bedroom door. "That detective wants to talk to you guys," Max said in a raspy whisper.

"We'll be right down," Nick said. "Who's with you?"

"Right this very second, nobody. I gave my bodyguard a coffee break."

I started for the door, but Nick held on to me. "Serena," he said, "we're going to find her. Focus on Max. Please, hon."

I nodded. And then my mind raced straight to Tristan. Right now, maybe somehow, somewhere she was staring at her own picture on a TV screen. Maybe she was waiting for me to appear and plead for her return. Maybe the press conference Nick said we shouldn't do would give her something to hold on to.

"Please," I whispered. I just didn't know to whom.

If Ed Malone was disappointed that we weren't doing the press conference, he didn't show it. He said putting Tristan's picture on the news was having the desired effect. The police station had reported several calls already.

"Nothing much to go on yet," he said, "but it's still early."

He left with Nick to meet with two FBI agents and get their take on the possible kidnapping angle. Max reported from her post at the foyer window that the same cop from yesterday was out there in his car.

"What is he, twelve?" Aunt Pete said as she peered out the window. Then she went back to dusting the entire house with pink chenille.

Another detective, younger and, according to Max, geekier than Ed Malone, brought a copy of the flier they were distributing. I stood in the middle of the foyer and stared back at the girl who smiled from the page.

She couldn't have been Tristan. She had my daughter's bashful smile, her wide eyes, the wisps of hair that danced across her forehead. This girl lowered her chin the way my daughter did. But she couldn't be Tristan, not with the words in bold type beneath her picture: **Have You Seen This Child?**

The "pedigree information" was listed—her height, her weight, her Boardwalk Fries uniform. There was no mention of her bell of a laugh or the way she pirouetted across the kitchen or how much she loved mustard on a hot pretzel. If this girl was my Tristan, how could they find her without knowing those things?

"Jody Johnstone just called," Christine said. She'd materialized beside me, clipboard in hand. "She's mobilized a group of moms and daughters to help distribute fliers."

"I wanna go!" Max said.

"Over your father's dead body," Aunt Pete said. She was at the top of the stairs, polishing the railing.

I put an arm around Max and nudged her toward the living room. She flopped into one of the armless chairs, limbs sprawled.

"You guys always said if anybody ever stole *me*, they'd bring me right back, so I don't know what you're worried about."

"What makes you think we're afraid somebody's going to steal you?" I said in a too-high voice.

Max rolled her eyes. "I'm not a moron." She pulled her knees to her chest and stretched her shirt down to her toes. I realized she was wearing one of Tristan's tees. The one with Baryshnikov on it.

"Nobody's gonna take me, Mom. I'd kick and scream and bite. You know, be my usual charming self."

She grinned. I sat on the couch and held out my arms to her, and she came to me and curled up in my lap. She was solid in my hug, such a different feel from Tristan. The willowy Tristan who only two days ago had seemed to turn into a woman before my eyes. Now that loss of little-girlness made her look even more vulnerable in my mind, too fragile for whatever she was headed for.

We had been talking about her hair that night. That alone had nearly moved her to tears. I couldn't bear to think of her coping with anything worse. I couldn't bear it.

"I don't see why we can't at least go down to the beach," Max was saying. "You can watch me, and"—she leaned closer—"who's gonna come near us with Aunt Pete there? You gotta admit she's pretty scary looking."

"I heard that," Aunt Pete called from the kitchen.

Max concealed a grin with her hand.

"The kid's got a point." Aunt Pete appeared in the doorway, wiping her hands on the bathrobe. "We can watch her down on the beach as easy as we can in the house. Junior out there can stand guard instead of sleeping in that patrol car like he's doing now." She nodded toward the thumb I was gnawing. The nail was long gone, the cuticle bleeding. "If we don't get out of this place, we're all three gonna go batty."

I squeezed Max, anticipating something like "You're already gone, Aunt P." coming out of her mouth.

"Nick was pretty clear on our staying inside," I said.

"No, he wasn't," Max said. "He said to watch me like a hawk and stay by the phone. He didn't say it couldn't be the *cell* phone."

"Little pitchers have big ears," Aunt Pete said. "I'll pack a picnic."

"I'm not hungry," Max said quickly. She leaped from my lap. "Let's just go."

The young policeman was summoned. His name, Christine told us when she arrived to man the home phone, was Frankie Bales.

Aunt Pete loaded herself up with her personal beach chair, a thermos of her undrinkable iced tea, and the woven turquoise bag the size of a mail satchel that she spent most of her time on the beach digging through as if the secrets of the universe lay in the bottom.

I'd wondered several times that summer how Aunt Pete had ever managed when she and her husband, the legendary Uncle Hank Bernardi, used to travel. They'd never had children, which Max had pointed out to me was probably a good thing or she would have killed them with her cooking. Until Uncle Hank's death two years before, they had spent the years after his retirement "doing" every tourist attraction on four continents. She had sent us postcards that said variations of "We did the Louvre, Versailles, and the Eiffel Tower this morning. We'll do the Left Bank this afternoon." When Uncle Hank had died of a sudden massive heart attack at age eighty-two, Africa, South America, and Antarctica were left undone.

I didn't know Aunt Pete or Uncle Hank well back then; the postcards and boxes of magnets and T-shirts and salt and pepper shakers
shaped like English phone booths and Japanese pagodas were my only
contact with them. Most of what I knew of them came from Nick's
stories of his childhood. Back then, Uncle Hank owned two movie
theaters in Philadelphia and made sure Nick came up to visit from
Bethany Beach at least once a month to see as many showings of the
current films as he wanted and to consume popcorn and Milk Duds
until he was bloated or threw up, whichever came last. Aunt Pete did
the books and ordered the candy and generally minded the more mun-
dane aspects of the movie theater business. According to Nick, she also
minded everyone else's business. She hadn't lost her touch for that.

"You're going out too far!" she yelled at Max. She jabbed me with
her elbow. "She's going out too far, Serena."

Max was about two yards from shore with her back to us, dancing
in front of a wave and tugging one side of her polka-dotted bathing
suit down over her bottom only because she knew I'd be looking. Max
herself never cared that her suit stayed in a permanent wedgie. As we
watched, she plunged into the wave, headfirst, and swam out to con-
quer the next one.

I could almost see her out there at age four, when Nick taught her
and Tristan, then ten, how to ride the waves. Nick would stand before
the oncoming surf, a hand holding on to the back straps of their
bathing suits.

"This one, Daddy!" Max had squealed that first day.

"No!" Tristan cried. "It's too big!"

"Not big enough!" Nick said. He lifted them both above the wave with their slippery legs dangling in the air. Tristan's giggle rang on the breeze like a tiny bell.

"We have to wait for just the right one," Nick had told them. "And here it comes. Ready?"

"Yes!" Max squealed.

"No!" Tristan cried.

"Swim!" Nick shouted. "Swim till I tell you to stop!"

He swam between them as the girls wriggled through the water, Max free as a little fish, Tristan in a rhythm schooled by hours of swimming lessons. I stood up on the beach, shielding my eyes with my hand and assuring myself that Nick wouldn't let them drown. My babies looked so small out there—

"Okay, let go and ride it in!" Nick called to them.

Max let the wave carry her all the way to the shore, where her chunky little form bounced in a gale of giggles. Tristan stuck her arms out in front of her, straight and stiff. As she skimmed closer, I saw that her face was taut with the effort to get it just right.

I closed my eyes now. I could hear her chirping, "Was that good, Daddy?" I could smell her delicious concoction of sunblock and Lifesavers and cucumber-melon shampoo.

The only thing I couldn't do was ask her, "Tristan, baby girl, where are you?"

Now Max rode a breaker in, sliding over the soaked sand on her belly, and proclaimed, "Yes!"

"You were out too far," Aunt Pete said. She went back to rummaging through the woven bag and emerged with a huge, floppy-brimmed red hat. She situated it on her head and dug in again for the sarong she'd bought when she and Uncle Hank "did" New Delhi. It was as inevitable on the beach as the chenille bathrobe was in the house.

Max flung herself down on her knees in the soft part of the sand, lower legs splayed out behind her at forty-five-degree angles, and dug with a vengeance.

"Another sandcastle," Aunt Pete said. "I don't know why she keeps building them. Some jerk always comes along and ruins them."

"I don't know, either," I said. My hope was slipping again. I told myself it was from sleeping for only two hours just before dawn. But even as I clutched my cell phone between both hands, the hope of Tristan's calling was dwindling to nothing.

What would she say at this point? I'd already ruled out "Mom, I'm sorry. I did something stupid." And "Mom, please come get me. I'll never do this again." I couldn't allow myself to think "Mom, I'm okay. They haven't hurt me." Or "Mom, please do everything they say, or they'll do something terrible to me."

Tristan wouldn't be able to say those words anyway. If she *had* been abducted, the terror of it would have jolted her into shock. She would be doing what I wanted to do—shut down, close in, block out. She'd be mummified by fear.

I sat straight up and tried to breathe. I'd never known panic could be suffocating. But then I'd never felt panic like this before.

"Hey, Mom," Max called from the hole she was now thigh-deep in.

"Hay is for horses," Aunt Pete said. She produced a *People* magazine and an industrial-sized bottle of sunscreen from the bag.

"No, look." Max pointed toward the south end of "our" beach. "It's that Mylanta girl."

"Mylanta?" Aunt Pete said. "What are you talking about, child?"

Aylana. It was Aylana, standing on the other side of the fence with Officer Frankie. He beckoned me over with his hand, which was entirely unnecessary because I was already halfway there.

The sun glinted from Aylana's eyebrow ring and her earrings and the chain below her waist that followed the dangerous plunge of her white shorts. Her halter top was little more than a nod to the American custom of covering essential body parts on the beach. Officer Frankie was the color of a radish, and he kept his eyes fixed on me.

"Sorry for the interruption, Mrs. Soltani," he said. His voice squeaked into soprano range.

"It's okay," I said. "She's a friend."

As if to prove it, Aylana put her cheek next to mine. "I want to talk to you alone," she whispered.

"You need me?" Officer Frankie said. By now he could barely speak at all. Any other time, my imp-self would have wondered which was the bigger favor to him, having him stay or sending him away.

"We're okay," I said.

I glanced behind me. Aunt Pete was standing over Max, who appeared to be completely absorbed in the sandcastle. Neither of them was fooling me.

Aylana looked toward the house. "Her father isn't here, is he?"

"Tristan's father?" I said. "No—"

"Good. There is something I need to tell you, and I don't want him to hear. He's violent, your husband."

"He's just a little bit cranky right now," I said. That couldn't have sounded more ridiculous, I knew. It was just my automatic response when Nick snapped at one of the girls or Max pouted at the dinner table or Donald Rumsfeld cut somebody off at a news conference.

Nick had obviously redefined the word *cranky* for Aylana. "He scared me," she said. "I was afraid to tell what I know."

I felt myself going still. "What do you know?"

"That boy, the one I said comes just for fries—"

"What? What about him?"

"He came a lot. I mean, a *lot*." She shook her head, ponytail swinging. "I lied before. Fries, no fries—he came to talk to *her*. I told her he *liked* her. You know, he was *interested* in her, and at first, no, she said there was no way, all those things, because she doesn't know how beautiful she is."

"At first," I said. My lips barely parted to speak. I was afraid if I moved, some vital piece of this would fall away and be lost.

"He was into her," she went on. "He wasn't giving up, kept asking her to go on break with him, go on break. And finally one night she did."

"She left with him?"

"Just for fifteen minutes."

I wanted to tell her she was hallucinating. At the very least she was making it up. But I said, "When was that?"

Aylana toyed with a hoop earring and gazed at the sand. Her face was lit up, as if she were enchanting me with a fairy tale.

"Not very long after she started to work there," she said finally. "Maybe two weeks."

"So this was three months ago?" I said. Hope dropped out of sight once more. "If it was that long ago, then he probably didn't have anything to do with Tristan's disappearance."

Aylana's brows drew together as if I'd just missed the point of the story entirely. "He didn't go away after that. Tristan came back the first night that she went with him, eyes all shiny, smiling in that way."

"What way?"

She touched my elbow. "That way you looked at your husband when you were young and in love."

"In *love?*"

"This is a surprise to you." Aylana nodded. "Tristan told me her father wouldn't let her date. She wasn't *exactly* dating him. I don't think so. She just spent her breaks with him."

"Tristan?" I said. "Are you *sure?*"

"Oh, yes."

I pressed my temples with my fingertips. Images flashed, foreign images—Tristan leaning over the counter, smiling coyly at a stranger; Tristan slipping out the side door of Boardwalk Fries and lacing her fingers through his as they stole down the steps; Tristan running to meet him on the boardwalk Thursday night and disappearing into some dark corner of his life. Even in my mind, she was no one I recognized.

"You okay?"

I opened my eyes. "You're sure?" I said. "Inga and Yuri never mentioned him. Her best friend didn't tell me."

"No one else knew," Aylana said. "I only guessed because I know about these things."

"Who is he?"

Aylana looked startled, as if she was realizing for the first time that this was not once upon a time, that it might not be happily ever after.

"I don't know his name for sure."

She glanced down at my hand, which was currently squeezing her arm. I didn't know how it had gotten there, and I didn't let go.

"She said his name sometimes when he teased her, but it wasn't a real name. It was something he was called—"

"A nickname?" I said.

"Yes! It began with…" She made a hissing sound. "Scooter. Snake. No. I can't remember!"

She put her hand over mine. Her eyes were enormous and pleading. "I am so sorry. It was innocent, I thought."

"So he didn't seem dangerous to you? Not threatening?"

"No, no! He was…" She pulled gently away and held her hands out from her face as if she were shaping an aura. "Dark sometimes. Then sometimes not. What do you call that?"

"Moody?" I said.

She snapped her fingers. "Right. Guys are like that, but he was more."

"You said you didn't know what he looked like, but do you really?"

Aylana deflated. "No. I never looked at him close. He was not my type, you know? Too skinny. Too much lips. And"—she leaned in—"he used bleach on his hair. I hate that."

I did too. I hated everything about him.

"Please," I said, "will you tell the detective all this?" I saw her hesitation. "Please. We have to find her."

I covered my mouth, and she folded her arms around me, the scantily clad girl with the eyebrow ring who knew a secret my daughter hadn't told me.

"I'll help," she said.

When Ed Malone arrived to question Aylana, Nick wasn't with him. He didn't get home until both of them were gone. By then, I was actually dozing on the family-room couch. Some of the anxiety had ebbed away when Ed told me that even though a secret boyfriend whose nickname started with an *S* didn't give them much to go on, they would follow up. The space that a piece of hopelessness left filled up with fatigue too big to deny. Nick found me just on the edge of a nap.

"Don't go waking her up, Nicky," I heard Aunt Pete say.

"I'm not asleep." I propped up on an elbow. Nick strode across the room and dragged one of the wicker chairs closer to the couch. His face was pinching something back.

"What?" I said.

"Aunt Pete told me about Aylana."

"It could be a good thing, couldn't it?" I said.

"We don't even know if it's true."

I blinked at him. He ran the telltale hand down the back of his head. "Hon, why didn't you call me before you brought Malone back over here to question her again?"

"I don't understand."

"You're already upset. Then the girl shows up again with this story about Tristan having a boyfriend." He stopped to crinkle his face in disbelief. "I wish you'd called me first."

I could only stare at him.

"From now on, let's discuss things." He kissed my forehead and then dropped himself against the back of the chair. The weariness was palpable. "Is this really happening, Serena?"

Judging from the fear that was once again pressing down on me, I had to say yes.

The rest of the afternoon and evening held enough distractions to keep me from flattening completely. Tristan's dance teacher brought over a larger-than-life homemade card from the girls in the studio. An older couple from church delivered a bushel each of corn and toma-toes. Ring-to-ring phone calls offered everything from prayers to tranquilizers.

But the quiet of the night was brutal. Around 4:00 a.m. it finally beat me into an exhausted sleep, riddled with dreams of a hissing boy with huge lips and Tristan dressed in Aylana's halter top and Nick telling Rebecca to hit me over the head with the cast-iron skillet if I wasn't asleep in twenty minutes. Just as the frying pan was coming at me, I sat straight up in bed and cried out, "I can't help it! I can't sleep until she comes home!"

There was no one there to argue with me. Slats of sunlight striped the hardwood floor, and the clock winked a digital 9:15. Propped against it was a note:

Hon, we've gone to church. You needed to sleep. You're safe—someone's watching the house.

Nicky

I touched the paper, touched the pillow where his head had been. His troubled head. He'd muttered things in his sleep before I finally drifted off, and although I couldn't decipher the words, the threatening tone was more than clear. I'd seldom heard Nick go beyond "a little bit cranky." He gritted his teeth at times, tightened his jaw muscles, and then he usually dug in for the fix. Nothing was worth yelling about or punching at when a solution was just a calm thought away.

That wasn't working for Nick now. My usual smile and reduction to "just a little bit scary" wasn't working for me, either. Alien tactics were rising up in both of us.

As alien as some part of Tristan now was. If Aylana was telling the truth, my daughter must know how to talk to a boy and how to make fifteen minutes with him put a glow on her face. That was hard to fathom.

Just three years before, when Tristan was barely thirteen, she'd climbed off the bus one day, puffy eyed and silent. All the way home from the bus stop, I tried to coax out of her what was wrong, but she wouldn't even confess to being upset, as if I might have somehow missed her spine curved miserably into a question mark and the vulnerable looseness around her mouth. I found her sobbing in her room an hour later.

"I hate boys," she said.

This was nothing new. Boys had been tormenting her since kindergarten with their nose picking and their alphabet burping and their armpit noise making. There had been several traumas over pre-adolescent males who wouldn't cooperate on group projects and who laughed high and silly when she practiced en pointe on the playground. But she'd never carried on like this before.

"Why do we hate boys today?" I said. I motioned for her to roll over so I could rub her back.

"They won't leave me alone, especially Ian."

"What's he doing?"

"Writing me notes. Following me around. *Talking* to me all the time."

"That jackal," I said.

"Mo-om, I'm serious!" Tristan flipped herself over to face me, and I stifled a grin.

"Is he being mean?" I said.

She flattened her hands, fingers spread jazz style against the bedspread and gave an exasperated sigh. "No! But he's being weird." She came up on her elbows, brown eyes large as moons. "He's all 'Do you like me?' and 'Do you want to go out?'" The eyes grew wider. "Honest, Mom, I didn't do anything to make him do that. I know I'm not allowed to like boys. And I *so* don't!"

"Honey, we never said you couldn't like boys."

"Daddy did. He said they were all absurd little creeps and to stay away from them."

I had to work at not laughing. "Daddy was kidding, baby girl. You can't date, but, honey, you're precious. Why wouldn't some boy like you?"

"He can't!" she cried. And then her wonderful, wide-open face crumpled into pubescent agony. "I don't know what to do about it!"

"You don't have to do anything," I said. "Just be your nice, sweet self, okay?"

There hadn't been any complaints about Ian after that. Jessica went boy crazy the next year, and I heard references from her to this hottie and that loser. Tristan told her more than once in my presence to give it a rest.

It was painful to think that something, or someone, had changed her mind.

The bed was suddenly a mattress of tacks again. I climbed out and pulled on Capris and a top before I pushed aside the sheers at our reading-nook window to see who was "watching the house." Ed Malone looked up from a newspaper he appeared to be reading standing up. He lowered one foot from the parking lot curb and waved. I waved back and pointed downstairs.

I met him on the side porch with two cups of coffee. Nick had obviously beaten Aunt Pete to the pot because it was several shades lighter than mud. Ed took one cup and smiled sheepishly down at his cutoff sweat shorts and sleeveless T-shirt. At one time it had probably said "Bethany Beach" on the front, but the letters were cracked and disintegrating into faded blue confetti.

"I'm off-duty," he said. "I was out taking a bike ride and thought I'd let the uni take off. He was here all night."

"Uni?" I said.

"Uniformed officer." Ed gave me a sad look. "I guess you haven't had much reason to learn police lingo, have you?"

"I've never even had a speeding ticket."

He put his fist softly to his mouth. There was no wedding ring, but I asked anyway, "Do you have kids?"

"No. I can't come close to imagining what you folks are going through."

His eyes belied that. I suspected that even now they were drawing up a pretty clear image of our agony. Especially when he once again tilted his head.

"What?" I said.

He set the mug on the porch railing and leaned, ankles crossed. "Mrs. Soltani—"

"Serena."

"Serena. Look, I want to make sure you know we're still treating Tristan's disappearance like an abduction." I looked down into the blackness of my coffee. "The good news is—"

My head came up, and he winced. *Good* was obviously too strong a word.

"I don't want to give you false hope," he said. "But we did find out when we canvassed the boardwalk again that every lifeguard on the eastern shore has a nickname."

"What's the bad news?" I said.

He smiled at me. "It's not that bad. So far nobody on the Bethany Beach squad has a nickname that starts with *S*, but this isn't the only beach. He could be from Ocean City, Fenwick—"

"And that could be why Aylana didn't know him," I said.

Ed grinned again. I noticed this time that his two front teeth overlapped slightly. "Yeah, I get the feeling she's pretty much checked out every male in this territory."

My eyes stung. "I hope you don't think that about Tristan. It's hard for us to believe she even had *one* boyfriend."

"Here's the deal," he said. "I've spent the better part of the last forty-eight hours with the Soltanis. I think I have a pretty good feel for your family. You're not parents who raised"—his lips twitched— "an Aylana."

I tried to say "thank you," but my throat had closed off.

"It's okay," he said.

It seemed impossible that the workweek could start without a trace of Tristan.

Not a call. Not a scrap of a clue. Max wanted to know why nobody had asked for Tristan's comb or her toothbrush so they would have her DNA.

"Where does she get this stuff?" Nick asked me Monday morning as we sat at the kitchen bar while Aunt Pete charred the bacon.

"She might be watching just a bit too much TV right now," I said.

Nick nodded. "Poor kid. I guess there isn't much to do when you're ten and you can hardly go outside."

"Which is ridiculous," Aunt Pete said. She rapped her knuckles on the window. "We've got Junior staked out in the parking lot and that detective hovering around like Sherlock Holmes. Why can't one of them give us an escort?" She walked back to the stove, eyes squinting down to nothing. "I've got half a mind to stick Maxine in sunglasses and a wig and at least take her down the boardwalk—"

"*No* boardwalk," Nick said.

Aunt Pete turned and shoved the bacon around in the pan. Nick stared at his hands.

Shortly thereafter he left to check in at the office and make sure things were taken care of. I promised three times to call him on his cell phone if anything at all came up before he got back. As he drove away, I secretly wished I had somewhere to go, some activity that would keep me sane. There was nothing to do but wait.

Aunt Pete, however, had other ideas. Around nine, she folded the newspaper with a vengeance and said, "Nobody told me *I* couldn't leave the house." She disappeared into her room and came down twenty minutes later wearing the red hat and the sarong with a Phillies T-shirt and carrying the ubiquitous woven bag.

"Where are you going?" I said.

"I don't know," she said. "I just know it's not here."

Max was still asleep. The laundry was folded Rebecca-neat in drawers. We had enough prepared meals to last us until Halloween. No horizontal plane in the house had ever been so dust free. I was about to take another dive into panic when someone knocked on the front door. I peeked out, Max-style, to see Officer Frankie with a woman who looked vaguely familiar. Since every new face was a possibility, I whipped open the door.

It took me a full ten seconds to realize the woman was Hazel, from Thursday night's moms' meeting. It seemed to take her equally long to recognize me.

"Geez," she said, "you look terrible."

Officer Frankie straightened his shoulders, his pimpled face already on its way to scarlet. He looked a little bit huffy.

"It's okay," I said to him.

He looked doubtfully at Hazel as I let her in.

"I'd feel *real* protected by Officer Clearasil there," she said, jerking her thumb toward the closed door. She sounded as if she'd smoked a pack of Marlboros already that morning. The blue-against-leather eyes scanned what she could see of the house and came back to me.

"I read it in the paper this morning," she said. "Have you flipped out yet? I'd have flipped out."

"I can't flip out," I said.

She surveyed me for a long moment. "I highly recommend it," she said. "Looks like you've got all your emotions stuffed into those carry-on bags under your eyes."

I heard myself laugh. It was a pale, wan rendition of my Marlene Dietrich guffaw, but it was the first one that had come out of me since the last time I'd talked to Hazel. Ten minutes before I had discovered my daughter was gone.

"You want some coffee?" I said.

At first Hazel turned down my offer. "The brood's out in the car," she said.

"They can come in," I said, trying to remember how many children she'd reported having. She must have told us that night; she'd shared everything else about her life.

"You got a yard?" she said. She gazed around at the foyer. "They could trash this place in about seven seconds."

I was about to give her an automatic "They can't hurt anything in here" when a horn blared from the direction of the parking lot, too long and obnoxious to be a car alarm.

"I'm about to bust some behinds," Hazel said and flung open the front door.

I stood on the porch while she marched to an ancient Suburban that might once have been red. It was now a milky pink in the places where rust hadn't eaten it away. Officer Frankie was bent at the waist, peering in and knocking on the driver's side window. I could just make out a bouncing brown shape behind the wheel.

"Hey, knock it off!" Hazel yelled. "Or so help me I'll take you down."

I thought at first she was talking to Officer Frankie until she all but shoved him out of the way and yanked the door open, releasing a metal-on-metal screech and a small, mocha-colored boy who bolted across the parking lot.

"Grab him, would you?" Hazel hollered at Officer Frankie. Her inflection implied that he should have foreseen the child's escape and been ready with the SWAT team.

She had her hands full with the two who erupted from the second seat—a chunky nine-ish boy with spikes of hair I was sure Hazel had colored from her own bottle and a frighteningly thin preadolescent girl in Raggedy Ann tresses whose legs seemed to sprout directly out of her neck like a three-year-old's drawing.

"Don't let those dogs out," Hazel growled at them. But two lanky

Irish setters spilled onto the parking lot, rolled entangled in each other several times, and shook free to chase the little horn honker as he made for the beach with Officer Frankie in hot pursuit.

Yes, Hazel, I thought, *I do have a yard. But I don't think it's big enough.*

She turned to me, one hand clamped around the blond tank-shaped boy she had secured under her arm, the other poised to smack the almost nonexistent behind of the girl.

"You can change your mind about that coffee," she said.

I considered it. Watch a junior wrecking crew demolish my backyard? Or spend the day shoving my fears into corners until one of them finally sprang loose and mauled me? It didn't take much for me to make a decision.

Not that there was much of one to make. When Officer Frankie tackled the getaway child at the top of the steps leading to the beach, the setters, seeing that they were no longer vital to the rescue, took a hard left and floated like deer over our privacy fence. I heard two splashes.

"You got a pool?" Hazel said. She was now at the bottom of the porch steps, squirming offspring still in tow.

"We do," I said.

"Then they're in it. You're gonna have to call the Humane Society if you want them out. I got no control over those two."

I wasn't sure which two she was talking about. The girl and the chunky boy she currently had in headlocks were struggling to get loose. The boy gnawed on Hazel's forearm.

We got everyone into the backyard, and I sent Officer Frankie to his patrol car with a sack of muffins from one of the several Rubbermaid containers in our recently overstocked pantry. By then, Max had stumbled downstairs, and she stood, gaping, at the top of the back-porch steps.

Tristan's T-shirt, which Max hadn't taken off for two days, hung off one shoulder and down to her knees. She shook the hair that suffered from terminal bed-head and ventured down the steps on bare tiptoes. She craned her neck toward the pool, where the two red dogs were doing laps.

"Shut *up!*" she said. "Can I swim with them?"

The question was obviously meant for me, but before I could answer, Hazel's girl said, "Sure. They won't hurt you. See?" And she jumped in, fully clothed. Granted, the denim shorts with the two-inch inseam and the spaghetti-strapped tank top didn't necessarily qualify as *fully.* I waved Max toward the pool house before she could do likewise. She emerged seconds later, still pulling on her bathing suit top, and dove headfirst between the two setters.

"I'm goin' in too," the chunky blond boy said and executed a cannonball that nearly emptied the pool.

"You going for it?" Hazel said to the remaining member of the tribe. He took a momentary break from kicking an inflated dolphin and shook his head.

"He's pouting," Hazel said. "I never had a pouter before. Sun's a whiner. Tri's a biter. If the truth's known, I prefer pouters. They're quieter, and they don't draw blood."

"So," I said, "um, their names are Sun and Tri?"

"Yeah, well, Sunrise. She was the one I had in the log cabin. Her father named her that because she was born at dawn." She put up a hand, which, I noticed, had a ring on every finger and one pierced into the pinky nail. "Don't take me there," she said. "Tri's short for Triumph. My second husband was a biker, rode a Triumph 750. I'm glad he didn't have a Harley, or he would have named him Hog. I'm not kidding you."

I was sure she wasn't. I was afraid to ask the third one's name. I'd mentally switched him from Horn Honker to the Terminator. The dolphin now lay limp and shriveled on the deck, and he'd started on the pink turtle. Decapitation was imminent.

"Man, I'm sorry," Hazel said.

"Nobody ever plays with that one anymore anyway," I said.

But Hazel launched herself from the Adirondack chair to snatch the turtle out of the child's hand.

"Knock it off!" she said, just before bopping him on the head with it. "Get in the pool with your brother and sister. I want to see you swim."

The boy slapped his arms into a fold and stuck out his lower lip, brows straining down to meet it. Hazel tugged at one of his cornrows, the color of corn itself. I guessed that husband number three had been African American but that Hazel's genes were as invincible as the rest of her. All three children had her startling blue eyes.

"Okay, Desi," she said to him. "Just sit there, then. Don't have any fun."

"Desi?" I said. "As in Arnaz?"

"Desmond," Hazel said. "I think it's a sissy name." She snorted. "But it was that or Tutu."

I was about to ask why she had let her husbands name her kids, but she pounded her forehead with the heel of her hand.

"Listen to me," she said. "I'm going on about my kids, and you've got one missing."

"Yeah," I said, "I do."

For a few minutes I had let my imp-self nudge in. Fear smacked her aside now with a little help from guilt. How could I have been distracted from thinking about Tristan?

"So what are we doing about it?" Hazel said. "That's why I came by, to see how I can help." She narrowed her eyes at the squeals rising from the pool. "Not doing too much so far, am I?"

Max popped up over the side, with the customary yank of her bathing suit bottom. Her hair was slicked back from her face, her grin like a slice of watermelon. The water that curled down her arms and legs glowed on her skin.

"I'm gonna get our thingies we dive for," she said. "We can see if the dogs'll fetch them."

"They'll fetch anything," Tri bellowed at her.

"Yeah, but we can't throw just anything in," Max said. She was walking backward toward the pool house, shaking her arms out like cooked noodles. "My dad would have a coronary."

As if he weren't already going to have one when he found several pounds of red dog hair clogging up the filter. But as Max darted into the pool house, face alive with a plan, I shook my head at Hazel.

"You're already doing a lot," I said. "You have no idea."

Chapter Six

H azel, I discovered that day, could not sit still. "You need to put me to work," she said after she refilled our coffee cups for the third time.

"I don't know what you could do—"

"For openers I could redo that lame excuse for a flier they're posting. There's too much stuff on it. It needs to pack more of a punch. I'm a graphic artist. I'll give it a go."

"That would be—"

"What I'd really like to do is get a bunch of mothers together and go out and find this kid-snatching psycho ourselves so he doesn't get off on some technicality. If the police nab him, the courts will be all about protecting his rights."

Hazel pushed her bracelets up her arms in the absence of sleeves to roll up for the fight. I couldn't even imagine Hazel in sleeves. She had on a tank top again, which was barely holding her inside it.

"A bunch of us mothers wouldn't care about the dude's rights," she went on. "Who cares if he's a Little League coach or some mental patient that got out of the institution because he'd stopped banging his head for two days?" She patted the pockets of her fatigue green hiking shorts that strained at the seams. "We wouldn't hang around to find out if he was a sociopath who hated his mother so he took it out on you by stealing your kid. We'd take a machete to him first and send him to a shrink later." She patted her pockets again and stood up. "Hey, Sun, you seen my cigarettes?"

"They're in your purse," Sun shouted from the pool. "But you don't need one right now."

"Get off me, kid." Hazel reached for a jungle-print bag and glanced at me. "She hides them from me. Thinks she's gonna get me to quit." She pulled a rhinestone-encrusted case from the bag. "If I tried to quit, they'd be hunting *me* down—for homicide. 'Nicotine Deprived Mother Strangles Children.'" She gave me a pained look. "And now I'm gonna step outside before I get my *other* foot wedged in my mouth."

"You *are* outside," I said.

Hazel panned the newly stained deck, the columned porch, the thickly padded patio furniture, and grunted. "This isn't 'outside.' This is 'gracious outdoor living.'" She shook her head and went out the gate.

I gripped the arms of the Adirondack and pressed my back against its sun-warmed boards. What *would* it feel like to personally rip Tristan from the clutches of one of the sick, heinous monsters Hazel had described? I couldn't conjure up anything more lethal to use than a serrated bread knife, but even that image surged through me with an unfamiliar force. Maybe something would take over and I could rake his face with my fingernails, tear off an ear with the sheer force of maternal instinct, stamp on the hands that had touched my daughter.

But the wave of energy slammed into a wall. Even if that kind of hate was me—and nothing in my beige past had ever indicated that it was—it definitely wasn't God. Not the God I was trying to talk to. Whatever was clamping my hands to the arms of the chair and welding my teeth together wasn't the God I knew. But then neither was the fear or the guilt or the hopelessness that painted over everything else.

So where was He in this? Was He not what I thought He was? And if not, then who was He?

The fact that I even had those questions added to the guilt that was already smothering me.

"You must be drawing out the town kooks," Hazel called from the other side of the gate. "Get a load of this show."

I peeled myself out of the chair and stepped over a prostrate Desmond to join her.

"Isn't Officer Clearasil supposed to keep the freaks away?" Hazel said. "Look at him. He's letting this woman come right to your door." Hazel shoved the bracelets up again. "You want me to take care of it?"

I stood on tiptoe and looked over the gate. Aunt Pete was crossing the driveway, stiff-legged as a stork, sarong threatening to slide off one hip.

"She *is* a kook," I whispered to Hazel. "But she's my husband's great-aunt. She's staying with us."

Hazel slid her sunglasses down her nose to look at me over the top. She must have donned them when she'd gone "outside." Furry leopard fabric covered the frames. "You let her out of the house?" she said.

"She wanted to walk on the beach or something. She was a little bit stir-crazy."

"That's scary." Hazel dropped her cigarette onto the gravel and ground it out with the sole of a tiger-striped flip-flop. "Looks like she found something for you on the beach. Too bad he's a little young. Nice body."

I pushed open the gate and stepped out to where Hazel was standing. She pointed to Officer Frankie, who appeared to be deep in conversation with a tanned young guy in red Bethany Beach lifeguard swim trunks.

"Would you please watch the kids?" I said to Hazel and took the driveway at a jog without waiting for an answer.

"All right, enough with the horsing around in the pool," I heard her yell. "Tri, you drown that dog and I'll drown you."

Officer Frankie nodded at the lifeguard when he saw me. The young male face that turned to me was on the far side of adolescence, jaw cut confidently out of fuzzy teen-ness, cheekbones freshly polished with the cloth of his emerging sexuality. Smooth, muscled arms hung carelessly at his sides, but I saw Tristan in them, pounding on his pectorals, pulling her face from the attack of his lips—

My last flash before I stopped in front of him was the serrated edge of a bread knife.

"This is Mrs. Soltani," Officer Frankie said. He inched toward me, close enough for me to see the muffin crumbs that hung on the buttons of his shirt. "This is Jeff Cousins. Your aunt says—"

"He might know something, Serena," Aunt Pete called from the side porch. "You talk to him. I have to go inside. Some kid ran over my foot with his skateboard. I think he broke my toe." She wiggled her index finger at me. "You talk to the kid."

I looked again at the young man, who was rubbing the side of his nose with his thumb.

"The lady said you were looking for a lifeguard," he said. "Nickname starts with *S*?"

"Do you know one?" I said.

"What's *your* nickname?" Officer Frankie said. He'd taken a wide stance and lowered his voice, but his last syllable squeaked despite his best effort.

"Fried," Jeff said. He gave a self-deprecating smile that covered his cockiness not a whit. "My first summer guarding I refused to use sunblock. I fried the first week and ended up in the hospital." He stopped and wiped his mouth with his palm as if to erase all levity. "Sorry," he said. "I do know a guy that guards down at Fenwick—or he *did*. His name's Spider."

The name crawled across my skin.

"He *did* lifeguard at Fenwick Island?" Officer Frankie said. He hooked his thumbs in his belt and jerked his chin at Fried. "What does *that* mean?"

"It means I heard he's getting fired. He must have ticked off somebody down there." Fried tossed the answer sideways without looking at Frankie. He obviously wasn't impressed with his interrogation skills.

"Ticked 'em off how?"

Fried shrugged. "Probably by being a jerk. He had that down to an art form."

"So you know him?" I said.

"Not any more than I have to. He started hanging out up here this summer. I guess nobody in Fenwick Island wanted to have anything to do with him. I was at a couple of parties he came to up here, and I'm like, 'Keep this dude away from me, man.' He's the kinda guy I eventually would've taken down. Still might." He twitched his shoulders as if he were gearing up should Spider suddenly appear over the dunes.

I wished he would.

Officer Frankie pawed at his shirt pockets, and for a confused moment I thought he was looking for cigarettes.

"Wait here," he said. "I gotta get my pad."

He trotted heavily toward the patrol car. The dark blob of sweat on Frankie's back stuck his shirt to him like the skin of a plum. Fried fixed a smirk on his mouth.

"Do you know where he is now?" I said. "This Spider?"

"I haven't seen him lately. I never found out his real name. Didn't want to. All I can tell you is, he's not from here."

"Is he mean?" I said. "Do you think he would hurt...a girl?"

Fried's arms suddenly seemed too long for him, and he planted his hands under the opposite armpits.

"I never saw him be violent or nothin' like that," he said. "He's got this obnoxious thing—like he tries to be funny, but all he does is insult people. He acts like he's this macho stud, but I never knew a girl to even go out with him." He tightened his arms. "You think Spider had something to do with your daughter being gone?"

"I don't know what to think," I said.

He glanced toward Officer Frankie, who was hurrying in our direction empty handed. "I saw your daughter at Boardwalk Fries all the time," Fried said. "She was a nice kid. *Is* a nice kid."

He gave me a pained look. Officer Frankie reached us, face neon pink, breathing like the little engine that could.

"Couldn't find my pad," he said. "You should probably talk to Detective Malone anyway." He patted his pockets again. "Cell phone's in the car."

"I'll call him," I said. I pulled my cell from the pocket of my cargo shorts. "As soon as, well, I'll call him."

"You sure?" he said. He puffed out his chest, still panting, and jerked his chin up at Fried.

"Just contact me through Fenwick Beach Patrol." Fried had recovered his superiority and reached out a magnanimous hand to Frankie. "Glad I could help, buddy," he said.

I called Nick as I headed back to the pool. His voice mail picked up almost immediately, informing me seamlessly that he couldn't take my call right now.

Anxiety threatened again, or was it annoyance? He had his phone turned off right *now*?

Okay, stop, I told myself. *He's not getting reception. He's on another call. He's in the bathroom. The kidnappers have taken him too...*

But that particular conclusion didn't have the power it would have had an hour ago. Not with the more disturbing possibility that some person named Spider had lured my child into a web. The thought skittered through me. I tried Maya, Nick's assistant. She said she hadn't seen Nick yet today.

But he'd left the house hours ago.

By the time I let myself back in the gate, Aunt Pete was in the hammock under the overhang with a bag of ice on her foot. Hazel was perched on the edge of a canvas deck chair a few feet away, leaning her forearms on her knees and dangling an unlit cigarette from one hand. Body language told me Aunt Pete was giving her a full report over the constant squeals coming from the pool.

"Well?" they said unanimously. Having met only moments before, they were already speaking in one voice.

I filled them in, detail by detail. Talking kept me from ripping right out of my skin.

"Did you call Malone?" Aunt Pete said.

"Nick wants to handle that," I said. "But I can't reach him."

Hazel looked at me over the tops of her leopard-skin glasses. "I don't get it."

I didn't attempt to explain it to her. My mind was spinning in another direction, which had me punching at my cell phone again.

"You calling Malone?" Aunt Pete said. "Thank heaven."

I shook my head and waited for Aylana to pick up. When the hip-hop version of the *Fiddler on the Roof* song started, I wanted to toss the phone in the pool.

"What gives?" Hazel said.

"I need to talk to Aylana," I said.

"Who?"

Aunt Pete was nodding at me. "See if Spider's the name of the guy who was hitting on Tristan."

"Did you just say 'hitting on'?" Hazel said.

"I'd go down and check it out for you, Serena," Aunt Pete said, "but…" She moved the ice bag to reveal two toes that could have been mistaken for Greek olives.

"Go where?" Hazel said. Actually, it didn't seem to matter where, because she was already standing up. "You want me to go?"

"Boardwalk Fries," I said.

"I'm there. I'll pick up some corn dogs while I'm out. They're all hollering they're hungry."

I shifted my gaze to the pool, where Max and Sun were each astride an Irish setter, and Tri was teetering at the edge with Desmond thrown over his shoulder. I couldn't decipher what Desmond was screaming, but it clearly had nothing to do with food. Aunt Pete and I exchanged glances. Hers read, *Let her leave here without those children, and your name is going to be Mud.*

Snatches of conversations whipped past me on the wind as I wove my way up the boardwalk.

"I'm not paying for that…"

"I bought you three tacos and a cotton candy, and I'm a terrible mother?"

"I don't want to hear it. I told you to wear your shoes."

But the words were almost foreign. They had to be code for something more important, like "I saw Tristan just ten minutes ago having a frozen custard" or "We all have to stop what we're doing and look until we find her. What's a taco when a child is missing?"

The colors shouting "Hawaiian Shaved Ice" and "Exotic Eats" were too loud, the push to get them unreal. I felt as if I could walk straight through the old men with binoculars dangling from their necks and the prep-school boys with iPods hanging from theirs.

The only thing that came into focus was Boardwalk Fries, its cheerful yellow sign mocking me from the corner. And why wouldn't it? The last time I was there, the place had told me that it had failed to protect my daughter and had no information to give me. Until maybe now.

A narrow tunnel of reality opened up. I didn't have a serrated knife, but I had the energy to push myself past all that didn't matter to get to the only thing that did.

The signs above the open counter windows told me I could have lemonade, Popsicles, and frozen drinks, but when Inga greeted me, her face visibly searching for something appropriate to say, I asked for Aylana.

While Inga was getting her, I stared at the closed window to my right until I realized I was looking at Tristan's face as rendered by a school photographer, staring emptily back at me from the police flier. I hadn't even recognized her, because she wasn't where she was supposed to be. She should be on the deck at home, coaxing little Desmond into the water. And Hazel should be watching in amazement.

And I should be explaining that Tristan was wonderful with children, that in the church nursery they practically hopped into her pocket like baby kangaroos, that the very softness of her being was a lullaby in itself.

The pear-smooth arms of a female came around me from behind, and I clutched them, eyes closed, for several seconds before I realized it wasn't my daughter.

"You are so sad," Aylana said. The esses sang like silver. Her cheek was warm against mine. Yet for a moment I hated her because she wasn't Tristan. I turned to face her.

"Was it Spider?" I said.

She stared at me blankly for a few seconds before her eyes sparked. "The lifeguard? Yes!" She pulled both my hands into hers. "His name *is* Spider."

"And he knew Tristan?" I said.

Yuri leaned out the window at the end. "*That* boy?" He shook the coffee can. "He will never leave the tip."

"You mean that guy who was always trying to get Tristan to give him free fries?" Inga said. She stuck a container of said fries on her counter as if the harried-looking father on the other side had made the same brazen request. "He's a creep."

I put my hand up to my mouth.

"Why are we talking about him?" Inga said. "Did he do something? It wouldn't surprise me."

I darted to Inga's counter as the father faded into the buzz behind us.

"Did you see him that night she disappeared?" I said. "Thursday night, did you see him here?"

One fine line appeared between her eyebrows. I put all my hopes into it. But she shook her head.

"No," she said.

Yuri, too, shook his head. I knew if there were anything else they could tell me, they would. I could see that in the longing in their eyes.

At least they had all agreed that Spider was the one. But the one who what? The one who tried to hit Tristan up for illicit french fries? The one who lingered at the counter and—did what? Made rude remarks like Fried said? Tried to impress her with his manufactured machismo?

Or was he the one who had snapped his spidery fingers and made her disappear?

I untangled myself from Aylana and somehow thanked them before I stumbled back up the boardwalk, groping in my pocket for my cell phone. I still got Nick's voice mail and then Maya's. There was no one to whom I could pass on the thin, mean confirmation that might tell us nothing at all and yet might show us everything. I broke into a run and kept my eyes ahead until the white gate to my own backyard was in front of me.

Hazel pulled it open as I reached for it, and I pitched forward, flailing for something to grab, for a place to put my words.

"Spider…he's the same one…and I can't find Nick—"

But I stopped. There was a sudden silence, the kind of stillness only children can achieve when a grownup breaks the trusted adultness and becomes a child herself. A voice called from the pool, a voice that was usually husky and that now stretched thin, as if she'd been betrayed.

"Mom?" Max said. "Are you okay?"

I was already nodding, already frantically gathering up the pieces of myself when I turned to her.

"I'm okay," I lied. "I ran all the way up the boardwalk. I'm just a little bit out of shape."

Tri's head bobbed up beside Max's. "Did you bring us any corn dogs?"

I snapped my fingers. "I knew I forgot something," I said.

"What are we gonna have for lunch, then?" he said.

"You're not gonna starve to death, Tri," Hazel barked from behind me. "Go play."

Amazingly, he did. Through it all, Max didn't take her eyes off me. In their soft, squinty pouches, they were waiting for a better answer.

"I'm finding out more about who...who Tristan knew that we didn't know about...so maybe he can help us."

It was only half-true, and she obviously believed only that much of it. She raised an eyebrow at me.

"What are you going to do?" she said.

"I'm going to call Daddy," I said.

I watched her process that. She finally gave a nod and disappeared under the water.

I tried to walk solidly to the deck chair Hazel had vacated next to the hammock. Aunt Pete tossed the bag of what was now water onto the deck and sat up to glare at me like a barnyard goose.

"You're going to call 'Daddy'?" she said.

"He wants me to—"

"Why don't you just call Ed Malone? We're burning daylight here!"

"Nick told me…"

Aunt Pete leaned forward, eyes down to slits. "For crying out loud, Serena," she said, "can't you even go to the bathroom without asking that man's permission?"

I closed my eyes, and there was Tristan, dragging her nervous, brown-eyed gaze from the glistening pile of fries in their tub on the counter to the moneyless hands of the man-child with spidery fingers.

There is only one choice you can make, Tristan, I wanted to whisper to her.

But to my horror I saw her glancing over her shoulder and sliding the unpaid-for fries toward him. He pushed them aside and wove his fingers through hers. And she let him.

I keyed in Ed Malone's number.

Chapter Seven

Within an hour Ed had Aylana at the Fenwick Island Beach Patrol office looking at photos of their lifeguards. He called to tell me she had picked out Spider without hesitation.

"His real name's Ricky Zabriski," he said. "He hasn't reported for work since he got off Thursday afternoon. The Fenwick police are trying to get a warrant to search the trailer he's been renting."

"Maybe she's there!" I said.

"They've already checked it from the outside. Nobody was around."

Before another hour passed, Ed called again. The kids had started up a game of Marco Polo in the pool, so I took the phone outside the gate and pressed my hand above my eyes to block out the sun, which was blistering everything that couldn't run for cover.

"The place was left like he intended to come back," Ed said. "According to the other lifeguards they questioned, he wasn't one to leave an expensive stereo system and a refrigerator full of Bud Light. We have a call out to bring him in for questioning."

"Do you think—"

"I think it's the first strong lead we've had." Ed's voice still surprised me with its lack of stress. If the words he said couldn't be soft, at least the delivery was. I moved to the side porch and sat on the bottom step next to a pot of geraniums that were mockingly merry.

"The *good* news is," Ed went on, "nobody we've talked to has ever seen him do anything violent. His worst fault seems to be a bloated sense of entitlement."

"Meaning?"

"He wants something for nothing. Thinks the world owes him everything. They're firing him in Fenwick, but nobody seems concerned that he's going to go postal on them or anything."

"But you think he'll be back for his things?"

"We hope so. Fenwick PD will keep watching his place. The AMBER Alert now has his license number and a description of his car: blue '94 Buick. Hard to miss."

A stream of sweat ran down my back, but I couldn't move up into the shade of the porch. I wasn't sure whether it was the humidity or the unsaid part of Ed's report that was making me feel as if I were trapped inside a pillow.

"So what's the *bad* news?" I said.

"Not as bad as it could be. Depends how you look at it." I could see him inclining his head. "In a sense this is good news too, Serena. The possibility is getting stronger that Tristan wasn't taken against her will. That maybe she chose to go off with this guy."

How, I wanted to ask him—wanted to scream at him from the suffocating center of myself—how could something impossible be a possibility?

"I don't think that personally," Ed said, "not after what you've told me about your Tristan. But if she did, there's a better chance that she's not hurt. That has to give you some hope."

I shook my head as if he could see me. I couldn't put faith in something I knew wasn't true.

"It would be hard to accept," he said, "but it would be a whole lot easier than any other scenario. Let me ask you this: do you remember your last conversation with Tristan?"

I'd already been over it at least fifty times in my mind. "We talked about her hair," I said. "She wanted to cut it, and Nick wouldn't let her."

"Did she seem upset?"

"A little, but Tristan's sensitive."

"So, no more upset than usual?"

"No."

"I know this is hard, but can you think back? Did she give you any indication at all that she wasn't going to see you for a while?"

I forced the scene into view yet again. Tristan being quiet, feet propped on the seat. Resigning herself to Nick's no about the haircut. Refusing my offer of ice cream. Assuring me she wouldn't change her mind.

"No," I said. "I told her Nick would be there to pick her up at nine, and that was it."

Until she walked straight from the Blazer to a blue Buick? I thought.

Turning from my child into an unknown young woman as she went? Was
that what had happened?

"No," I said again.

"Okay," Ed said. "Now, I'm just going to put this one more thing
out there, and then I'll leave it alone. In most cases of runaways, when
the situation at home is basically good, the kids return after a few
hours or days." His voice went soft. "I think your home goes way
beyond 'basically good,' don't you?"

"Do four days count as a few?" I winced. I felt as if I'd just betrayed
my daughter by even asking the question.

Ed didn't answer.

"His name is Ricky Zabriski," I told Aunt Pete and Hazel on the back
porch.

"Well, there's your trouble," Hazel said. "With a name like that,
no wonder he's screwed up."

Aunt Pete looked from her to the four children sitting in a line at
the edge of the deck, towels shawled around their shoulders, licking
banana Popsicles. She'd evidently learned the names of Hazel's three.

Hazel nudged me with the side of the hand still holding an unlit
Marlboro. "Whatever his name is," she said, "at least you know it
now. That's something."

"I guess it is," I said. "But we don't know where he is or whether
he's with Tristan or, if he is, what he's doing with her—"

"Who are you talking about?'

My voice broke off as I looked up at Max. She was suddenly beside me, hair plastered back, leaving her face wide open to whatever havoc my answer could wreak on it.

"Nobody, Maxine," Aunt Pete said. "Look, you're dripping your Popsicle all over."

But I shook my head at Aunt Pete and said to Max, "We're talking about a boy Tristan knew that she didn't tell us about."

"No way," Max said.

"Yes, way," I said.

"So he's the one who took her?" Max said.

"Maybe," I said.

"Why?"

I tugged at the towel she was hugging around her. Despite the heat, the sun-browned skin on her legs had erupted in gooseflesh. I couldn't sit there and watch her take on my anguish.

"We don't know, honey," I told her. "Maybe he didn't take her. Maybe she just went with him."

Max tucked in her chin. "You are *not* serious, Mom," she said. "Those cops need to get a major clue, because Tristan *so* did not do that."

I had to smile. Everyone should remain ten years old, where the obvious could be stated and all else dismissed with a roll of the eyes.

Nick had a similar reaction when he called a few minutes later, almost frantically apologetic because his phone battery had gone dead, and I reported to him, word for word, what Detective Malone had told me. I slipped inside the house as his voice threatened to go beyond the boundary of the phone. I could tell Max was listening from where she reclined, head on the flanks of an exhausted Irish setter.

"Malone can just take that runaway theory and put it in the shredder," Nick said. The expected sigh was deep and weary. "You okay, hon?"

"I don't know. If it's true, then she's probably safe, and I can hang on to that, but I know it *isn't* true, and that makes me—"

"Okay, I know. The thing is, it's a lead, and that's what we've been hoping for. What else did Malone say?"

I went over it again, every word, every pause, every nuance, just as I had before. Each time I told it, I felt momentarily more real. It seemed to hold me together.

"All right. You're not alone, are you?" Nick said.

"No, Aunt Pete's here and Maxie and Hazel and her kids."

"Who?"

"Hazel. She came to my moms' group last week—"

"Serena, this is not the time to be entertaining. That's too much for you right now."

"No, it's helping—"

"I don't want you getting more stressed out. Why don't you send them home? I'm about fifteen minutes out. I beat the worst of the traffic, so I'm practically there. I'm going to call Ed Malone."

I bristled a little as I hung up, but I rushed to make it okay. Naturally he wanted to hear everything for himself. Hear it from Ed, who might have an update by now. Who had a voice that wasn't wound tight with terror. Who might tell him something I'd left out—or Ed had left out. Nick was just a little bit... What? Frustrated? Terrified?

Certain he would disintegrate if Tristan didn't come back at once and pirouette across the kitchen?

Just as I needed to say it all, over and over, he needed to hear it. That was it. I had to stuff the needling resentment away.

And indeed Ed did have more to tell Nick when he phoned him. Ricky Zabriski was from Georgetown, a little more than an hour away. His mother said she hadn't heard from him in two weeks, but that wasn't unusual. When asked to call Detective Malone if she heard from her son, she said it shouldn't be long. If he was true to form, he'd be calling within the week to ask for money.

But Spider Zabriski didn't call his mother that day. Or the next. Or the next. And Tristan Soltani didn't call hers, either.

I was tucking Max into bed the next Monday night, after more than a week without Tristan, when she said to me, "I want to talk about Sun and those guys and Regis and Kelly."

"Regis and Kelly?"

"The dogs."

"Oh."

"Is it okay that I have fun when they all come over?"

"Honey!" I said. I ran my hand across the folded top of the sheet that pocketed her shoulders. "Why would you ask me that? Of course it's okay. They're a little, um, different, but they like you—"

"No, I mean…" Her brow puckered. "Should I be having fun when something bad could be happening to Sissy?" And then her face crumpled, and she started to cry, husky, rasping sobs that went on until she fell asleep in my arms. I spent that night in her bed, making a bowl of my body and holding her in it so she couldn't spill over again.

I was in a fog the next morning when Hazel appeared with the brood. I managed to emerge from it when she handed me a sheet with a picture of Tristan on it, dressed in her Boardwalk Fries uniform, executing a deerlike leap down our front steps.

I stroked the graceful little chin. "This was taken right before she went to her first day of work."

"It was in this bunch of pictures you gave me," Hazel said, waving a bulging brown envelope.

I couldn't remember giving her pictures, but, then, as sleep deprived as I was, I couldn't remember whether I'd brushed my teeth most days.

"So what do you think?" Hazel said.

I realized for the first time that it was a new flier, less cluttered than the one the police had done and more certain, with its startling font, to draw the eye to this vibrant teenager who was still missing.

Still missing. Maybe leaping farther and farther away every moment of every day.

"It's beautiful, Hazel," I said. "It's great."

"And you wish we didn't have to do it in the first place."

We looked at each other until I couldn't see her through my tears.

"Go get Mrs. Soltani a tissue, Sun," Hazel said. "And don't be snooping in her medicine cabinet."

As all three kids took off, sliding on the hardwood floor and fighting over who was going to hand me the Kleenex, I sank into a kitchen chair, still holding the flier.

"I brought the rest back," Hazel said. She spilled the contents of the envelope onto the table and fanned out the photos. "I gotta ask. Who took these?"

"Nick," I said. "He's the camera bug in our family."

"He's more than that. These are professional quality."

Hazel picked up one and held it deftly without touching the surface. It was a closeup of Tristan and Max together, sitting on a bench on the boardwalk, each with an ice-cream cone. Max wore a chocolate-chip-cookie-dough mustache. A vanilla dribble ran over her fingers as her eyes followed some off-camera fascination. Tristan was studying her cone with the intensity of a brain surgeon. It had been licked smooth as satin.

"See, this is a real kid," Hazel said. "Those cookie-cutter shots they take at school make them all look alike. Sun and Tri are like identical twins in last year's. But this—" She tapped the picture with a gold-striped fingernail. "Look at the way he caught her."

"She never lost a drop," I said.

"It's not only that. I mean, look at her. That isn't just ice cream to her. There's a whole other world in there."

She was right. It was as if Tristan was neatly licking her way to the dreams that lay within swirls of chocolate and vanilla.

"We gotta get your girl back," Hazel said.

I looked up into the too-blue eyes. She blinked them furiously.

"The kids and I are going to plaster these everywhere from Ocean City to Bowers Beach and inland as far as the Maryland border."

"I wanna help." Max's voice was froggy, and her eyes were sleep-puffy. "Can I go, Mom?"

"It's okay with me," Hazel said. "What difference is one more kid?"

But I was already shaking my head.

"Mo-om!" Max said.

"Honey, Daddy would have a fit."

"Can't you call him?"

"Not when I already know what he's going to say. We'll do something else fun."

"Yeah," Max said. "Right." Sarcasm still dripping from her lips, she stomped out of the kitchen.

"O-kay," Hazel said. "I don't get that, but I'm gonna keep my big mouth shut."

I kept mine shut too. I couldn't explain to Hazel that Nick wasn't happy about her presence, although I was sure she noticed him stiffening every time he came home to find her there. Nor could I explain to Nick what she brought to us, besides junk food and children whose every utterance seemed to be delivered through a megaphone. If somebody made Max smile, do her hip-hop routine, and think about something besides her lost sister, I had to let her in the front door. Even if Nick did say she was "not a good influence."

Max pouted about having to stay home until Hazel and the kids came back the following morning, announcing that *everybody* was going to know Tristan's face now.

"I still wish I could've gone," Max said, glaring at me.

"It really wasn't that much fun," Sun told her.

"You said it was yesterday," Tri said.

"Shut *up!*" Sun said and pushed him into the pool.

Ed Malone came by later, full of compliments about the flier. "Maybe the phone will start ringing again."

"So, can I just ask you a question, Mr. Detective?" Hazel said.

I squirmed, but Ed gave her a slow smile. "I don't think I can stop you. And call me Ed."

"Okay, Ed." Hazel directed her eyes at him. "How hard are you leaning on Mama Zabriski?"

"Ricky's mother?"

"That's the one."

Ed took a sip of the coffee Aunt Pete had put in front of him and winced. "We've questioned her. I'm convinced she's told us everything she knows."

"Right," Hazel said.

"We didn't put any bamboo shoots under her fingernails," Ed said. "But I just didn't get the sense that she was lying."

Hazel looked ready to put a few sharp items under *his* fingernails, but he was saved by the arrival of Christine, dressed in an Evan-

Picone suit and obviously with an agenda. Ed excused himself while Hazel kept Desi from climbing into Baby Mitchell's stroller with him.

"I can't stay long," Christine said. Her eyes trailed warily to the stroller. "I just brought you a cheese platter."

Max wrinkled her nose at the plate Aunt Pete was toting off to the kitchen.

"What's that *smell*?" Tri said.

"It's your manners," Hazel said.

Christine edged closer to the stroller. "Oh, and I wanted to let you know that I'm putting together a Web site, just so we can keep people apprised of what's happening with the search."

"Oh," I said.

"That way you won't have people constantly asking you questions. And, of course, then we'll know how to pray."

How to pray. I wasn't sure I knew myself anymore.

"I don't know what kind of cheese that is," Aunt Pete said when Christine and Mitchell were gone and Hazel had herded the kids out to the pool. "But Tri's right about the stink."

"Christine eats goat cheese," I said.

Hazel pushed open the door to the deck for me. "She eats something that doesn't agree with her. Must be why she has that nervous tic in her eye."

"Christine has a nervous tic?" I said.

"It's probably because this whole thing freaks her out."

"I'd think she was nuts if it didn't," Aunt Pete said. She gave me a look I didn't understand. I didn't have the energy to try to figure it out.

"She hasn't been around since last week, for one thing," Hazel said.

"She's so busy," I said as I dropped into a chair. "She has her job, the baby, her husband. I don't expect everybody to drop everything."

Hazel leaned against the porch railing and patted her pockets. "I know. I'm just ticked because those cops aren't doing enough."

"That's exactly what I think," Aunt Pete said. "You can bet your boots if I could drive, I'd have been in Georgetown already."

"Getting right in that Zabriski woman's face," Hazel said. She gave up her search for cigarettes and jerked her chin at me. "You and I ought to be on our way there right now."

"What?"

"We need to go talk to her. I might *want* to pin her against the wall until she gives up her kid, but with you there, I'll restrain myself."

"I can watch the kids," Aunt Pete said. "They know they can't get away with anything with their Aunt Pete."

"Just wait," I said.

"See, that's the problem," Hazel said. "You've *been* waiting, and it hasn't gotten you any closer to your kid." She grabbed my hand and pulled me to my feet. "I've had my dealings with law enforcement, okay? There comes a time when you have to take matters into your own hands."

"I can't do this, Hazel. Nick would—"

"Nick would what?" Aunt Pete said. "You think he's gonna take away your birthday?"

"He doesn't hit you, does he?" Hazel said.

"No!"

"Then I don't see the problem."

I shrank back from her. "I don't think you understand—"

"Do you want to get your daughter back or not?"

I couldn't pull myself away from her eyes. They had the spark and fight in them that I had only felt in surges.

"We can take my car," I said, "if you'll drive."

"I can't believe I'm doing this," I said.

"You've already said that six times, and we're barely out of Bethany Beach," Hazel said. "Either you take one of my Xanax, or we talk about how you're going to handle this. Otherwise you're going to drive me nuts."

"How *I'm* going to handle it?" I said. "You said you've had experience with 'taking things into your own hands.'"

"I don't think you're going to have to handle this situation the way I had to deal with mine."

"What was yours?" I wasn't sure I really wanted to know, but if she didn't do something to distract me, I didn't think I'd make it.

"My third ex," Hazel said, "Desi's father. He was a monster, and I had him arrested. When he weaseled his way out of that, I got a restraining order. He ignored that, so I broke a leg off the dining room table and chased him off with it. Shocked the macho out of him." She gave me a triumphant look. "I haven't seen him since."

"Are you serious?"

"Beyond. I'm not suggesting we break up Mama Zabriski's furniture, but you may have to get tough."

My mouth felt like desert terrain. "I can't call her Mama Zabriski," I said.

"Then I guess we better find out her name," Hazel said. "Her address wouldn't be a bad idea, either."

The terrified part of me hoped the Georgetown phone book wouldn't give up Mrs. Zabriski, but it did. When Hazel swung the Blazer into the driveway of the gray ranch house, that same terrified part hoped it was the wrong house or at least that Sarah Zabriski wasn't home.

"I don't know if I can do this, Hazel," I said.

"Just go in there and be Tristan's mother." She took off the leopard-skin sunglasses to look at me. "Seems like that's what you do best."

I let Hazel ring the doorbell, and on her instructions I stood a few steps behind her.

"We don't know what kind of wacko she might be," she had told me in the car.

I was ready for anything from the barrel of a semiautomatic weapon (Hazel's image) to a blast of insults about my daughter (my image). I did not expect the woman who opened the door to be wearing flowered scrubs and a guarded smile.

"I'm glad you found the place," she said. Her voice was almost shrill. "Come on in."

I looked at her stupidly as she opened the door and motioned us inside. Hazel went right in, dragging me by the sleeve.

The tall, wiry woman patted the sides of her hair. Its blond was fading rather than graying, much like everything else on her seemed to be doing. I sensed that I was watching someone slowly disappear.

"Giselle's in the back," she said. "I'm sure you can hear her." She gave a nervous laugh, which accompanied the high-pitched barking that came from behind a closed door somewhere.

"Do you think this will take longer than a half hour?" she said. "I have to leave for work."

In spite of Hazel poking my arm, I shook my head. "I'm afraid you have us mixed up with somebody else."

The woman looked at my hands. "Where's all your stuff? You aren't the dog groomers?"

"No," I said. "I'm Serena Soltani. Are you Sarah Zabriski?"

The woman erased her smile and went stiff.

"What do you want?" she said. "Don't think you're going to come in here and make accusations about my boy. I've had enough of it. I don't know what happened to your daughter—I've told them all that—and I'll tell you what I told them: My Ricky didn't do anything to her. Giselle, shut *up*!"

The barking stopped, although it was hard to tell the dog's voice from hers. Hazel poked me in the back, but I couldn't say anything. I was afraid Sarah Zabriski would tremble into pieces if I did.

"Mrs. Soltani isn't here to accuse you of anything," Hazel said.

"Who are you?"

Hazel put out her hand. "Hazel Jefferson. I'm here for moral support. Looks like you could both use some."

Sarah didn't shake Hazel's hand, but she stepped away from the wall she'd plastered herself to and nodded toward a shadowy room. "Five minutes," she said. "If you don't leave then, I'll scream for those cops out there."

"What cops?" I said.

"You mean those two in the unmarked car across the street?" Hazel said. "Could they be any more obvious?"

"They're watching the house in case Ricky comes back here." Sarah pointed us to the couch and perched on the edge of a rocking chair. She was so thin it barely moved. Everything in the room matched her—breakable and frail and obsessively tidy.

"I'm going to tell you what I keep telling them," she said when Hazel and I had seated ourselves on a Queen Anne replica that I was afraid would crack beneath us. "I do *not* know where Ricky is. Has it occurred to anybody that he's missing too? What if something happened to both of them?"

The thought was more chilling than almost any I'd entertained yet.

"Then you really don't know where he is?" I said. "You haven't heard from him?"

Sarah closed her eyes. "Why doesn't anyone believe me? I want him home—just like any mother would."

"I'm so sorry," I said. "Mrs. Zabriski, I know exactly how you feel."

She gripped the arms of the rocking chair. "Do you? Are people saying your child is a kidnapper and a rapist and maybe even a murderer? Are they hunting her down like she's a serial killer?"

I could only shake my head.

"Is this Ricky?" Hazel said. She held a framed photograph she'd obviously picked up from the end table. For a moment I thought

Sarah was going to fly across the room and snatch it out of Hazel's hands.

"Nice-looking kid," Hazel said.

She tilted the picture toward me. Either Hazel was lying, or I didn't see what she saw. The boy inside the frame sneered at me with the big lips Aylana had described. They looked ready to say, "You want a piece of me?"

"I didn't want him to bleach his hair like that," Sarah said. "But he thought a lifeguard had to be more blond." Her voice softened into motherly pride. "Other than that, he still looks just like his father."

Ricky's father must have had a straight nose and sharp green eyes and a sinister cut to his cheekbones. In spite of every effort not to, I imagined Tristan cuddled up next to him. He looked down at her, lip curled, with the same contempt in his eyes that he had for the camera.

"Where's his dad?" Hazel said.

"He died when Ricky was only five," Sarah said. "It's been just the two of us ever since. We're so close. That's why I know something has happened to him. He would never let me worry like this."

The dog in the back began to howl.

"It's all right, Giselle," Sarah called out. "She's been having a fit ever since Ricky went missing. It's like she knows something's happened to him. She's his dog; he had to have a schnoodle."

"A schnoodle?" Hazel said.

"It's a poodle-schnauzer mix. She loves him so much."

She looked down at the hands she was knotting together in her lap. Her misery was as palpable as my own.

"Nice tattoo," Hazel said, tapping the picture. "Looks new."

I forced myself to look back at it. I didn't know how I'd missed the black and red spider on Ricky's left arm. He was obviously displaying it for the camera.

"It was new then. That was taken back at the beginning of June. He couldn't wait until the next time he came home for me to see it, so he sent me the picture. He designed the spider himself."

"He's quite the artist," Hazel said.

"I think he is. I wish he hadn't wasted his talent on a tattoo, though. The pierced ear I didn't mind, but I just don't like body art." Sarah sighed. "I'm glad now that I didn't tell him that. I would hate for one of our last conversations to be me giving him a bad time."

"I know," I said. "The last time I talked to Tristan, it was about our not letting her get her hair cut. It seems so ridiculous now."

Sarah nodded. "You just go over every word you said and every word they said, looking for some kind of clue."

"I do." I drew in a deep breath. "When you talked to Ricky, did he ever mention Tristan?"

"He never talks to me about his girlfriends. I'm sure he's had them, cute as he is, but I guess boys don't discuss those things with their mothers."

Even though you're close? I wanted to say, but I couldn't push the knife into this woman's heart any further.

"We should probably go," I said. "Let you go to work."

"You in the medical profession?" Hazel said.

"I'm a nurse's aide in a convalescent home." She sounded almost apologetic. "It isn't much. I wish I made better money so I could do more for Ricky. I hate that he has to drive that old beat-up car."

I wondered if she knew that old beat-up car was now infamous on the AMBER Alert. Somehow, I hoped not.

"Listen," she said as she led us to the front door. "I'm sorry I was so rude to you when you first got here. I've just been harassed so much—first the Georgetown police, then the Bethany Beach police, then the private detective—"

"Somebody hired a private investigator?" I said.

Sarah blinked at me. "Well, yeah. You did."

"Excuse me?"

"He said the Soltanis sent him. I guess I would do the same thing if I could afford it."

Giselle set up another wail, and Hazel took me by the arm.

"We'll let you go take care of the schnoodle," she said. "Thanks for your time."

Chapter Eight

I couldn't talk on the way home. It was all too much: the idea that something could have happened to both Tristan and Ricky, that without him we might never find her, that another woman's heart was breaking just like mine was. And that Nick had hired a private investigator—that he, too, had taken matters into his own hands.

Hazel left me alone until we were only a block from my house. "Something struck me when I was looking at that tattoo," she said then, "and I think we oughta check it— What the…"

Gravel sprayed as she skidded the Blazer to a stop on the side of the road. I could feel the color draining from my face.

There was an ambulance in our driveway, lights flashing. Ed Malone's cruiser was parked askew on the grass, and a beach patrol Jeep sat halfway on the curb beyond them both. Nick hadn't even gotten his Nissan all the way off the road, and the door on the driver's side was hanging open.

I screamed Hazel's name, but she was already out of the car, tearing toward the house. I followed blindly. Terror sheared every thought from my head.

By the time I got to Hazel, she was coming back through the pool gate, eyes wild.

"Where are they?" she demanded of me. "Sunrise! Tri!"

"Down here!" The voice came from the beach.

"Dear God, no." I turned toward it, toward the figures emerging up the steps from the shore.

By the time I got to them, Hazel already had a paramedic by the collar.

"Where are my kids? You better have saved my kids—"

"Yo, lady." A second paramedic wedged an arm between them. "Your kids are fine."

Behind him, a soaked lifeguard grinned. "It's those dogs you oughta be worried about."

Hazel let go of the medic. "What? My setters?"

The lifeguard jerked his head toward the steps. Another lifeguard stumbled into view, barely holding on to Regis and Kelly by a pair of ropes. Drenched and sandy, they paused at the top of the stairs and shook themselves out in unison.

"Everybody stop when you get up there," I heard Nick say. "Don't go another step."

The tops of four little heads appeared above the steps—Max, Sun,

Tri, and Desi. Aunt Pete followed, looking as much like a whipped puppy as they did.

When Nick got to the top, a paramedic cleared his throat. "Looks like you don't need us anymore. Glad everybody's okay."

"They won't be for long," one of the lifeguards muttered.

The four of them exited, leaving the dogs with Hazel. She passed them off to Ed Malone, who was the last to make it up from the beach and marched over to the remorseful-looking lineup in front of Nick. When Desi saw her, he burst into tears and hid behind Max.

"What just happened?" she said to them.

"That's what I'm trying to find out," Nick said through his teeth.

"What did you guys do?"

"It wasn't my idea," Tri said.

"Shut *up!*" Sun said.

"Excellent plan," Nick said. "Now, Aunt Pete, you want to explain this to me?"

"Yes," Aunt Pete said, "if you'll put that finger away."

She glared until he jammed his hand into his pocket. She was recovering fast.

"We were down there on the beach. Everybody was playing nice, and the next thing I knew, those two dogs were out so far I could barely see them."

Nick stared. "So you called 911?"

"Yes, I did. Maxine was determined she was going out there to save them, and when I wouldn't let her, she got hysterical."

"She really did," Tri said. "Her face turned all purple and everything."

"Shut—"

"Enough." Nick put his hand up in Sun's direction and looked at Max. "What were you so upset for? Look at all this madness you brought on."

"It was my fault the dogs were out there," Max said.

She had her arms wrapped around her wet self, and her lips were verging on blue. Nobody had even put a towel around her. I started toward her, but Nick put the hand up to me this time.

"What do you mean it was your fault?" he said to Max.

"It was my idea to play Search and Rescue. They sniffed out everything we sent them for, only I didn't know they'd go that far out."

"Don't cover up for him, Max," Sunrise said. "Tri was the one that threw the package of hot dogs out there."

Hazel caught Tri's fist before he could land it on Sun's arm.

"It's still my fault," Max said. The chin she tilted up at Nick was quivering. "I couldn't stand it if anything happened to Regis and Kelly. I don't want anybody else getting lost."

Her face crumpled, and she ran to me. Nick was in danger of rubbing the hair right off the back of his head. He looked at Ed, who was still flanked by the panting Irish setters.

"I'm sorry you had to come over here for this."

"Actually, I wasn't invited to this party," Ed said. He looked uncomfortable. "I came about something else."

Nick put his hand on Max's shoulder. "Okay, go on in and get cleaned up. We'll talk about this later."

"Hey, anybody home?"

Gary Dalberg walked toward us up the driveway, carrying a galvanized tub nearly as big as he was. Lissa bounced behind him.

"Anybody up for some fresh crabs?" she said.

"Are they alive?" Tri said.

"Come check it out."

The children surrounded Gary, squealing like piglets. Even Aunt Pete craned for a good view of reaching claws.

Nick stepped closer to Ed. "What's up?" he said.

I had never seen Ed look embarrassed.

"I got a call from Georgetown," Ed said, "and I'm sure there's a perfectly good explanation for it—"

"For what?" Nick said.

"For why the police saw Serena at the Zabriski house this afternoon."

I bit into my lip.

"Like I said, I'm sure there's a perfectly good explanation."

"There better be," Nick said.

"I'll cook these crabs for anybody who's hungry," Gary called to us.

Lissa bobbed her head "I brought coleslaw and bread."

"Tri, Sun, in the car. Let's go," Hazel said. She already had Desi on her shoulders.

"Don't go," I said. "Stay and eat with us." I could feel Nick's glare through the back of my head. I turned to face Ed. "I hope I didn't mess anything up. I just had to talk to Ricky's mother."

"Serena, for the love of Mike," Nick said.

"And you know what?" I said. "That poor woman is as miserable as we are."

The kids nodded off one by one in the family room when the chaos of the crab dinner died down. Lissa and Aunt Pete banned me from the kitchen while they cleaned up, and Gary and Hazel adjourned to the side porch after Hazel asked him whether they would boot her out of the church if she came, seeing how she had "a past more checkered than those curtains you got hanging in that hall."

Nick looked at me and said, "We're going for a walk. I want to talk to you."

A late afternoon breeze was coming off the ocean when we reached the beach, but I felt strangely claustrophobic. Nick held my hand firmly and talked as I scurried to keep up with his long stride.

"I don't even know where to start, Serena. You left Max with Aunt Pete, which I asked you not to do. You went off with Hazel, who you know I don't approve of. And what were you thinking? You had no idea what you were going to run into at that house."

I didn't try to respond. It was clear he wasn't interested in answers. My mind darted to a man ahead who threw a stick into the ocean for his loping yellow Lab. At the water's edge, fishermen were setting up, and noise spilled out from the boardwalk. All these things I loved, and yet I had come to fear them. This place had stolen Tristan, and it wouldn't give her back.

"That just seals my decision," Nick said.

I willed myself to focus on him.

"I don't want Max going to Lord Baltimore School," he said. "I've been looking at Bethany Home School, and I think it would be better for her under the circumstances if you'd teach her at home. It's like a co-op. They have—"

I came to life. "Under what circumstances?"

Nick stopped and faced me.

"You don't think all of this is affecting Max? Look what happened today when you left her with Aunt Pete. Playing Search and Rescue? Hyperventilating over a couple of dogs? That can't be healthy."

"What circumstances?" I said again.

"You just have to trust me when I say we have to be very, very careful about Max."

"Did that private investigator tell you something?"

Nick slowly folded his arms. "How did you find out about that?"

"Sarah Zabriski told me," I said.

Nick's eyes grew filmy. "Serena, I want you to take care of Max, and I'll handle the rest of it. I'm not afraid just for Tristan. I'm afraid for you and Max too." He put his hand on the back of my head and tried to pull me into his chest. When I stiffened my neck, he stuck his hand in his pocket.

"I want Max in a school closer to us than the one in Ocean View. And do not leave her alone with Aunt Pete in the meantime."

I looked at him so deep and so long his face began to morph—from my guide and my rock to my master and commander, the one who made the rules and delegated the authority.

As I watched his mouth remain firm and his eyes wait for my expected reply, I realized that it wasn't the first time I'd seen that expression. It had just never mattered before.

Nick touched my elbow and steered me back toward the house. "Aunt Pete's leaving the day after Labor Day, so—"

"She's leaving?"

"That was always the plan. I think she's getting antsy to be back in Philly. Anyway, it will be safer if it's just you and Max, staying close to home while I'm away. "

I dug my feet into the sand. Nick stumbled and caught himself neatly.

"Where are you going?" I said.

Nick tried to nudge me forward, but I didn't move. I couldn't move. He gave a sigh ragged with impatience, which he was clearly trying to keep stowed.

"All right, look. Ed Malone is stalled. The PI got a lead, but he's taken it as far as he can. I feel like I have to follow up on it."

"What lead?"

"Serena—"

"Nicky, please."

He scraped his hand down the back of his head. "I'm going to Los Angeles. The PI traced a guy there, one I let go a couple of months ago. He made a lot of noise around the plant about putting it to me the way I put it to him. I know the guy; he's all talk. If he has Tristan, it's just to spite me, not to hurt her."

I held back my questions: *Why is it okay for you to follow your heart and go looking for her, but it's not okay for me? Why is it all right for me not to know where you are when I can't reach you, but you have to know my every move?*

"Ed doesn't know anything about this," Nick said, "and I don't want him to."

"But he said to tell him everything—"

"And what's he done with it, Serena? The police are no closer to finding Tristan than they were the night she disappeared. You felt like *you* had to go to Zabriski's mother, for Pete's sake. It's up to me now, and I *will* find her." His voice broke. "I'm her father."

It was the first time I had seen him come close to crying since our crisis had begun. His pain swelled in me, and I reached for his cheek with my palm. When he spoke again, his voice was flat and hard.

"Now that's all I'm going to say about it. I'll handle everything with Aunt Pete and Max, and I know you'll stand behind me."

There was a time when I would have quietly taken my place in that spot behind him, where I'd belonged, where I'd felt safe. But there was no security there now. My image of a strong, wise Nick Soltani, who could protect and provide and prevent, shattered in a blast of doubt. And somehow with it went my image of a strong, safe Father who would never have let any of this happen if He had been the God I thought He was.

A different Nick led me through the dropping dusk. I followed him because I didn't know what else to do, because it was what I'd always done. But the distance between us lengthened with the shadows until I could barely see him anymore.

Chapter Nine

Four days later, the night before he left for California, Nick summoned Max to the family room, where he had the Bethany Home School brochure spread on the coffee table, secured by the heavy stone coasters with sailboats bobbing happily on them. His explanation was clear and crisp and left no room for discussion. Evidently, Max missed that part.

She glared at the brochure and said, "I don't see why I have to be punished for something Tristan did."

She scrunched herself into a corner of the couch, arms slapped into place across her chest. Her face was pulled so far down it was almost comical, but Nick wasn't laughing.

"In the first place, young lady," he said, "this isn't a punishment. And in the second place, your sister didn't *do* anything. It was done *to* her."

"Maybe," Max said.

It was the first time Max had conceded the possibility that Tristan wasn't abducted, and I knew it was only because she saw a chance to use it to her own advantage. It might have annoyed me if I hadn't felt sorry for her.

"It's not fair!" she said. "And don't say 'life isn't fair,' because that never helps."

To my surprise, Nick visibly swallowed his annoyance and sat on the arm of the couch, arm slung across the back. Max refused to look up at him.

"What *would* help, Max?" he said. "Besides me just letting you get on the bus for Lord Baltimore like you always have. That's not gonna happen."

A gleam came into Max's eyes. "I don't have to ride the bus," she said. "Mom could drive me to school in the mornings and pick me up in the afternoons. That way you'd be sure nobody was going to nab me—like they *would*—" Eye roll. "That's the only thing you're really worried about. This way I could still go to a real school and get a decent education."

I knew Nick was going to veto that proposal, and for that at least I was grateful. Lord Baltimore was only in Ocean View—fifteen minutes away in traffic. But I hadn't driven the car since Tristan's disappearance. What if I had a panic attack right on Route 26? I was already envisioning the Blazer squealing into oncoming traffic when Nick said, "All right."

My head snapped toward him.

"Are you serious?" Max said. She came up onto her knees on the sofa.

"We'll try it. If it's too much for your mother, all bets are off."

It was a full fifteen seconds before Nick looked at me. I was incredulous. There was no sign of a question: *Do you mind, hon? Would this work for you?* I pushed my fingertips into the palms of my hands. If I'd had any nails left, I would have shredded myself.

"It won't be too much, will it, Mom?"

I could feel Max searching my face. I pulled my gaze from Nick's unflappable one and turned to tell her that indeed it would be too much. Getting out of bed these days was almost too much. But the face I looked at was as soft and yearning as a puppy's. I hadn't seen that much trust there since Max had turned four and had begun to know everything.

"It won't be too much, right?" she said again.

My heart twisted. How could I squeeze out what was left of the normalcy in this child's life when all she wanted was her world the way she'd always known it? And how could I stand the distance that a simple no would create between Max and me? I had to have one daughter I could still hold in my arms.

"Sure," I lied. "I'll be fine."

Nick gave Max a resoundingly juicy kiss on the side of her face.

"That is so gross, Dad," Max said. She dragged her hand down her cheek. "You know I'm not a baby anymore, right? You know I can take care of myself on the bus if this doesn't work out."

"Not a chance, short stuff," Nick said.

When she'd reluctantly given up getting him to budge on that and went back to her room, Nick turned to me. "I think that's a pretty good compromise, don't you? She's happy, you're happy, and even though it still worries me, I'm not *un*happy." Without waiting for an answer, he kissed the top of my head. "I'm going to get us through this, hon," he said. "I have to pack."

I slept in a fist-shape that night. Max must have too, because when she got up the next morning, long after Nick had left for the airport, she took one look at me and exploded in the middle of the kitchen, in front of Rebecca and Hazel.

"Dad's treating me like a baby!" she said. She knocked a bowl of plums off the snack bar. As it rolled faster and faster, spewing fruit like a pitching machine, my mind rolled with it. The Soltanis didn't hurl things—insults or fruit or feelings. Yet it looked as if it would feel good to throw a fit like that.

Rebecca watched it all, raisin faced, and I had a fleeting image of myself slamming a plum at her. It was a shocking little blip on my screen. After all, Rebecca had been there almost every day since Tristan's disappearance, bringing food and pieces of Scripture and sometimes her mother—a plumper, grayer version of herself. I stuffed the plum-pitching image and ushered Max out of the kitchen.

"Go on up to your room, honey," I said to her at the bottom of the stairs. "I'll be up in a minute."

"I want to ride the bus with my friends, Mom," she said. "It's not fair, and I don't care what Dad says, it *oughta* be."

I couldn't give her an honest answer, and I was sure she knew that before she charged up the steps and slammed her bedroom door.

"I'm glad to see she's a normal kid," Hazel said when I returned to the kitchen.

Rebecca straightened from retrieving the bruised fruit. "That's not normal for Serena's children."

Neither was taking off with the boyfriend you weren't supposed to have.

I was immediately on myself, chastising my psyche for going there, for even driving by, as Max would say. Tristan hadn't run away with Spider Zabriski.

But because the alternative was worse—that he might have forced her to go—I sagged into a chair at the table and tried to go numb. It didn't work. Anxiety seeped in through the cracks right along with Rebecca's voice.

"She'll go up there and straighten Max out," she was informing Hazel, "but you won't hear any yelling and back talk." The implied *You could learn a thing or two from her, Hazel,* wasn't well concealed. Rebecca pushed a plate of Aunt Pete's charbroiled toast toward me. "Have you heard any more about that lifeguard?"

I shook my head.

"Serena, I know I've said this before, but it's impossible that Tristan went off with some boy of her own free will. Not the way you've raised her."

"Huh," Hazel said.

"What was that for?" Aunt Pete said from the stove.

"It just seems to me that once a kid gets to be sixteen, there are more influences on her than just her parents. Like hormones, for starters."

I didn't have to see Rebecca to know her posture was improving by the second. In another time I would have asked if anybody wanted more coffee, but I didn't have the urge to smooth it over.

"Well, that's it right there," Rebecca said. "It seems to *you*. But *we* know that the most important influence on a child is her parents, especially if they're Christians." She swept a hand toward me.

"So Serena's Exhibit A," Hazel said.

"Serena has an amazing faith in the Lord. You don't see her breaking down, do you? Look how strong she is."

Aunt Pete shuffled over from the counter and sloshed more muddy coffee into my cup. "She's a little too strong if you ask me." Her eyes cut to me. "I don't hear you crying. I don't see you gettin' mad. I mean, if I was you, I'd have shoved Nicky's orders right back down his throat about six times by now."

Hazel clapped.

"You're not serious," Rebecca said.

"I'm serious as a heart attack," Aunt Pete said.

Rebecca put her hand on top of mine. "We just don't do things that way. That's why Serena can be so calm. She depends on Nick and on the Lord."

I slid my hand away. "Rebecca," I said, "would you do me a favor?"

"Anything. You know that."

"Would you go pick up the dry cleaning? Nicky's almost out of shirts."

"That was on my list." She scraped back her chair and looked at Hazel. "I'd like to finish this conversation sometime."

"Oh," Hazel said, "were we having a conversation?" She hoisted her purse over her shoulder and headed for the door behind Rebecca. When Rebecca had disappeared through it, Hazel poked her head back in and whispered hoarsely, "Way to clear the room, Serena. I have to run an errand. I'll be back."

"Nothing gets past that Hazel," Aunt Pete said after they'd both left. She got up from the table.

"Don't go," I said.

"I'm just gonna put on another pot of coffee."

"No, I mean don't go back to Philadelphia. Please."

She turned to me, eyes glassy in her life-dried face. "Who said I was going back to Philly? I'm staying till Tristan comes home or until you—not Nicky—throw me out." Her breath was uneven for a minute while she filled the coffeepot at the sink. "I'm going to tell him that too," she said. She let the water overflow as she dabbed at her eyes. "That and a few other things."

Hazel came back that afternoon to find me pacing around the house. She parked the kids in the family room with a DVD and a package of Oreos and sequestered the two of us in the library.

"Okay," she said, "I would have taken you with me, but Aunt Pete said you're under house arrest right now, so I had to go without you."

"Go where?"

"The tattoo parlor." Hazel tossed her bangs back. "It took me awhile to find the one where Little Ricky got his done, but I have connections. Anyway, you remember I asked his mother if that tattoo in the picture was new?"

"She said it was."

"That was three months ago. Which means right about now, he'd be going back in to have it touched up."

"How do you know that?" I said.

"I used to work at a tattoo place. I told you I was a graphic artist."

"You went there?" I bolted from the chaise longue. "Has he been back? Have they seen him?"

Hazel shook her head. "No. I hate it, but…I did find out something, and I'm not sure how it's going to hit you, so—"

"What is it, Hazel?" My hands were tightened into little balls. "Just tell me. I'm so tired of people not telling me."

"Attagirl, Serena. Okay. The guy at the Lone Wolf told me he hasn't seen Ricky Zabriski since mid-July, when he came in with his girlfriend."

"Tristan?"

"I showed him her picture, and he said it was her. He said the Zabriski kid was trying to talk her into getting a tattoo on her ankle. She said no, but this guy was surprised they didn't come back in to have it done anyway."

"Why?" I said.

Hazel grimaced. "He said either she was in love with him or she was scared to death of him, but one thing was for sure: she would have done anything he asked her to."

⌇

At nine I was lying on my bed suffering through the vision of Tristan crawling to please Ricky Zabriski when Aunt Pete brought me the phone.

"Nicky got to L.A.," she said.

Evidently she'd told him "a few things" during their conversation.

"I don't like this," he said to me, "but I guess I can't kick her out of the house."

"I want her here," I said. "She's keeping me from losing my mind. I can talk to her."

"Talk to her all you want," he said. "Just don't listen to her." He sighed. "I guess she's better for you than that Hazel character."

I had a flash of myself hurtling a plum right at his forehead.

Maybe I really am losing my mind, I thought after we hung up. I was having bizarre images of assaulting my loved ones with rotten fruit, but I couldn't bring into focus the one thing that had always kept me sane before.

Perhaps that was a good thing, I decided. The sight of God as Christ comforting a lapful of trusting children raised too many ugly questions I wasn't allowed to ask. What had He done with *my* child? What about the comfort *I* needed? How was I supposed to trust Him now?

The comfort and the safety and the trust had disappeared. Just like Tristan. And I didn't know where any of it was.

Although Nick's stay in L.A. lengthened to more than a week, he gave me no information about searching for the disgruntled employee who he thought had Tristan. All he would say was that he was working on it and not to worry. I held back so many retorts of "How can I not worry?" and "Don't I have a right to know?" that by the Friday of Labor Day weekend, I was stuffed with them. I thought if I spoke at all, I would lose what little control I had. Lissa took one look at me that morning and called in "the Girls."

"You don't have to do that, sweetie," I told her. "I'm fine."

"You need your friends with you, Serena. We can't fix you, but I think you need some support."

Pastor Gary took all the kids to a movie in Fenwick. We gathered, childless, in my family room—Hazel, Aunt Pete, Rebecca, Christine, Lissa, and Rebecca's mother, Peg—while Baby Mitchell napped in the library. Peg passed around a mound of homemade gingersnaps, and Rebecca told them about my new chauffeuring duties.

"You're amazing, Serena," Christine said. "Seriously. You have all this on you, and you can still focus on Max."

"It's not that amazing, really," Peg said. She stroked the turkey skin on her neck. "Serena just trusts in the Lord. You can keep going when you have that kind of faith." She nodded conspiratorially at me, as if she and I were among the very few who possessed it.

"I was saying this to Hazel the other day," Rebecca said. "Serena's not falling apart. She just keeps being this amazing mother. I bet she could tell you exactly what verse is holding her together." She nodded to me as if she'd just given me a cue.

The expectation was like a pinch, and I pulled back from it.

Hazel, who had been oddly quiet until then, said, "So, is there a verse for every situation?"

"If you know your Bible," Peg said.

"Or someone else can show you," Lissa said.

"So, okay, here's what I'm hearing," Hazel said.

Shut up, Hazel, I wanted to say to her. *All of you shut up.* My imp self scowled—as if while I'd been ignoring her, she'd turned into an ugly troll. I stayed still, lest she suddenly get away from me.

Hazel pushed her bracelets up her arms. "I'm hearing you say that if you know your Bible or somebody can give you the right verses, your natural feelings will go away, and you can handle everything without ever getting your panties in a bunch."

Peg scowled, skin sagging down from her forehead. She began to remind me of Duke, the police bloodhound. "That isn't what we're saying at all."

"Then what are you saying?"

"That when we have bad feelings, we can turn them over to the Lord." Rebecca nodded toward me. "Like Serena's doing."

"Is that what you're doing?" Hazel said, riveting her blazing blues to me.

Peg reached her hand toward Hazel and patted the air since Hazel was too far away to be patted. "This is probably hard for you to grasp, Harriet, since you don't have the background—"

"Hazel," Lissa muttered.

"Yeah, thanks, Lissa, but I can speak for myself," Hazel said. "The question is, can Serena? You're all talking for her like you know what she's thinking."

"We probably do," Rebecca said.

Aunt Pete muttered something. Christine excused herself to go check on Mitchell's nap situation. Lissa ran her hand up and down my arm. It was all I could do not to jerk it away.

"You know what?" Hazel said. "I don't believe that."

Peg gasped.

"I want to hear it from Serena," Hazel said.

They all turned to me, and I could almost hear them saying, *Tell her, Serena. Set her straight.*

Yet even as I opened my mouth, I couldn't say it. I couldn't validate them all with the reassurance that, indeed, I had turned all my "bad feelings" over to God. I wanted to say, "He sure hasn't done much with them." I was dying to say, "Who cares about my feelings? I want my daughter back." All I could manage to say was, "I don't want to."

"You're tired." Lissa stroked my arm and turned on Hazel, "Let's not push it, okay?"

"Okay," Hazel said, "then I'll tell you what *I* think you're thinking, Serena." Hazel moved her substantial self to the edge of the Papasan chair, tipping it up behind her. "You're thinking, 'If only I hadn't let Tristan get that job. This is my fault. I'm supposed to be Supermom, and I screwed up.'"

"Oh, honestly," Peg said.

"You're dying inside because you want to kill the monster that took your kid, whether she wanted to go or not. You want to chew out the cops because they haven't found her yet. Heck, not just the cops. The mayor. The city council. The governor."

"Serena, do you want me to stop her?" Lissa said.

"You can't sleep at night because you're afraid you'll dream things that might drive you straight out of your mind—"

"I'm sorry, but you don't know what you're talking about," Peg said.

"Maybe that's how *you* would feel, Hazel," Rebecca said.

Hazel didn't take her eyes off of me. "You can hardly even think about your husband because you want to smack his face."

"Where are you getting all this stuff?" Lissa said.

"I'm paying attention." Hazel pointed straight at me. "I look at you, girl, and I don't see you being all strong and holy. I see you pretending you don't hate life itself right now. You're about to crack open like an egg."

I turned from her and tried to find something to look at that would keep her from being right. I found the stack of stone coasters on the coffee table, the ones with the happy sailboats on them. I hated them. I, Serena Soltani, hated, and I hadn't even known that I knew how to hate.

"I think we should change the subject," Lissa said.

"I don't," Hazel said. "It's just starting to get real."

"You don't know what real is, Hazel," Rebecca said.

"What is it?" Hazel said.

"Real is that God is sovereign, and even though we don't always understand what He's doing—"

"I hate what He's doing," I said.

The air in the room went dead.

"I hate it," I said. "I *hate* it."

"Serena!" Rebecca said.

I pulled a coaster off the top of the stack, like a card off a deck, and, getting to my feet, hurled it. It sang past Rebecca's ear and landed with a thud in a basket of cotton throws.

"Hon? What's going on?" Lissa said.

I dodged the hand that tried to grab my arm. "I hate everything that's keeping Tristan away from me." I chucked a coaster at the ceiling and dislodged the plaster. And then another at the floor and another, with the hate that poured from my cracked shell.

"I hate Spider Zabriski. I hate myself. I hate being told what a wonderful *mother* I am. I *hate* hearing that 'God is good all the time; all the time God is good,' because He let her be taken, and He won't bring her back, and I don't see anything *good* in that!"

The last coaster smashed into the telescope and knocked it against the window.

Peg shoved past Lissa to get to me. "Now you just sit down, Serena. And you get hold of yourself. This isn't you talking; this is Satan, and we need to put an end to it."

"Stop it," I said.

"We need to pray, and we need to pray deep—"

"Stop—"

"Serena, now—"

"Get off me! All of you, just get *out!*"

I snatched up the table lamp and screamed again into their shocked faces.

"Get out. Get *out!*" Then I let go of my weapon and heard it crash to the floor. Smothering my face with both hands, I followed it.

Sobs came out so hard they hurt. When someone tried to put her arms around me, I shook her off. It was all coming out now, and I didn't want anybody to stop it. The one thing I knew for sure was that if I shoved it back down, it would be there forever, and it would destroy me.

Beyond me, Baby Mitchell's frightened cries faded out the front door. I heard snatches of Lissa on the phone and Peg still declaring that they needed to pray for a deeper faith for me so Satan couldn't get to me and Aunt Pete muttering to Rebecca to get her mother out of there before she herself started hurling crockery.

I just kept rocking and retching up sobs. When there was nothing left but little-girl hiccups, I raised my head. The room was empty except for a familiar smell that wrapped itself around me.

"Aunt Pete's making coffee," a gravel voice said. "Personally, I think you need something stronger than that."

Hazel was on the couch above me, restacking the coasters. The lines radiating from her eyes were deep, like wisdom.

"You okay?" she said.

"No," I said.

"Good answer. If you'd said yes, I would have socked you."

I looked warily at the doorway. "Is everybody gone?"

"You think? Christine and Lissa couldn't get out of here fast enough. Aunt Pete ran the other two off with her broomstick."

"I was just a little bit hard on them."

"A little? You were better than Judge Judy." Hazel grinned. "I was proud of you. I knew you had it in you, though."

"*I* didn't." I stretched my legs out and rubbed my shins. A creeping sense of regret was edging in on me.

Hazel nudged me on the shoulder with her toe. "Don't go getting all remorseful. If they're your friends, they'll get it. You've been storing up that stuff for too long. It had to come out."

"Why did it have to come out in front of them?"

"Who cares?" Aunt Pete said. She carried in a tray of mugs that, in her own words, could have walked in from the kitchen by themselves. I'd have bet she made the coffee triple strength.

"Look, I'm sure they mean well and all that," Hazel said, "but they don't let you act like a human being." She frowned into the mug of mud. "You don't even let *yourself* act like a human being."

I started to cry again. "I don't mean to be mad at God, you know, but where *is* He? And where was *I,* and where's Tristan?" I doubled up into my knees. "Oh, my *gosh,* this hurts."

"Get it all out, Serena," Aunt Pete said. "Get all that stuff out of there."

"I don't know how!"

"Looks like you're doing a pretty good job of it to me."

"Want another stack of coasters?" Hazel said.

Chapter Ten

Hazel stayed until Gary brought her kids over. I sorted through the group on the porch and said, "Where's Max?" I caught Gary's sleeve. "Where's *Max*?"

"She's at our house," Gary said. "Nick asked if we'd keep her overnight, give you a chance to—"

"Nick?" I said.

"Much as I'd love to stay and hear the end of *this* tale," Hazel said, "I better get these guys home."

Sun put her hands on her nonexistent hips. "I wanted to stay with Max. It's not fair."

"Who ever promised you fair, kid?" Hazel said.

I gazed after them as Hazel piled everyone into the Suburban. Nick had said something like that to Max dozens of times, but the way Hazel put it—"Who ever promised you fair?"—wedged itself into me. I'd honestly thought Somebody *had* promised me fair.

"I felt like I had to call Nick, Serena," Gary said to me as Hazel drove off. "Lissa said you were so upset."

I set my teeth. "Did she tell you I lost it?"

"Something like that. I suspected you were just having a normal reaction to an abnormal situation. Looks like I was right." His freckles crinkled as he smiled. "I'll tell Nick he doesn't need to fly home."

"What?"

"He wanted me to check on you and tell him whether I thought he should cut his trip short and come back."

I tried to imagine Nick pulling into the driveway just then, spraying gravel but smoothing himself down before he emerged from the car to come and put me back together.

But according to Gary, I hadn't fallen apart. He was the pastor, and he should know. Now he could tell Nick, and Nick would know I was fine. Nobody asked me.

"No," I said, "I'll go get Max. Let me just get my purse."

"She's having fun at our place. They're ordering pizza."

I knew Max wasn't having fun. She thought Justin was "the boringest boy on the planet."

"Why don't you give yourself a little space at least until tomorrow morning?" Gary said.

"I want her home."

"Okay." Gary motioned to the wicker chairs. "Let's just talk for a few minutes first, huh?"

"Are you going to tell me I don't have enough faith, so Satan's attacking me?" I said. "Because I don't want to hear any more of that, Gary. I can't."

If he was shocked, he didn't show it. He just sat down and studied his hands, folded between his knees. "Lissa says you're having
some issues with God right now, and before you answer, just know
that I think it's perfectly understandable." He nodded at me. "So
does God."

It was still so raw, this coming out with the unspeakable. I wasn't
sure I could trust it. I sat down.

"Let's not call them issues," I said carefully. "Let's call them questions."

"Okay. Now's a good time to ask."

"As long as you don't answer with 'God is good all the time. All
the time God is good.'" Now that I'd let the imp loose, she was obviously taking over.

But Gary only nodded again. "Depends on our definition of
good. If *good* to us means everything the way we want it or the way
we think it should be, then it's not the answer."

"Did God ever promise us fair?" I said.

He released a slow grin. "You gotta love that Hazel, don't you? She
hit it right on the nose." Gary shook his head. "No parents in their
right mind promise their kids fair, at least not fair the way kids see it.
Kids think something's unfair because they didn't deserve it or it
wasn't the same as what somebody else got. That's because they can't
see the big picture."

"I don't care what the big picture is; somebody taking Tristan
away is not fair. That's why I'm having issues with God, Gary. I'm
sorry, but I am." I smeared at my tears with my fingers.

"Now *that* I might be able to help you with," Gary said. "Most of the time when we have 'issues' with God, it's because we expect God to be something He never was in the first place."

"He's *not* loving and gentle? He *doesn't* protect us when we're faithful?" I didn't even bother wiping my eyes this time. "Then I've been sold a bill of goods."

"He's that, but that isn't all He is. Expecting Him to be soft and comforting when it's something else you need is setting yourself up for separation from Him."

"What I need is Tristan."

Gary leaned toward me. "Maybe whatever it's going to take to bring her home is what you need."

"I don't know what that is."

"God does."

I sank back in the chair and closed my eyes. It was dark and still inside my head. There was no vision of my Father. But at least there was nothing there to mock me. At least there was room for something I didn't know. It was very small, but it was something.

"Why didn't you tell me all this before?" I said.

Gary gave me a long and serious look. "Because you never got angry enough to ask," he said.

Tuesday morning, the first day of school, Max was in a black mood when she came downstairs for breakfast. Her eyes could have cut glass.

Part of it, I knew, was that we hadn't had our annual Labor Day party, the one we'd always planned as if it were the last party we would ever have. The end of summer always called for an all-out fiesta before the boardwalk shops nailed down their shutters and the beach umbrellas withdrew their flapping colors and the smell of cotton candy faded from the air.

Although Max had said very little to me all weekend, I'd heard snatches of the earfuls Aunt Pete had gotten in the kitchen, on the side porch, in Aunt Pete's room. Anywhere I wasn't.

"It rocked. There would be cars parked all down Ocean View Parkway… I know it can't happen this year. Nothing can happen… Sometimes I hate Tristan for getting taken. And don't say I'm a horrible person, because I already know it."

That, I assumed Tuesday morning, was the other reason for the deep crevices Max formed between her eyes as she toyed with a bowl of Cheerios. I knew what it was like to be a "horrible person."

"I bet you wish we'd had a party this weekend, huh?" I said.

She didn't look at me. "We couldn't."

"I know. But did you wish we could?"

"What difference does it make?" Her shoulders flicked, like a horse twitching at a fly. "No offense," she added.

"It makes a difference, because nothing's the same as it was before, and it seems like it never will be. It's okay to hate that."

She tapped her spoon and swung her legs and did everything but answer me.

"You wanna know what *I* hate?" I said.

Max shrugged.

"I hate that I can't make things okay for you."

The shoulders twitched again.

"I'm so sorry, Maxie," I said.

"It's not your fault," she said. The words were adult, but the voice quavered with childhood fear.

The phone rang, and I choked back tears to answer it. It was Nick.

"I just wanted to tell our girl to have a good first day of school," he said.

"It's Daddy," I said to Max. I tried to make my voice as bright as Nick was trying to make his, but all I could hear was the absence of Tristan's name, of a good luck wish for her too.

"I have to go brush my teeth," Max said and left the table.

I let her go.

"I heard," Nick said.

"She's having a hard time."

"I still wish she was staying home with you."

Silence fell between us, yawning wider than the miles.

"You okay?" I said finally.

"I'm just trying to deal with all this," he said. I could tell he was barely opening his mouth. "I'm just putting one foot in front of the other."

"Have you found out anything?"

"It was a dead end. Look, don't worry about it. You just try to hold yourself together for Max until I get home. I'm flying out today."

When we hung up, I went in the bathroom and sobbed, because I didn't know what else to do. Then I put on sunglasses for the drive, even though the sky was overcast. It was already drizzling as we headed for Ocean View.

For a while Max stayed quiet, hugging the new backpack Lissa had taken her shopping for on Saturday. My hands were white knuckled on the steering wheel.

Finally she said, "Everybody says fifth grade's hard because they're getting you ready for middle school."

"Is that our subject?" I said.

"Huh?"

"Our subject. School. Boys are all shoot spitballs across the room, and girls are—"

Max shrank down behind her backpack. "I don't feel like playing," she said. She turned on the radio and was silent the rest of the way.

When we pulled into the line of cars at the front of Lord Baltimore, I said, "You want me to come in with you?"

Max's eyes rolled up. "Mo-om! No way. It's not like I'm some first grader."

"How silly of me," I said.

I drove home in tears, because she didn't want me there, because I would have been a blubbering idiot in front of her new teacher, because I skidded into Garfield Parkway and careened dangerously close to Chief Little Owl, the twenty-six-foot totem pole that marked the entrance to "downtown" Bethany Beach.

By the time I pulled up to the house, I was shaking. Aunt Pete met me on the porch.

"The school called," she said.

"Already?" I said. "I just dropped her off."

"Not Max's school. Tristan's. This lady wants you to call her back."

I shook my head at the piece of notepaper she waved under my nose. "Didn't you tell her Tristan won't be there?"

Aunt Pete grunted. "Oh, she knew. She said it was urgent. You better call her."

She all but pulled my cell phone out of my purse for me.

"I'm gonna fix you some toast," she said and disappeared into the house.

I stared at the numbers written with Aunt Pete's unsteady hand and at the name she'd painstakingly printed: Virginia Hatch. That wasn't the principal. The name didn't ring a bell as one of Tristan's teachers. A lump formed in my throat as I realized I didn't know who her new teachers were, the ones she would slave for her junior year. Or not.

I looked dismally at the rain and resisted the urge to crumple the paper in my hand and pretend Tristan would come home today and tell me all about this Ms. Hatch, who was going to be brutal and make her study so hard…

I punched in the numbers and hoped I'd get voice mail. I didn't feel like trying to explain what I myself didn't understand.

"Virginia Hatch."

"Oh," I said.

"How can I help you?"

You can't, I thought. But I said, "This is Serena Soltani."

"Ah."

The brisk quality of Virginia Hatch's voice softened in one syllable. *Please don't do that,* I thought. My tongue was already getting thick.

"Mrs. Soltani," she said, "I'm Tristan's guidance counselor here at Indian River. I apologize for not getting in touch with you sooner, but I've been out of the country. In fact, I just got back in time for school to start, and I heard about Tristan's disappearance."

"We really don't know much—"

"But I think *I* know something."

I moved the phone to my other ear and raked my hand through my hair. "I don't understand."

"Maybe we can figure it out together. There are some things I think you should know." She didn't give me a chance to question. "Can you come see me?"

"When?" I said.

"I think the sooner the better."

"I'll be right there," I said.

I closed the phone, and Aunt Pete put a charred bacon sandwich in my other hand. "For the road," she said.

I was barely aware of the rain as I drove the seven miles to Indian River High School in Frankford. I was barely aware of anything except the questions that nearly battered me to a pulp by the time I pulled into the visitors' parking lot. I had to take a minute to peer into the rearview mirror and make sure I didn't look like an escapee from the state hospital. I was very nearly coming apart, and I had to glue myself back together at least long enough to find out if this counselor, this Virginia Hatch, really did know something about my Tristan.

I can do this, I told myself. *God, just help me do this.*

I was fine approaching the columned old brick building, a larger version of Max's Lord Baltimore. It had managed to maintain its dignity, even as the newer additions had been tacked on through the years wherever they could be attached, like new words on a Scrabble board. The times I'd been there, I had always found it idyllic when the last bell of the day rang and the students poured out the front door and down the steps, as they had for decades. Even if half of them had nose rings and had lost their virginity in middle school, I could still imagine girls in poodle skirts, boys in crew cuts—or both in tie-dyed T-shirts—all ghosts from High School Past.

But as I stepped into the main hallway, the figures around me were all too real. Teenagers. Sixteen-year-olds. Girls with long dark hair and eyes like young does, doing pliés in front of their lockers.

I covered my mouth with my hand to keep from crying out, "Tristan! Where have you been?" and made my way to the office.

A woman with a nametag that said "Virginia Hatch" was at the counter fending off a mob of students all waving schedules that they claimed were "screwed up."

"I'll take care of these later," she said when she saw me.

"Come on, Mrs. H.!" was the unanimous response.

"It isn't like you're that anxious to start your classes," she said in the brisk voice I'd first heard on the phone.

She left them muttering and led me into her office—a narrow room overlooking the parking lot and overflowing with papers and folders.

"I almost need counseling myself by the time the first week is over," she said as she cleared a place for me on a red-checked love seat that was obviously not the property of the Indian River School District. I took in Virginia Hatch's face, which was evenly tanned and framed in a stylish wispy cut of gray hair. Her eyes nearly matched it, and yet her face was far from colorless. She had a warmth that came from her smile, a smile that she banished as if it was somehow inappropriate right now. I was left looking into the countenance of compassion.

She pulled a director's chair, covered in red canvas, near the love seat and sat facing me.

"I don't know if Tristan told you," she said, "but for the last few months of last year, I was seeing her here in my office every week."

"You mean for counseling?" I said. I shook my head. "Of course it would be. You're a counselor. It's just that Tristan wasn't—"

"The kind of girl you'd ever think would have a problem."

I stared down at the checked fabric, which seemed to come up and slam me in the face.

"Normally I wouldn't break her confidence," she said, "but—"

"This isn't 'normally.'"

"No, and I think what I have to share with you might explain some things."

"Please, tell me anything you think would help," I said.

She steepled her fingers under her nose before she began. "I first saw Tristan at the end of March. She had burst into tears in the middle of English class, and the teacher sent her in with a note saying Tristan was a perfectionist and maybe she was cracking under the pressure of tests and papers."

"That could be," I said. "She has to do everything just right, or she gets so upset. She's been like that since kindergarten."

"I thought that was the problem when we first talked, especially after she told me how many dance classes she was taking a week and that she was also in student government and on the dance team here at school, not to mention French club." Virginia smiled faintly. "I needed a nap just listening to her."

"I thought maybe she was doing too much," I said. "But she wanted to do everything." My voice sounded pinched, defensive.

"She did want to," Virginia said. "And as we talked more, I found out why." She directed her eyes at the ceiling. "She craved approval, especially from her parents, mostly her father." She looked at me. "She was sure you would love her even if she'd held up the school store, but she felt like she had to prove her worth to her dad."

I shook my head.

"I'm sorry," she said. "I know this isn't easy for you."

I rubbed at the pain that was gathering in my chest and nodded for her to go on.

"Tristan involved herself in an impossible number of activities so that every minute was filled with something, and in everything she did, she toed the line obsessively, again because she equated approval with worth, and because it helped her deal with the pressure."

"What pressure?"

"The pressure she was putting on herself and the pressure she felt she was getting at home."

"Pressure?" I said again. It was like a foreign word I couldn't translate.

"She felt like she wasn't allowed to be a normal teenager," Virginia said. "And part of the reason she packed her schedule was so she could limit her interactions with you and her dad."

She was obviously choosing her words carefully, but I wanted to knock the whole precise stack of them over with a swipe of my hand. Yet even as she placed one on top of the other, they formed a truth I couldn't turn away from. I could only stare at it and wish it weren't there.

"We had a faculty briefing this morning before classes," Virginia said. "From what I pieced together, Tristan was last seen with a lifeguard."

"Ricky Zabriski," I said. "Spider." The word came out like a spit. "Doesn't he sound heinous?"

"He does. The whole thing is heinous; that's the perfect word." Virginia leaned forward, and I could see tired etchings around her eyes. "The police think he abducted her, yes?"

"Yes."

"What do you think?"

I couldn't blurt out what I wanted to be true. Not with Virginia's words still trying to arrange themselves in my head: *Tristan felt like she had to prove her worth to her dad. She wasn't allowed to be a normal teenager. She wanted to limit her interactions with us.*

Virginia looked at me directly, as if I could handle one more blow. "Have you considered the possibility that Tristan may have run away with this boy?" she said.

"It's been suggested." My voice went tight. "But I keep thinking it's impossible. That's just not Tristan."

Virginia got up and went to her desk. I resented her for knowing things about my daughter that I didn't, even while I hoped she would pull something out of her drawer that would take me to Tristan.

She handed me a piece of paper. "Tristan expressed her feelings in her poetry."

I stared at the paper. "She wrote poetry?"

"She only told me the last week of school, and this is the only poem she shared with me." Her voice softened as if she were afraid she might break me. "If I can't convince you, maybe Tristan can."

She stood up and moved toward the door. "I'm sure the natives are getting restless out there. I'm going to check on them."

As the door clicked shut behind her, I ran a finger down the page in my lap, over the thoughts my daughter had written there, the words she'd never intended for me to see.

"Into the Day"
by Tristan Soltani

I move into the day
Like heavy
Like lead
Like hauling the load that's assigned.

I move into the day
With orders
With dictates
With voices I know are not mine.

I move into the day
Just smiling
Just dancing
Just knowing that I am not free.

I move into the day
No flying
No singing
No light for a glimmer of me.

I move into the day
With wishes
With glimpses
With dreams that only I find

Of a time when I'll shed
All the shoulds
All the musts
And move into a day that is mine.

I felt as if I'd been stabbed, and yet I kept reading it over and over until the rhythm of my daughter's pain was in my breath, in my heartbeat.

"How could I not have known?" I said when I heard the door again.

Virginia moved soundlessly to her chair. Her eyes had the sheer matte finish of almost-tears.

"The important thing is that you do now," she said. "And the more you know, the better chance you have of finding her and bringing her back. I'm convinced of that."

I pressed the poem to my chest. "You said this is the only one she gave you."

"She said there are more, but she didn't tell me where. I suggested that she keep them in a special book, but she said no—you and her dad would find them."

"I never went through her things!"

"In her mind there were no boundaries. She did tell me that she put them in various secret places."

"More secrets," I said.

"Now might be a good time to *start* going through her things," Virginia said. "You can help her."

I looked ruefully at the poem. "Can I?"

"I think you're the only one who can," she said.

Chapter Eleven

How I got home, I didn't know. I suddenly found myself sitting in the car in our driveway listening to the windshield wipers taunt me with every slap.

> *Like heavy*
> *Like lead*
> *Like hauling the load that's assigned.*

They could have been my own thoughts right then. Thoughts I'd never had before and yet were somehow familiar. The same thoughts that had made my precious daughter so unhappy. Thoughts she couldn't share with me.

The stabbing pain in my chest took my breath away. Had it felt this bad to Tristan? Had she gotten to the place where she wanted to hurl the family-room knickknacks or spit in people's faces? *Our* faces?

With orders
With dictates
With voices I know are not mine.

She must have. And yet she smiled. And she danced. And she went to her room and wrote poems.

There were more, Virginia Hatch had told me. She kept them in "various secret places."

I shut off the motor, leaving the wipers suspended in the middle of the windshield. I had to find those places. I had to know the secrets, or I might never get her back.

I could hear Aunt Pete snoring in the recliner as I climbed to the second floor, and I was grateful for that now. I didn't want her on this mission with me, dragging the turquoise beach bag behind her and pouring muddy coffee down my throat. I stood outside Tristan's room for several minutes, hand on the doorknob. I'd sailed into that room a thousand times or more with a basket of folded laundry or a snack to get her through studying for finals or a reminder to turn out her light by nine thirty. I usually entered without so much as a knock. In fact, the girls' doors were almost always left ajar except when they were getting dressed.

"Let's keep the open-door policy," Nick had told me six months before when I'd reported that Max had registered a complaint about having "like, zero privacy."

"If she doesn't have anything to hide," he said, "why does she need the door closed? You don't hear Tristan complaining about it."

Just smiling
Just dancing
Just knowing that I am not free.

Now as I stood pressing my forehead against Tristan's door, I struggled with going in. I was barging into the room of someone I didn't know, about to rummage through things not meant for my eyes. It was like going through a stranger's purse.

"I have to do this, Tristan," I said out loud, "because I have to find you."

That tiny point of focus could hold nothing else. I went with that and opened the door.

I'd been in her bedroom at least once a day since she'd disappeared, but I hadn't touched a thing except the bed, which I often crawled into in the crazy-making hours of the night. I wanted her room to be exactly the way she left it so that when she came home, she could step right back into her life, unscathed by whatever she'd been through.

As I dragged my gaze across the perfectly stacked wicker trunks and the gauzy curtains that softened the glare of the sun, I felt completely foolish. Was this room her life? Did she want to step back into it and pick up where she'd left off?

No light for a glimmer of me.

I marched to the windows that covered the beachside wall and shoved the curtains back one by one until the walls were drenched in sunlight. It made the room, with its subtle shades of gray, seem stark—the edge of the oak dressers too sharp, the lines of the bedposts too severe. Everything was so tidy and tucked. Where could she possibly have hidden secret poems?

My hands ached as I opened a drawer and slid them between the precisely folded pairs of socks and then the cotton panties, the T-shirts, the dance togs. My shoulders throbbed as I pulled each muslin-lined basket from the closet shelves and turned every page of every notebook and emptied the contents of every folder. My neck was a solid rod of pain by the time I put each torn movie ticket and dance recital program back into the exact place I'd found it.

Aunt Pete woke up around noon and brought me a tuna on pumpernickel that I never touched. To my utter amazement, she didn't ask me what I was doing. I heard her on the phone to someone—probably Hazel—saying, "I wondered when she was gonna start digging. I was giving her another week, and then I was going through that bedroom myself."

She left me alone—to dig—until two thirty, when she poked her head in and asked if I was going to pick Max up at school.

"Oh, no!" I said. I started to scramble up from the stacks of books I was going through page by page, but Aunt Pete waved me back down.

"Sit still," she said. "Hazel said if you were in the middle of something she'd pick up Max for you. She's picking up her two anyway."

"Why?" I said. "Don't they take the bus home?"

"Tri's banned from the bus," Aunt Pete said. "Something about Supergluing some kid's rear end to a seat last year."

I looked helplessly at the pile of books that had so far given me nothing. I had convinced myself that one of them would cough up a poem if I just kept searching. Nothing else in the room had.

"She offered," Aunt Pete said. "Personally, I don't think you'd make it out of the driveway before you hit something."

"Nick wouldn't like it."

"The mood he was in when he called, he doesn't like anything today, so it's six of one, a half dozen of another if you ask me."

"He called again?" I said.

"From the L.A. airport. From the Denver airport. I told him you were busy, and you still are. I'm calling Hazel back."

I let her.

There were only three books left to go through: *Anne of Green Gables, Little Women,* and *Jane Eyre.* I opted for Jane. I didn't even know Tristan owned a copy. I had only read it in the modern British literature course I'd taken in college. It seemed a little dark for her innocent taste.

The book looked as if it had been read more than once and with vigor. Several signatures had pulled away from the binding, and there was a chocolate stain on the page it fell open to. A stain and a slip of paper folded in half.

I tried to convince myself it was just a note from somebody. Maybe Jessica. Maybe Spider Zabriski. I unfolded it and forced myself to scan it. If it didn't look like a poem, I would put it back.

"Numbers 30," it said at the top. "By Tristan Soltani." The words were arranged on the page in careful blocks. I could already feel their rhythm in my pulse.

My lungs have no breath as I watch him descend,
Face transformed from listening to Him.
I have waited my childhood to hear it.

Who knows what God thinks,
Makes the heart of pow'r yearn?
This man, I trust.

My heart has no beat as I hear him intone
Words like tablets carved in stone.
I have promised my lifetime to heed them.

Who knows what God loves,
Makes the soul of Him burn?
This man, I hope.

My mind has no thought as I take in the Law,
Accept with automatic awe.
I have promised my future to hold it.

Who knows what God wants,
Makes the hand of Him touch me?
This man? I thought so.

My soul has no rest as I chafe at the rock.
This man can undo my promise knots?
I vow my womanhood to shun it!

Who knows what God says,
What He whispers to me?
No man. I feel that.

My self has no nerve as I grope in the dark.
Try, with no guide, to make my mark.
I have no knowledge to do it.

Who knows where God is,
How to follow His lead?
Not this man.

Then who does?

The words made no sense, but I was chilled, as if my soul already understood them.

This man. Who was that? *This man* who descends with the Law?

"Moses?" I said to the room.

No, Mom.

I jumped and looked, terrified, at the door. Of course she wasn't there. For an insane second I was relieved that Tristan hadn't found me searching through her secrets.

But I'd heard it so clearly. *No, Mom. Not Moses.*

I pored over the poem again. "Numbers 30." Numbers, in the Old Testament?

I crawled between the heaps of books to the bedside table where I'd already come across Tristan's Bible earlier. I found myself shivering as I thumbed the thin, feminine pages. The book had the smell of little girl hands. She'd had enough Sunday school and Vacation Bible School and won enough memory-verse prizes to practically head up the Christian education program at church before she was fourteen. But as I located Numbers chapter 30, I saw that the pages to this book were stiff. This book, unlike *Jane Eyre,* was not my daughter's friend.

I was surprised to find whole verses underlined and exclamation points drawn sharply in the margins. The lines were nearly engraved into the paper, as if they'd been put there in anger.

> When a young woman still living in her father's house
> makes a vow to the LORD or obligates herself by a pledge
> and her father hears about her vow or pledge but says
> nothing to her, then all her vows and every pledge by
> which she obligated herself will stand. But if her father
> forbids her when he hears about it, none of her vows or
> the pledges by which she obligated herself will stand.

I looked back at the poem. Where was this Scripture in what she had written? I sat cross-legged and leaned against the bed.

Okay, *Face transformed from listening to Him.* That had to be Moses's face transformed, didn't it? And *Words like tablets carved in stone.* That was the Law. I got that.

My eyes snagged on the next verse. *He can undo my promise knots?* He who? And what promise knots?

I traced Tristan's underlining in the Bible with my finger. Vows, pledges. That was where the promise knots came in, and she obviously didn't like the idea of somebody untying them. My finger stopped, and with the stub of what fingernail I had left, I felt something I hadn't noticed until then. Tristan had drawn an extra line under every reference to "her father" in the passage.

But if her father forbids her when he hears about it, none of her vows or the pledges by which she obligated herself will stand.

I went back to the poem. *This man can undo my promise knots?* Her father?

My back came away from the bed, and I pulled the sides of the paper until a bitelike piece came off in my fingers. Was *this man* her father?

Suddenly, frantically, I tried to fit the torn piece back into its space. My thoughts raced like screaming cars. *God! God, please don't let her be talking about Nick! He's a good father! He loves her! He protects her.*

The mental race screeched to a halt as if it had been flagged down.

Nick told her and told her: "Listen to me. I know what's best for you. I'll decide." *I hear him intone / Words like tablets carved in stone.*

Nick laid out the rules so clearly: "We follow the Bible at our house. I'm the spiritual head of the household. Let's look at what God wants us to do." *I take in the Law, / Accept with automatic awe.*

But something had happened to make her *chafe at the rock.* So much that she couldn't stand it anymore? So much that she had to get away from it?

"God, is that it?"

The sound of my own voice startled me, and yet hearing it made me feel, again, as if someone were in the room with me, someone I was really talking to, who was listening.

"God," I said, "if it is—if we drove her from home—please, please show us how to bring her back. Please."

It was the clearest thought I'd had in weeks.

There was a brittle rap on the door. "You might want to wrap it up," Aunt Pete said from the other side. "Hazel just drove up with the kids."

I tucked the poem into my pocket and lined the books back up in the bookcase. I didn't want Max to know I'd been going through Tristan's things, at least not until I'd had a chance to talk to Nick. I was just closing the door behind me when Max reached the top of the stairs.

"Hey!" I said too cheerfully. "How was your first day in fifth grade?"

She stamped past me, eyebrows knotted as she struggled to get free of her backpack. "It was only the worst day of my entire life."

"Honey!" I said. "Why?"

Max hurled the backpack into her room and watched it slide across the hardwood floor. I heard it crash into the dresser between the twin beds.

"Madison and Ashley and all of them," she said. She still wasn't looking at me. "They started a club on the bus this morning. Only I can't be in it, because I don't ride the bus." Her voice spiraled up. "They're supposed to be my friends!"

I sagged. "I'm so sorry," I said.

She finally turned to me, eyes filming over. "Can you ask Dad to let me ride the bus?" she said, and then she threw up her arms. "Forget it. He'll just say no."

"Hey, Max! You comin'?"

It was Sun, shrieking from the bottom of the stairs.

"Yeah, hang on," Max called down to her. To me she said, "I'm going swimming with her and Tri and the dogs." She started into her room and then stopped and as an afterthought added, "Is that okay?"

There wasn't much I would have refused her right then.

It was good to see Hazel. I let her regale us with stories of Tri, who got his name written on the board, and Desi, who tore off the pocket of Hazel's jeans when the kindergarten teacher peeled him from Hazel's leg. Still, it was hard to keep from silently reciting Tristan's poems.

Hazel and her brood were leaving when Nick pulled in. His scowl told me he wasn't happy to see her there again, and he excused himself to go upstairs to change.

"Happy homecoming," Hazel muttered to me.

I asked Aunt Pete to give Max some supper, and I followed him up to our room.

"You okay?" I called to him.

He answered from inside the walk-in closet. "The question is, are you?" He stuck his head out and looked at me as I tucked myself into the chaise longue. I was shivering again.

"You've been crying," he said.

It was almost an accusation. I hugged my arms around myself.

He started back into the closet, but I said, "We need to talk, Nicky. I found out some things today—about Tristan."

Nick was immediately on me, standing over me, hands twitching on his hips. "What things?" he said. "Why didn't you call me?"

"Because it took awhile to figure them out."

"What? What was there to figure out?"

His irritation was so pointed, I could have reached out and pricked my finger on it. I watched him take a minute to smooth his hackles with his hand and lean against the bedpost, hands shoved into his pockets.

"Okay, I'm sorry," he said. "Tell me."

Actually, I would rather have done anything else. As I laid out the pieces of what Virginia Hatch had told me, new lines carved themselves into his face. When I started to read Tristan's first poem, he yanked it out of my hand after two verses.

"What on earth is she talking about?" His eyes moved down the page as if he were poking holes in it.

"She was unhappy, Nicky," I said.

"What did she have to be unhappy about?" He waved a hand obviously intended to take in our entire life. "She had everything. She was bright, she was popular, she was—" He looked momentarily stricken. "She *is* all those things." He crumpled the poem in one hand. "I don't know what this is about."

"I think this one will tell you," I said.

I extricated "Numbers 30" out of my pocket, and then I pressed it down on my thigh. I was about to hand him a knife to stab himself with, right in the heart.

"Is that another one?" Nick said.

I nodded.

"Let me see it."

"This one's going to hurt you," I said. "But I think we have to pay attention to what she's saying."

"Well, let me see it." Nick stuck out a demanding hand.

I wanted to slap it. As it was, I pressed the poem down against my thighbone. Giving it to him suddenly felt like another betrayal of my daughter.

"Serena, let me see it!"

"Not if you're going to call her a liar," I said.

It stopped both of us in midbreath. My heart was pounding, but I couldn't let go of the paper. Nick looked at me as if I had just walked in off the street. I watched him calm himself.

"Okay, hon, let's not blow this out of proportion. These are the writings of a mixed-up kid."

"Our kid!" I said. I pressed the poem to my chest.

"Sure doesn't sound like our kid. This counselor probably had her digging around for what made her flip out in the classroom, and you know Tristan. She was just trying to please."

Just smiling
Just dancing
Just knowing that I am not free.

"I think that's the problem," I said.

"What problem?" Nick held out the poem he'd crumpled. "This

is something she made up when all that was really going on with her was probably hormones."

"PMS did *not* make our daughter run away!" I said.

"Who said she ran away? The counselor? The lady with all the answers?"

Nick hurled Tristan's balled-up poem across the room. It hit the window and dropped to the floor. I went to it and smoothed it out and folded it with the other one. With both of them held to my lips, I cried silently out at the ocean. Nick's arms came around me.

"I'm sorry, hon." The words were murmured and thick. "I hate to see you grasping at straws. It's just getting you all upset, and you can't even think straight."

I pushed his hands away with my forearms and moved out of his reach. "No, Nicky," I said. "For the first time since this happened, I *am* thinking straight. I don't like what I'm finding out, but we have to face it. It could lead us to Tristan."

"There's nothing to face." Nick's mouth stiffened. "Somebody took Tristan against her will—whether it was that kid Zabriski or somebody trying to get me. We're trying to hunt him down and bring her home."

"You and your private investigator?" I said.

Nick's eyes flicked away. "I'm in touch with Ed Malone daily too."

"And what does he say?"

"Not much. But we will find her, Serena, and reading things into it that just aren't there isn't going to help."

"Why haven't you told me you talk to Detective Malone every

day?" I was shouting, and my voice was so unaccustomed to that volume that it was wobbling like toddler legs.

"Because I was afraid of *this*!"

"What?"

"This." Nick held out both hands. "You getting yourself all upset and losing control—"

"Don't tell me I'm losing control! My daughter has been missing for a month. Nobody knows where she is, and now I'm finding out maybe she doesn't *want* to come home!"

"Don't go there, Serena." Nick's jaw muscles flexed. "And don't go back into Tristan's room. It's not good for you, and it's not telling us anything."

I stared at him. I didn't say a word. He tried to reach for me, but I turned away.

"Why don't you give me that stuff?" he said.

"What stuff?" I said.

"Those poems or whatever they are."

"Why, if they aren't going to tell you anything?"

"Mom?" Max said from the other side of the door.

I gave Nick a long look before he went to open it.

"Hey, short stuff," he said.

"Hi. Is Mom here?"

I waved to her from the window.

"Nice to see you again too," Nick said.

"I said hi." She turned to me. "Is it okay if I write on my old T-shirts?"

The pure simplicity of it brought me to tears. "What's up?" I said.

"Me and Sun are starting our own club."

"Me and Sun?" Nick said. "What kind of grammar is that?"

The hairs on the back of my neck bristled. "You're making club T-shirts?" I said to Max.

"*And* secret cards. Our club's gonna be way cooler than Ashley's."

"Way cooler," I said. "Sure. Go for it."

"Excuse me," Max said to Nick. She stepped around him.

"I don't like her attitude," Nick said when she was gone.

I stepped around him too.

Chapter Twelve

Nick and I spoke very little over the next few days. I went through Tristan's room several more times but didn't uncover any more poems, so I spent a lot of time studying the two I had. I used the iron to press the wrinkles out of the one Nick had crumpled.

"*Now* what are you doing, Serena?" Aunt Pete said when she found me at the ironing board in the laundry room on Thursday.

I told her. After all the ways she'd supported me, she had a right to know. I even let her read both poems.

"It doesn't surprise me at all," she said when she was through. "Nicky runs those girls like a Gestapo."

"He's not that bad!" I said.

"Look out, now. You don't want to burn that." Aunt Pete pulled up the corner of her bathrobe and put it over the paper. "Now press," she said. "And no, he's not that bad, but he doesn't need to be so hard on Tristan. She's the closest thing to perfect in a kid I ever saw. I told her that too."

I pulled up the iron and stared at her. "I didn't know you had conversations like that with Tristan."

Aunt Pete shrugged. "She was sitting down there on the beach one day, writing something in a notebook. You could practically see the smoke comin' out of her pen."

"Did you see what she was writing?"

"She didn't offer to show me, and I didn't ask. Matter of fact, she stuffed it in her bag like she was afraid I was gonna grab it from her."

Aunt Pete pulled her bathrobe off the ironing board and held it out from her until it cooled. Her legs, spindly and white and veined in purple, were exposed, and it struck me how very old she was.

"I told her," she went on, " 'I'm not gonna pry into your business,' and she kind of grunted and said, 'You'd be the only one.' "

My insides sagged.

"She said her father had to know everything she was doing and who she was with every second. She said it probably ticked him off that he couldn't read her mind. I said to her, 'I bet it's a good thing he can't,' and she said, 'Yeah.' "

I set the iron down. "You knew and I didn't."

"Yeah, well, don't go beatin' yourself up. The question is, what are you gonna do with this?" She nodded toward the poem. "Did you call that detective?"

"No. I'm afraid if he thinks this is evidence that she ran away, he'll call off the search. We still have to find her, even if she did go because she wanted to." I yanked the iron's plug out of the outlet.

"If you're not calling that detective just because you think Nicky's going to be mad at you, forget it," Aunt Pete said. She wandered into the kitchen, and I followed her. She poured us each a cup of coffee. "It isn't gonna hurt him, and it's not gonna hurt you, either. You should be mad at him, the way he's acting."

"I know he's scared."

"He's terrified! But he's too stubborn to admit it, and that's gonna keep him from seein' things you've got your eyes wide open to now." Aunt Pete gave me the Soltani squint over the top of her mug. "Which is why you should be the one talkin' to Malone."

I considered that. "I could just ask him what they would do if we discovered Tristan really had run off with Spider Zabriski."

"You got nothin' to lose," she said.

"Where's the number?" I said.

"It's 555-0102," Aunt Pete said.

I looked at her.

"I've just been waitin' for you to ask," she said.

Ed Malone wasn't at the station when I called, but the officer I talked to, who spoke as if he had something heavy attached to his tongue, said he'd have Ed get in touch with me. Ten minutes later Ed was knocking on the front door.

"Is this a good time?" he said when I opened it.

He looked thinner than the last time I'd seen him, and the tiny lines around his eyes were more pronounced, the eyes themselves set deeper into their golden greenness. And yet he still managed a smile.

"Coffee's hot," Aunt Pete squawked from the kitchen.

"Shovel me out a cup," Ed called back to her as I led him into the library.

He grinned at me and waited while I perched, one leg under me, on a chair before he sat in the other one. "I could stand a little more hair on my chest," he said.

Aunt Pete brought the cups in on a tray and left, to my surprise, closing the french doors behind her.

"You have news?" Ed said to me.

"I have a question." I looked down at my toes poking out of my sandals.

"Hope I have an answer," Ed said. His voice was so kind it hurt.

"I just want to know," I said, "if we found out that Tristan ran away with that Spider guy—you know, if he didn't drag her off—"

"Right."

"Would that mean that you—the police—would stop looking for her?"

"Absolutely not." Ed blew into his coffee. "It would just mean we'd change her classification on the NCIC, identify her as a runaway."

"Oh," I said.

The fight against tears was pointless. Ed handed me a napkin from the tray.

"I'm not going to stop looking for Tristan, Serena," he said. "Because if she did run away, by now I'm sure she's forgotten what prompted her to do it and she wants to come home."

"Then why doesn't she?"

"We don't know, and that's why we'll keep looking—in case it's something she has no control over."

"Like what?"

Ed laced his fingers together and put them behind his head. He kept his eyes on me.

"Maybe Spider, if he's still with her, won't let her come home. Not that he's abusing her or anything, but he might not give her the means to get back here or let her use a phone—that kind of thing." He waited for me to nod again. "Maybe she's not with Spider anymore. Maybe she tried to get back home and got into some other trouble."

"What kind of trouble?"

Ed brought his hands down to his knees and looked at them. "It's rough out there on your own when you're sixteen, especially when you've never had to fend for yourself. She might have trusted somebody who offered to help and wound up in a deeper trap."

"What kind of trap?"

Ed's eyes grew quizzical, and I couldn't blame him. Until that day I'd done almost nothing except nod at him. But now the questions were popping from me as if something inside me was snapping its fingers.

"Drugs, maybe," Ed said. "Not necessarily taking them but running them, for food and shelter."

"She could be living on the street?" I said.

Ed leaned toward me. "Serena, if you have reason to think she ran away, please tell me, because that will change the nature of our search. We'll stand a better chance of finding her if we have all the information."

Shoulders shaking, I pulled the folded poems out of my pocket and handed them to him. While he read, I curled up in the chair and closed my eyes.

It was a while before he said, "Serena."

I looked up. The veins in his eyes were red and blurred.

"I'd like to make copies of these," he said. "They don't prove that she ran away, but they're enough to warrant broadening our search. There's a good chance she's gone to a shelter. Plus there are other places where runaways congregate."

I touched the pages in his hand. "These were her secrets," I said.

"I'll take good care of them. In fact, do you want to come with me to the station? I'll make the copies while you're standing there, and you can have them right back."

I shook my head. "I trust you. I think... I don't know!"

Ed squeezed my hand before he stood up. "You're doing the right thing," he said.

I half hoped Nick would think so. The other half of me didn't care whether he did or not. I wanted my unhappy daughter home, where maybe we could start over.

Now that Nick was back, there was no way to get out of going to church that Sunday, as much as I wanted to avoid Rebecca and her mother. Lissa hugged me before I went into the sanctuary and whispered, "You don't have to be embarrassed about what happened that day at your house. None of us have told anybody."

I just looked at her.

"I'm so glad you're here," she said. "We need you."

I sat through the service between Aunt Pete and Max, wondering what I had to give at that point. Before the final hymn was over, I escaped to the rest room. I'd barely started a good cry when Hazel filled the doorway.

"Want a ride home?" she said. "Sun's watching Tri and Desi, and I've got the getaway car outside."

It wasn't until I was in the front seat of her Suburban with Regis and Kelly drooling on my head that it occurred to me to ask, "Were you in church, Hazel?"

"I've been there the last two Sundays. Somebody had to keep the rumors from getting out of hand. Those church ladies can be vicious." Hazel fumbled in her purse for something as she drove and then gave up. "Lissa, now she's not bad. But I think she's scared of them. What, do they give a lot of money to the church or something?"

I surprised myself by laughing. It was as much of a pain reliever as crying.

"So what did Nick say when you told him you showed the poems to Ed?"

"I didn't tell him."

Hazel took her eyes from the road to stare at me. "Okay, who are you, and what have you done with Serena?"

I laughed again, but it wasn't the first time over the last few days that I'd thought about how easy it was not to share information with Nick. Why wouldn't it be? I realized that I never told him I always kept Max quiet in church by feeding her clandestine candy or that I let Tristan stay up until ten to study when he was out of town.

"I guess sometimes I just take the easy way out," I said.

"Huh," Hazel said. "So it's going to be easy to explain why you just skipped out on the fellowship hour?"

I shrugged. Maybe it was getting easier to argue with Nicky too.

When we got in the house, Hazel put her purse on the kitchen counter and pulled out her cell phone. "This stupid thing," she said. "Battery's dead again. Can I see if Sun left a message on your phone?"

"Already?" I said. But then I nodded. She *was* watching Desi, after all.

Hazel pushed the button while I pulled a pitcher of orange juice out of the refrigerator. When I heard Tristan's voice on the machine, I let the pitcher slip to the floor, where it shattered.

"Hi, Mama. Hi, Daddy. It's me."

I tore for the phone and skidded on the wet floor, crashing sideways into Hazel. She pushed me the rest of the way to the answering machine. The voice coming from it was fragile and thin, but it was her. It was Tristan.

"I'm sorry I didn't call before," she said. "But I'm okay. I just wanted you to know."

"Where are you?" I said.

Of course there was no answer. There was only her trembling close: "Well, I guess that's all. I have to go."

"No! Don't go! Tristan, where are you?"

I fumbled with the buttons until Hazel pulled my hand back.

"Let me. You're liable to erase it doing that." The tape rewound, and she played it again.

"Hi, Mama. Hi, Daddy. It's me. I'm sorry I didn't call before. But

I'm okay. I just wanted you to know. Well, I guess that's all. I have to go."

I played it again and counted the words. There were thirty of them. Thirty fragile words from my daughter—who was alive.

"Thank you, God," I said over and over. "Oh, Tristan. Baby girl."

I made Hazel play it at least ten times while I strained to hear what she didn't say, what might be hiding in the creases of her voice. We were on our eleventh round when the front door slammed, and Nick was suddenly there.

His face was a livid scarlet until he registered what he was hearing. His angry eyes went from me to the machine where Tristan was speaking to him. "Hi, Daddy. It's me."

"Is that Sissy?" Max said from behind him.

Nick waved her to silence and leaned over the machine, just as I'd done. I cried as I watched him swallow hard.

"She's okay," I said.

"Where is she, Mom?" Max said.

"I don't know," I said. I pulled her off her feet into my arms. "But she's okay!"

"I can't hear," Nick shouted at us.

Hazel hustled Max out of the kitchen, nearly knocking Aunt Pete over. I heard them whispering in the foyer.

Nick let the tape rewind and slowly straightened.

"Nicky," I said, "this is *good* news."

"Yeah," he said. His face was ashen as he ran his hand down the back of his head. "This means she's alive." He shook his head and swallowed again, and I was sure he was going to cry. But before I could get my arms around him, he drove his fist into the snack bar. The salt and pepper shakers jittered in their places.

"She knew we'd be at church," he said. "She purposely called when she knew we wouldn't be here."

My thoughts ran into each other.

"I don't think she did it on purpose," I said. "Maybe it was the first chance she had to call. She said she was sorry—"

"She said she was sorry she *didn't* call sooner. She didn't say she *couldn't.* Why didn't she tell us where she is? Or how we can reach her?"

When the words "star six nine" formed in my head, I was still way behind Nick.

He was already pounding the keys on the phone as if they alone were responsible for what Tristan didn't say. He listened for a few seconds and then slammed the phone down. "The number can't be reached that way," he said.

"Maybe Ed can tell where she is from background noises," I said.

"I didn't hear any background noises," Nick said. "This isn't *CSI,* Serena."

"We have to take this tape to Ed Malone," I said.

"Fine. Do what you want, since that's your new lifestyle." Nick glared toward the foyer and lowered his voice to a deep growl. "As far as I'm concerned, if Tristan wants us to find her, then she can tell us where she is."

He turned away, but I grabbed his sleeve and curled it into my fingers. "What are you saying?"

"She's playing a little game now." Nick's lips barely moved. "I thought I raised her different from that, but evidently not. She knows where she lives. Let her find her own way home."

When his tires had squealed off down Ocean View Parkway, Max crept into the kitchen, face the color of Cream of Wheat. "What's going on?" she said.

"Daddy's just a little bit upset," I said.

"Ya think?" Max said. She pointed to the answering machine. "I wanna hear my sister."

I nodded to Hazel, who pushed the button and stood by her.

Aunt Pete motioned for me to join her in the foyer.

"His pride's wounded," she said. "He'll see the light, but you can't wait for that."

"I know," I said. "I'm taking the tape to Ed tomorrow."

"What's wrong with today?"

I just shook my head. Maybe I thought Nick would "see the light" before then and go with me when I handed it over. Maybe I thought Tristan would call back. Maybe she was disappointed that we hadn't been there.

Maybe if I *had* been, she'd be on her way home right now. No. I'd be on my way to get her.

"Mom?"

I jumped.

"Tristan sounds scared," Max said at my elbow. "Wherever she is, I don't think she wants to be there."

I held on to her, and we both cried. Max cried because her big sister was afraid. I cried because, as much as Tristan didn't want to be where she was, she didn't want to be home, either.

Chapter Thirteen

Max informed me late that afternoon that Nick was down on the beach.

"What's he doing?" I said.

"I don't think he's building sandcastles," she said. "Can me and Sun have a secret club meeting in the big room?"

When the two of them were tucked away in the rec room on the third floor, I ventured down to the beach. I felt like a small child, watching Nick as I drew closer, looking for twitches and tightenings that would signal I should run. But he turned from his stance at the water's edge and saw me first. There was only regret on his face.

He looked down when I got to him, his shoed toe skimming the shallows that lapped at his feet.

"I was a jerk today," he said. "I'm sorry."

I didn't know how to respond to "I'm sorry." I only nodded.

"I know it's not like Tristan to scheme," he said. "I just want somebody to blame."

"You can't blame *her*," I said.

"I know that, Serena." His voice was strained. "I called the private investigator back in. I'm more convinced than ever now that someone has her who isn't going to hurt her. He just wants to make me suffer."

"For how long?"

"Now, how would I know that?"

"It just doesn't make sense to me, Nicky. And what about the poems?"

"The poems. You talk about something that doesn't make sense." Nick's face darkened, and he looked away. "She and I will have a talk about that when she comes home."

I had a flash of him stabbing a finger at Tristan's poems while she looked on in tears.

"What kind of talk?" I said.

"I don't *know*. What have I been trying to tell you for the last five weeks, Serena? All I can think about is hunting this person down and getting my daughter back. Now that's *it*."

"Conversation over?" I said.

His whole face squinted. "Don't get smart. Look, we can't have this thing happening between us. We have to stay united, or I can't do what I have to do."

And then the man who wanted me to stay united with him stormed off to the house. I waited a long time before I followed him inside.

I was at the police station at seven o'clock the next morning. Ed listened to the tape with me five times. When he stopped it for the last time, he said, "How does she sound to you?"

"Afraid," I said. "Not hysterical, not like something horrible is about to happen to her. But she's scared."

There was something else, something I'd heard at three o'clock that morning when a sullen Nick had finally fallen asleep and I'd crept down to the kitchen to listen to the tape again. I couldn't define it yet, though, so I shrugged at Ed.

"What do *you* think?" I said.

He shifted in his chair. Fluorescent light shone on his shaved head. "Let's just talk from the theory that Tristan wasn't abducted. From my experience with kids who have left home, I'd say it took a lot for her to get up the nerve to make that call. If that's the case, then the fear we're hearing is more from making the call than anything that's threatening her."

"She was afraid to *call us*?" I said.

He didn't have to answer. I knew we were both thinking about the poems.

"I didn't hear any background noise," he said, "at least nothing that would help us determine where she is. I'm going to send it to the crime lab in Dover, though. They have some pretty sensitive equipment—"

"You're going to take it away from me?" I said.

Ed's eyes went soft. "I'll make you a copy. Then you can listen to her as much as you want."

"I haven't heard her voice in so long," I said.

"Does it sound different to you?"

I was a little startled. It was the very thing I'd searched for in the tape last night.

"It does and it doesn't," I said. "Her voice itself hasn't changed, but it's like somebody else is using it."

"Like maybe someone was telling her what to say?"

I shook my head. I finally zeroed in on the feeling I hadn't been able to put into words. "It's more that now she's somebody I don't know," I said. My voice thickened. "She's a stranger."

"Hey," Ed said. "We're going to give you a chance to discover her all over again. This is a *very* good sign."

"Nick doesn't think so," I said.

Ed nodded. "He's pretty upset. Any father would be."

I didn't ask when Ed had talked to Nick. Instead I said, "I've never seen Nick angry like this. He's mad at me; he was mad at Tristan. This morning he cut himself shaving and threw the razor in the bathtub. Nick just doesn't do that."

"Just from a man's point of view," Ed said, "and I'm not a father, but it seems like he's angry with himself. He thought he could protect his family or at least beat the tar out of anybody who tried to hurt them. For you it's easier to accept that she ran away, because it might mean she's safer. For him—" Ed shrugged. "Maybe for him it's harder. If she left willingly, that destroys his whole image of himself as a father."

I had to agree. It wasn't doing much for my mother image, either.

"So what do we do now?" I said.

"I can actually point you in a direction." Ed swiveled in the chair, pulled out a piece of paper, and wrote down some instructions for us. If Tristan called again and we were there to answer, we were supposed to stay calm and tell her we wanted her home with us. We were to ask where she was but not lose patience if she wouldn't tell us.

"The idea is to let her know it's safe to come home," Ed said. "She's been gone long enough now that things may have become distorted in her mind."

"Or not," I said ruefully.

"Just don't let an argument develop over the phone."

I sighed deeply, out of the very emptiest place in myself. "You know something?" I said. "I've never had an argument with Tristan. I'd give my left arm to have one with her right now." My eyes blurred, and I nodded at the tape. "How long will that take?"

"A day or two."

"I shouldn't get my hopes up, should I?"

"Get them up as high as you want. What's the future in the alternative?"

There was a long, quiet space. Ed seemed to shake himself inwardly. "I know you're worried about how she's eating, whether she's got a roof over her head—"

"That's all I think about," I said.

"There are a lot of resources out there for her. There's the National Runaway Switchboard; they'd set her up with the Home Free bus service Greyhound's got—free transportation for runaway children returning home. Foundation 2 has shelters all over—"

I pulled my hands through my hair. "How is Tristan going to know about all that? She's never even been away from home before."

"Other kids will tell her," Ed said. "The National Youth Crisis Hotline has their number posted all over the place. Kids on the streets know it: 1-800-HIT-HOME."

"I don't even know if she had enough money with her to make a phone call."

Ed stopped midway into standing up and sat back on the edge of his chair. "What *did* Tristan do with the money she made?"

"Saved it. I don't think she bought herself one thing. It all went straight into her savings account."

Ed scratched his forehead. "We should have asked you before if she had access to money, but we were focused on the abduction theory. Why don't you—"

He didn't even have to suggest that I go to the bank. I stopped on my way home. Five dollars were left in Tristan's account. Her last, and only, withdrawal—$675—had been made at one thirty on August 2, the day before she disappeared. She'd worked the day shift that day. She must have made the withdrawal during her lunch break.

"There's no doubt now, Nicky," I whispered.

But the certainty didn't stab me as it might have a week, maybe even a day earlier. Instead, I felt a gathering in my chest, a tightness that told me the $675 was probably gone by now. I couldn't just wait for her to find her way home.

After I called Ed to report that news, I went up to Tristan's room and sat cross-legged in the middle of her bed, down comforter puffing up around me but offering me no comfort.

I had inspected every inch of that room, and yet I knew there was still something that would give another piece of her up to me. There had to be more poems.

I sank back against the pillows. If she'd planned ahead enough to take her money out of the bank, she'd probably taken her poems with her too. I tried to imagine her slipping from one secret place to another, pulling them out and tucking them safely into her pockets. I didn't get far with that vision. With the door open and our eyes always on her, how could she have done that without one of us noticing?

Or maybe somebody had and that somebody had just kept her mouth shut.

I hurried downstairs. Aunt Pete was on the back porch, attempting to cut her toenails. A delicious September breeze came up off the ocean. The passage of time it signaled went through me. It had been so stifling hot when Tristan left.

"It's getting harder and harder to reach these blasted things," Aunt Pete said. She snapped the clippers in the direction of her knotted toes.

"Let me do that," I said. I joined her on the deacon's bench and put her foot in my lap. Her leg went stiff.

"I'm not used to this," she said.

"You've been taking care of me for the last month," I said. "I owe you."

Besides, now I had her where she couldn't get away if she didn't like my questions.

"You told me Tristan confided in you, right?" I said.

"A little." Aunt Pete was way ahead of me. "If she'd told me something that could help you find her, don't you think I would've said something by now?"

"That's not where I was going," I said. I got a firm grip on her foot and positioned the clippers on her big toenail. It was as hard and brown as a horse's hoof.

"Did you see her poking into any strange places, maybe right before she, you know, went?"

"You still looking for more poems?" she said.

I crunched down hard, but the nail didn't budge. I moved to the next one.

"No, I didn't see her looking," Aunt Pete said, "but I been thinkin' about something."

"What?"

"That day I saw her writing on the beach. She had that beach bag with her, the one I sent her from the Riviera that time."

I pretended to concentrate on the little toenails, which were splitting in the wrong direction. Tristan had pulled the hideous rhinestone-encrusted bag down from the closet shortly after Aunt Pete's arrival in June. "I should use this while she's here," Tristan had told me, "so I don't hurt her feelings. I just hope none of my friends see it."

The last time I'd seen it, it was stuffed under the towels in the pool house. Her worst fear must have been realized, and she'd stashed it there to avoid the inevitable teasing—

I shoved Aunt Pete's legs off my lap and tossed the clippers on the seat. She was still muttering when I tore open the pool house door, pulled up the lid on the bench, and knocked the neatly rolled-up beach towels out of the way.

There it was, the seaweed green bag with the rhinestone fish swimming gaudily across it.

And inside was a blue spiral notebook, with a poem Tristan had forgotten to take with her. I looked around the scratched-out words and read the ones she'd allowed to stay.

"Sanctuary"
by Tristan Soltani

She was my safe place
She made it okay
"Kiss it better
Mommy's here
I love you. You're special, Tristan dear."

She was my God space
She taught me to pray
"Jesus loves you
God is great
Bless Daddy. Bless Maxie. Go night-night, it's late."

Until I grew ears
And I could hear:
"Yes, hon. No, hon. You are right
You have made me see the light.
She's just cranky, tired, pubescent.
I'll stay bright and effervescent."

Until I peeked out
And I could see
Serve the coffee. Calm the girls.
Bite your tongue and keep his world.
Bob your head. Don't rock the boat.
Say his words you've learned by rote.

The haven's grown plastic
She's taught ME to nod
"How's your day been?
Were you good?
Kept the rules, the smiles, the shoulds?"

She can't be my refuge—
No walls of her own
"I'll ask your daddy.
I'm not sure.
Who am I but sweet and pure?"

I look for shelter
And I find:
Potluck suppers. Smiley people.
"Thou shalt not doubt beneath this steeple."

I go to God
The way they say:
"Submit to husband, fathers, teachers.

Deny yourself and honor preachers.
God is love and Jesus Master."
Say the verses, say them faster.

Could love be my sanctuary?
He tells me it is.
"You're a woman.
They don't know.
Let me take you, let it show."

Is he my temple?
It's in his kiss
"I can free you
Spread your wings
Your heart, your arms, wide open fling.

Now I have heart
And I can feel
I am more than what they planned
Now the flames of love are fanned
There is warmth beside his fire
My old prison's now a pyre.

"God!" I cried out loud. "I failed her. Why did You let me fail her?"

The break in my heart was so painful I couldn't sit up. I closed the bench lid and lay down on top of it, still holding the poem that had just cut me in two.

I sobbed at the ceiling. "God? Did I do everything wrong? Why didn't You tell me? Why didn't You knock me over the head?"

But it hadn't seemed so wrong. I'd taught her to pray. "God is great, God is good" at the supper table. "Now I lay me down to sleep" every night as I tucked her in. Little whispers of "God bless Daddy and Maxie" as I tucked her in for night-night.

I taught her to pray the way I prayed, to a gentle and loving Jesus, who would always watch over her perfect little world. Did she know how to pray now? Was she badgering God the way I was, shouting at Him, throwing tantrums at His feet?

If she was, she hadn't learned it from me—not the way I was going to Him now, pounding my fists.

"Please teach her, God," I cried, "because I didn't."

"You all right in there?"

Aunt Pete's voice was crackly outside the door. She pushed through and let in a shaft of sunlight that didn't belong in the scene. I covered my eyes.

"You found one," she said. I heard her shuffle across the floor, felt her sit stiffly beside me. I tucked up my feet and pressed my face to my knees.

"This one was about me," I said. "Now I know how Nick felt."

"Come on, Serena. What teenage girl doesn't think her mother's ridiculous? I thought mine was an idiot until I turned twenty-five."

"You didn't run away from home."

"Not the way Tristan maybe did, but I left, went out on my own when I was barely eighteen. Thought I knew it all."

I lifted my face and waved the notebook. "I evidently didn't know a thing."

"And now you do."

I looked at her. "What do I know?"

"You know enough to pray the only prayer that's going to get you anywhere." She glanced toward the door. "I couldn't help hearing you talking to God, but, then, I did have my ear pressed against the crack."

"Did I sound like a moron?"

"No, you sounded like a woman who's finally come to her senses."

"Oh, then do tell me what I said!"

"You said something about God teaching her, because you screwed up. It was hard to tell exactly with all that bangin' goin' on."

I surveyed my fist and pressed it against my mouth.

"You never knew your mother-in-law, Maxina Soltani."

"No. She died before I met Nick."

"She was quite a woman, that one—better than my nephew deserved, I'll tell you that."

Aunt Pete had never "made any bones," as she put it, about the fact that she and Nick Soltani Sr. had never seen eye to eye. It still didn't take much to get her going about his alcoholism, the way he let the family business go, the way he neglected Nick after Maxina's death. I'd seen Aunt Pete pound a table in the telling more than once.

"Anyway," she went on, "I said to her when Nicky was going off to prep school, I said, 'Aren't you afraid to let him go? What if something happens to him?' and she said to me, 'Aunt Pete, I just pray for God to bridge the gap between what he needs and what I can give him.'"

"Really?"

"What? You think I'm makin' it up?"

"No!" I pushed my back against the wall and looked at my legs stuck out in front of me. My pants looked as if I'd slept in them. The heels of my sandals were worn down, and my own heels were almost as crusty as Aunt Pete's toenails. Stray dark hairs poked out from my ankles, where I'd missed shaving them.

"I just can't believe I'd have the same thought as Mama Maxina," I said. "I know if this had happened to her, she wouldn't have been as much of a mess as I am."

"You don't know from nothin'," Aunt Pete said. "She'd have died right on the spot if Nicky had disappeared. A mother's a mother. Point is, her prayer did the job. Nicky turned out pretty darn good, even if he is a man."

I had to grin.

"That's the prayer I think you oughta pray," Aunt Pete said. "Pray for the good Lord to bridge the gap between what Tristan needs and what you have to give her. And then, you give her all you have."

I looked down at the notebook, now resting in my lap, having done its worst to me. "I thought I did."

"So maybe she needs somethin' different. Like you findin' her."

I turned to face Aunt Pete squarely. "That keeps coming to me," I said. "That *I* have to find her."

"Makes sense to me. You're the only one getting any real clues."

"I just don't know what to do with them besides take them to

Ed." We both looked at the notebook, and I shook my head. "But not this one."

After all, what more could it tell him than he already knew? Tristan Soltani felt trapped by her parents and ran away to find refuge. Sanctuary.

I didn't show the poem to Nick, although I tried to cut him some slack over the next few days. I had a deeper knowledge of what it felt like to be informed that everything you'd done for your daughter had made her feel like she was imprisoned in your image of her. We'd both reacted in anger, Nick and I: he at Tristan, I at myself. At least we had that in common.

So I made Nick a bread pudding from Mama Maxina's old recipe and scratched his barrier of a back until he fell asleep at night and threw away the daily junk mail so he didn't have to go through it when he took the rest of the day's post into the library to read. Those were things I'd always done and always loved.

But never before had he ignored them completely.

Thursday night Nick and I were in the family room pretending to watch the news when Max took a couple of long-legged leaps across the floor and landed in front of us. It occurred to me that she'd grown while I wasn't looking.

"I made you guys something," she said. "Well, we did. Me and Sun. It's our first club project."

Nick flipped the TV off and frowned at her. "Sun and I."

"What is it, sweetie?" I said.

With a flourish she produced a notebook from behind her back. Its cover was decorated with a collage of teenage faces. On a strip of paper pasted across it were the words: BRH CLUB.

"What's the BRH Club, short stuff?" Nick said. He started to smile.

"Bring Runaways Home. This is all stuff we got off the Internet. We made it for you guys, but I'm gonna use it for my oral report too."

"No, you are not."

Nick's voice cut into me. Max clutched the book to her chest.

"Why not?" she said.

"Because I won't have our family business spread all over the world."

"It's not the whole world, Dad. It's just my class."

"Watch your tone, young lady."

It was my cue to chime in with support for Nick, but all I could think was how much I despised it when he called her "young lady."

"Who said you could spend all this time on the Internet?" Nick said. "Do I have to go over the rules with you again?"

"I guess so," Max said. The sarcasm was barely holding back the tears, I could tell. "I'm not as smart as Tristan; I have to hear them a thousand times before *I'm* perfect. She only had to hear them once. Oh, wait. Maybe she's not an angel. I mean, after all, didn't she run away?"

Nick's hand came out of nowhere. Only two words kept it from smacking into Max's cheek.

"Nick, *stop*," I said.

Nick closed his eyes. "Go to your room, Max."

She fled, sobbing.

I waited for her door to slam before I looked at him.

"I wasn't going to hit her," he said. He was barely audible.

"You threatened her."

"Because she's forgetting everything she's been taught about respect." His voice rose. "Serena, I am not going to let the rest of my family fall apart because of what we're going through over Tristan."

"Oh, Nicky," I said, "I think we started falling apart long before Tristan left."

The look that gripped his face frightened me, but I didn't move. He did, away from me, slamming doors behind him as he went.

Nick didn't come to bed that night. At one o'clock I crept down the stairs far enough to see that he was on the back porch, head turned stiffly toward the ocean. I went back to bed and spent the rest of the night going through the runaway information Max had printed out for us. Nick had been right about one thing: no ten-year-old should have to become aware of the facts she'd found.

One out of every seven children will run away sometime
between the ages of 10 and 18.

Over 40 percent of all youths cited family dynamics as the
reason they ran away.

Approximately 75 percent of all runaways are female.

In the next 24 hours, approximately 2,700 children and teens around the United States will run away from home.

As if that information weren't enough to rip my heart right out of my chest, there was more:

Most runaways living on the street find difficulty earning money to survive. They may panhandle for change and eventually find other means, such as prostitution, pornography, drugs, and stealing. Every year approximately 5,000 runaway and homeless youths die from assault, illness, and suicide.

I climbed out of bed and stood with one knee on the chaise longue, looking out into the same inky blackness my daughter was in, somewhere. It was impossible to envision her reaching from some corner of it, begging for nickels and dimes or cloaking herself in it to carry some packet of something heinous that I couldn't imagine because I'd never seen illegal drugs. I'd never even smoked a joint in college. I definitely had nothing to draw from to picture her as a prostitute, yet even the vaguest notion nauseated me.

No wonder Nick wanted to deny the whole thing.

But I couldn't do it anymore. And because looking at it hurt too much, I buried my face in the back of the chaise longue and said to

God, "Please bridge the gap between what she needs and what I have to give, because I have nothing."

I must have fallen asleep that way, because the phone woke me when the room was still gray. It rang only twice before I heard Nick's low voice and then his urgent footsteps on the stairs. I met him at the bedroom door.

"What is it?" I said.

"Ed Malone. They've got Ricky Zabriski at the station. I'm going down there. Why don't you—"

"I'm going with you," I said.

He didn't say a word.

Chapter Fourteen

I couldn't remember the last time I'd been out at four in the morning. Even quiet Bethany Beach had an eeriness about it. The streets were slick from an earlier rain, and the streetlamps dropped patches of ghostly white on the pavement. The only lights inside the shadowy shops were those left on to discourage burglars. I felt the need to glance over my shoulder as Nick and I made our way up the ramp to the front door of the police station.

Ed let us in. His face had the strained look of sleep deprivation, but he still smiled. The smile didn't reach his eyes.

"Sorry to roust you out in the middle of the night," he said.

Nick looked past him, as if Zabriski might be standing, unarmed, in a doorway. "I'd have been upset if you hadn't. I want to see this guy." His voice was coiled and menacing. I could see the muscles in his neck holding back words he didn't want to waste on anybody but the individual who had taken his daughter.

Ed nodded toward a frosted-glass door marked BBPD Personnel Only. Even with Ed's hand grazing the back of my arm as he gently ushered me into the room, I had the sickening feeling that I wasn't supposed to be there.

I wasn't. None of it should be happening.

Ed offered me a metal chair with olive green faux-leather cushioning, which I perched on, birdlike, and hooked my feet around the legs. Nick stood.

"Are they still processing him?" he said.

Ed sat on a corner of the long table and rubbed his hands together. "We haven't charged him with anything yet." He put up his hand as Nick took a step forward. "Right now he's telling us Tristan wanted to go with him to Baltimore—"

"He took her across the state line—"

"At sixteen, she's considered a consenting adult by Maryland law."

Nick's face darkened into the unshaven shadow of his beard. "He *tells* you she wanted to go, and you believe him."

"I didn't say that—"

"Then why haven't you charged him with kidnapping?"

"We haven't finished questioning him, Nick." Ed folded his hands on his thigh. "So far, he's being cooperative."

"He's told you where Tristan is?"

"He's told us where he last saw her." Ed looked at me. "A motel in Baltimore."

"He left her there?" Nick said. "A sixteen-year-old girl who's never been away from home without her family in her life?" Nick jerked his head toward the door as if he was ready to tear the station apart until he found Spider.

"According to his story," Ed said, "she left him."

"And since he's so credible… What are you *thinking*?"

"He hasn't asked for a lawyer. I'm thinking the longer we question him without charging him, the more information we'll get out of him."

"While my daughter's locked up someplace."

"You got a phone call from her, Nick."

"So? He could've been holding a gun to her head."

"There's no evidence of that. When the Georgetown police pulled Zabriski over, he was a block from his mother's house, driving that old Buick down a back street. He wasn't armed. He made no attempt to elude them." Ed tapped the table and sat up straight. "The only aggression he's shown since they turned him over to us was to ask for a Mountain Dew."

"Where's he been all this time?" Nick said.

I thought of Sarah Zabriski, stowing her son away in that fragile little house. I couldn't make it work.

"He told us he took off after he saw the AMBER Alert with his license number on it. Laid low with a cousin in West Virginia."

"Instead of coming forward," Nick said.

"He was afraid nobody would believe that he thought Tristan had just gone back home."

"You don't believe him, do you?"

"I do," I said.

Nick turned to me as if I'd just appeared on the scene. That wasn't surprising, since those two words were the first I'd spoken since we'd arrived. I unwrapped my ankles from the chair legs and sank against the leatherette. It was a cold slab through the thin cotton of my blouse, but I was already chilled to my core.

"I've read her poems over and over," I said. "It's all right there."

"Don't start with that, Serena," Nick said.

"It's been there, right in front of us, and we couldn't see it."

Nick slammed his hand against the table. "That's enough!"

"It's enough to convince me," I said.

"Good grief." Nick pulled back his tone, his hands, his eyes, and squatted in front of me. The effort it required not to take hold of me and shake me was twitching in his face. "I understand why you want that to be true. It means she's in less danger—"

"I don't want it to be true," I said. "I don't want to believe that our daughter felt like our home was such a prison that she had to run away with the first person who told her she could get free."

Nick's face went sour. "And you got all this from two poems."

"Three," I said.

Nick looked at Ed. "Sorry. Let's get back to this kid—"

"Reading Tristan's poems was probably the first time I ever really listened to her."

"Serena, just shut up!"

"No, Nick," I said. "I will not."

Nick turned to the wall and put one hand on it. I shook as I watched him, but I didn't go to him.

"All right," Ed said. "I think it would ease both your minds a little if you met Zabriski." He looked at Nick's back. "But only if you can keep your cool. If you go off on him, he's going to clam up."

"Then maybe it isn't such a good idea right now," I said.

Nick glared over his shoulder at me. "I'm fine. Bring him in."

Ed gave him a long look before he went to the door and motioned into the hall. Nick kept his back to the door, so I saw Ricky Zabriski first. Although Ed had told us they hadn't charged him with anything, I was still surprised that he wasn't in handcuffs and leg irons and guarded by two burly officers packing service revolvers. That wasn't the only thing that surprised me.

The boy who walked into the room looked almost nothing like the picture of the worldly tattooed son Sarah Zabriski had proudly shown Hazel and me. This boy had the look of a thirteen-year-old whose heft hadn't caught up with his height. He had a short, uncombed crop of bleached-out hair and patches of neglected stubble on his chin and jaw line, the only indication on his otherwise boyish, narrow face that he had actually reached puberty. Clad in camouflage-print cargo shorts and a *Star Wars Episode III* T-shirt with the sleeves cut out, he dropped into the chair Ed pointed him to and folded his hands on the table without looking at anyone. There was absolutely nothing frightening about him, including the spider tattoo on his arm.

"This is Mr. and Mrs. Soltani," Ed said. "Tristan's parents."

He didn't tell Ricky to pay us some passing form of courtesy, but it was in his voice. I'd never heard anything but Ed's calm, reassuring tone, yet the authority he was commanding sounded as if it belonged there. Ricky obviously sensed it because he looked up at me, not Nick, and nodded.

Ed took up his edge-of-the-table position again. "The Soltanis would like to hear what you have to say about Tristan."

Nick moved to the end of the table, still standing, but Ricky kept his eyes on me. They were green, framed with lashes too thick and curly to belong on any male. Those eyes were the first glimpse of anything I could imagine Tristan being attracted to. His voice was the second.

"I didn't do anything to her," he said to me. The words came out in a sultry bass that vibrated somewhere in my chest. It was as hypnotic as it was startling.

"Go on," Ed said.

"We been seeing each other all summer—"

"What do you mean 'seeing each other'?" Nick said.

Ed shot him a warning look, but Ricky shrugged again.

"I hung around Boardwalk Fries. We'd go talk when she went on break. A couple of times I took her to my trailer."

I caught my breath. Nick's seemed to pour out of his nostrils.

"That's a lie," Nick said. "We always knew where Tristan was."

Ricky sniffed, possibly his rendition of a laugh. "Evidently you didn't. She'd tell you she was working till closing when she actually got off at six. I'd take her to my trailer and bring her back in time for one of you to walk her home like she'd been working all night."

I thought Ricky's big lips smiled then, though it was hard to tell because the movement came and went so quickly. Nick didn't miss it.

"You think this is funny?" he said.

Ed held up a hand to Nick and told Ricky to keep talking. I

cringed into the fake leather. This was like unfolding one of Tristan's poems. I didn't want to know what I had to know.

"She talked about how strict you guys were with her," Ricky said. "I felt sorry for her, so I told her she oughta come with me."

"Come with you where?" Nick said.

"I don't know." Ricky still hadn't looked at Nick. His eyes were now focused on his hands on the table, where he picked at a piece of loose skin on his thumb until I felt nauseous. "I didn't know where I was headed, but she wanted to come with me."

"So you just let her," Nick said. "A sixteen-year-old girl—"

"Nick." Ed shifted on the corner of the table. "Let's hear the rest."

"That's basically it," Ricky said. "It was late that night, so we only went as far as Baltimore. I got us a motel room."

"My daughter slept in the same room with you?"

"Same room? Same bed."

I didn't understand what Nick said next. It was more a primal animal cry than words as he hurled himself at Ricky and grabbed the front of his T-shirt, strangling Darth Vader with his fingers. By the time Ed got his arms around Nick's shoulders to pull him off, Nick had Ricky up and off his feet, flailing like a hooked fish.

"Get off him!" Ed said as he spun Nick away.

Ricky backed up against the wall and smoothed his hand down the front of his shirt. His face was pinched and white.

Ricky Zabriski was rude and sullen, but he wasn't capable of the crimes we'd attributed to him.

In that moment, I knew he didn't have Tristan.

Once Ricky was hustled out of the room and Nick calmed down
enough to listen, Ed told us we could press charges against the kid but
he didn't think they could make it stick. With his eyes riveted to Nick,
he said they would check out the motel where Ricky said he'd last seen
Tristan and check out his alibi for the time since then. If nothing
stacked up against him, they'd have to let him go. Nick stormed out
of the station.

I started to follow, but Ed said my name. His voice returned to
the quiet level I could rest against and get my bearings.

"You okay?" he said.

"No," I said, "but at least I know he didn't hurt her."

He let himself smile. "Mother's intuition?"

"Maybe."

"Actually I think you're right. But as long as she's out there alone,
there's still the potential for danger."

"We have to find her."

"We're going to keep doing all we can," Ed said. "I'll call you as
soon as we learn anything from the motel."

As I walked toward the car where Nick was waiting in the first anxious light of morning, I felt that something had shifted. Maybe the
earth, maybe the tide. Maybe me. Whatever it was, I had to go with it.

Nick didn't speak as we drove the few blocks to the house. He
went straight upstairs to shower and left for work with only three
words for me.

"This isn't over."

To his retreating back, I whispered, "It won't be until I find her."

Hazel hailed me in the parking lot at Lord Baltimore, and I invited her over for coffee. I was in the middle of telling her and Aunt Pete about our meeting with Ricky when Ed called. His voice was so calm I knew he didn't have encouraging news.

"I talked to the manager at the North Avenue Motel," he said. "Couldn't get much out of him, but he said two kids registered there August 3 as Mr. and Mrs. Smith."

"And he didn't think—"

"Said he knew they were fake names, but what did he care. The girl had cash."

"The girl paid?" I said. My fingers tightened on the phone until they hurt.

"Yeah, this kid's a loser. Anyway, he said the boy checked out about noon the next day, but he didn't see the girl." Ed gave a soft grunt. "I'm sure he didn't watch over them from the window."

"How do we know it was Tristan and Ricky?" I said. And then I winced. It was the first time I'd used their names together. I hated the sound.

"I faxed them the flier and a photo of Zabriski," Ed said, almost reluctantly I thought. "He identified them."

Neither of us said anything for a moment. All I could do was ache.

"I wish I had more to tell you," Ed said finally. "Thing is, Zabriski's story checks out, including his claim that he was with a relative in West Virginia until she kicked him out. There's no evidence that he wasn't just going back to his mother because he was out of money."

"You have to let him go," I said.

When I hung up, I had a clear picture of Sarah Zabriski finally getting her child back. I wanted to be her.

"Not good, huh?" Between the early hour and Aunt Pete's brew, Hazel's voice was doubly gravelly.

"Not totally bad, either," I said. "She was there, at that motel, but the manager didn't see Ricky leave with her."

"What was the name of the place?" Hazel said.

I had to think. "North Avenue Motel."

She left the kitchen, and I sat back down at the table across from Aunt Pete.

"What are you gonna do now?" she said.

I stared miserably into my mug, watching the cream do its sickening swirl. "What can I do?"

"Well, you can't just sit here with your teeth in your mouth and one leg as long as the other." Aunt Pete's voice shook, and her eyes grew stormy, probably, I thought, at her failure to keep voice, tears, and my life under control.

"Believe me," I said, "if there was anything I *could* do, I'd be doing it. It's driving me crazy. She's alone."

"From what you've said about this kid, she's probably just as well off."

I pushed the mug away. "She even paid for their motel room."

"That's cause enough to put him behind bars if you ask me," Hazel growled from the doorway. She crossed to the table and put a map in front of me, printed out on the computer. She poked at a highlighted spot.

"What?" I said.

"North Avenue Motel. Not in the best part of Baltimore, but it shouldn't be that hard to find." Hazel produced another sheet of paper. "I printed out written directions too. I don't know which one's easier for you to follow."

I stared at the tangled maze of lines on the map and then at her. "What are you saying?"

"I'm saying what you're thinking." Hazel leaned on the table, bracelets clanking, talons tapping. "You want to go to this place and find out for yourself. There might be somebody else there who remembers Tristan."

"Maids," Aunt Pete put in. "Maintenance people."

"You think I should drive to Baltimore?"

"Don't you?" Hazel said.

I found myself nodding. "You'll go with me, won't you?" I said.

"Who's gonna pick the kids up from school?" Aunt Pete said. "If you get a lead, you might not make it back in time."

"I'll take care of the kids," Hazel said with a final glissando of her fingernails on the table. "You just go and don't think about anything else. Focus on Tristan."

I looked at the map again. Interstate signs and thick highway lines seemed raised like friezes. I never drove out of Sussex County if I could help it. Not alone. Not in traffic that made me feel as if I was suffocating.

"If you can make a cold call on Sarah Zabriski," Hazel said, "you can do this."

"I'll pack you some sandwiches," Aunt Pete said.

I had no choice. Not because they were ready to load me bodily into the car and follow me to the state line if necessary. Because my daughter's voice was on pieces of paper folded and tucked into my pockets. Because I could hear her whispering in my ear, *Come after me. No matter what it takes, come after me.*

I looked at Aunt Pete, who was piling salami onto kaiser rolls.

"If Nick calls—" I said.

"I'll tell him not to worry about you because God's bridging the gap."

I hugged her, and I took my sandwiches and my map, and with terror already pricking beads of sweat from the lines of my hands, I headed for Baltimore.

Chapter Fifteen

All the way there I shook every time I had to take the speedometer over forty-five and cringed when eighteen-wheelers sandwiched me between them. Only Hazel's map and Aunt Pete's prayer and Tristan's calling in my head got me to the North Avenue Motel without falling apart. But when I pulled into the parking lot, I almost did.

The motel was situated perpendicular to North Avenue, as if it were ashamed to face the street with its two double-story rows of beige dinginess. A dribble of cars between the buildings and a failing neon sign on an opaquely filthy office window were the only signs of life. Tristan would never have stayed in a place like this.

I could barely bring myself to get out of the car and push open the smeared glass door. The odor of cigarette smoke nearly knocked me backward. As I crossed to the counter, I saw the telltale gray curl rising in the air before I spotted the bald head of a man watching a black-and-white TV.

He punched it off when I said, "Excuse me," and turned to squint at me through the cloud he'd created.

"You want a room?" he said.

Are you kidding? I wanted to say to him.

"How many people?"

"None," I said.

He adjusted a murky pair of glasses to peer at me. His fingers were nicotine yellow to match the whites of his eyes.

"So?" he said.

"So." I fumbled in my purse and withdrew one of the fliers Hazel had made. "Have you seen this girl?"

He looked from me to the flier twice and then pawed through a pile of papers on the desk behind the counter. He pulled out a curled-up black-and-white version of the flier and flattened it onto the counter. There was a brown splash-shaped stain right next to Tristan's picture. I wanted to snatch it from him and clean it with my mother-saliva.

"She's the one the cop called about this morning," the man said. "She your kid?"

My eyes filled.

"I already told that cop everything I know. Came in here with some guy, registered as..."

I listened again to the story, straining to hear something, anything, that he hadn't told Ed. It was almost word for word what Ed had reported to me.

When he was finished, he retrieved the cigarette he'd left burning in an ashtray near the TV and stuck it in his mouth, complete with an inch of ash.

"Are you sure you didn't see her when he checked out?" I said.

He pulled the cigarette out and turned his head to exhale. A small fan on the desk blew it back at me.

"I never saw her after that night when she came down here asking for directions."

I gripped the counter with both hands. "Directions? To where?"

"I don't know." He looked at me as if I'd asked him to name the Supreme Court justices.

"Was it a store? A restaurant?"

"It was just an address." He took another pull on the cigarette and dropped it into a plastic foam cup on the counter. It sizzled in something. "Like I'm gonna remember."

"Please," I said. My voice broke, dropping my words helplessly onto the counter. "I have to find my daughter."

"So what do you want me to do, go under hypnosis? I'm telling you, I don't remember."

I watched the smoke from a new cigarette shoot out of his nose. Tristan must have come away from him with eyes stinging from the refuse of both his habit and his rudeness. To my knowledge, no one had ever spoken to my precious daughter this way.

"Thank you for your time," I said. I reached out to pick up the Tristan flier, which was lying next to the faxed one, her picture vibrant with color in contrast to the blurry black-and-white that matched everything in this place. The last time I'd seen her, she'd been the girl in the color photo. What about now? Had breathing smoke and suffering the contempt of people like this man faded her to gray?

I picked up the faxed copy and crumpled it in my hand.

"Will you please post this?" I said, nodding at the color one. "And put my phone number on it."

I recited my cell and our home phone numbers slowly while he wrote them down. He reached out and punched the paper into the wall by the counter with a thumbtack, clearly ready to be done with the conversation.

"Thank you," I said.

I pushed open the door, ready to take a gulp of fresh air, when he said, "Hey."

I turned.

"I think it was on North Howard. Near the hospital."

Then he turned away. I heard the television as I hurried to the car.

I locked myself inside the Blazer and blasted the air conditioner until I felt as if I could breathe again. The map shook in my hands as I searched for North Howard Street.

Maybe I should call Nicky. Soltani Casters was on the outskirts of Baltimore, only thirty minutes away.

Or maybe Ed. He needed to know what Mr. Chain Smoker had told me.

Some place on North Howard. Near some hospital. I didn't even know what to look for.

But I was going to look for it, whatever it was. I blinked my eyes clear and trailed my finger across the map until I found North Howard Street. It actually wasn't far and involved only one turn.

I looked once more at the shabby motel where my daughter's journey had begun.

"I hope it got better than this, Tristan," I whispered.

Come after me, she whispered back.

When Hazel had said I wasn't going to be in the best part of town, she wasn't exaggerating. I decided even *she* would double-check the locks as she passed what I was seeing now. Besides the greasy delis and grills and the offices that claimed to provide advances on paychecks weeks before payday, the street was lined with row houses. Most were boarded up, though some struggled bravely to be homes. The only building that didn't make me shiver was the sedate Seventh Baptist Church, which seemed to sigh sadly over the neighborhood, its sacred dignity still intact.

"God, this is heinous," I said to Him.

When I turned onto North Howard Street, I entered a world that made North Avenue look like suburban America. My faith in the locks on my car doors drained as I crawled past one abandoned storefront after another. Mr. Chain Smoker had been right about the hospital. Maryland General had made a valiant attempt at gentrification, but half a block down was an empty store with demonic images spray-painted over it with alarming precision. Beyond that was a shop possibly still in business with large ceramic masks in the window wearing vacant yet somehow disturbing expressions. Every building had bars on its windows and formidable locks halfway up its doors.

A horn blasted, and I jerked to attention. I pulled over to the curb to let a taxicab pass. The driver shouted something, but I turned my head.

He could insult me all he wanted. All I could hear were caustic voices cutting into my daughter as she walked down this street, clutching Mr. Chain Smoker's directions.

But what could she have been looking for? What could have been worth the risk that some creature would emerge from an alley—

Even as I cut off an image that threatened to undo me, a figure appeared in my rearview mirror and loped toward me wearing a ski cap and sunglasses. I squealed the car back onto the street and took off before he could get to me.

I only hoped Tristan had been able to do the same.

I cried all the way home as a new fear took hold. What if Tristan had left Ricky at the motel that morning to look for whatever it was she was searching for and someone *had* abducted her?

My only relief from that was Tristan's phone message. I went over and over it in my head. She hadn't sounded hysterical, had she? There was no reason to believe that somebody was holding her captive, was there?

I planned to go straight to the answering machine and play the tape again the minute I got home. But Nick met me in the driveway.

He opened the Blazer door and got a firm grip on my arm. The only thing that kept me from pulling away was the confusion in his eyes. His facial muscles were taut, his mouth line rigid, but his eyes didn't seem to know where to settle.

"I went to Baltimore," I said.

"I got that part, but for the love of Mike, Serena. You can barely cross the bridge without—"

"I went where Tristan went. The North Avenue Motel. I wanted to see for myself—"

"Oh, that's great. That's exquisite." Nick scoured the back of his head with his hand. "Do you know how many stabbings and shootings they have around there a *week*? You don't just go walking around in places like that."

"Tristan did," I said.

As I told him the motel manager's story and described my ride along Howard Street, I watched his face wrestle with the disbelief and the fear and the frustration I was stirring up in him.

"You can't do this," he said. "I can't lose you too."

"Tristan's calling to me, Nick," I said.

"I don't want to hear any more about those blasted poems!"

"It's not just the poems. It's like I can hear her in my head, begging me to come after her."

Nick let out a sigh that seemed to come from the pit of his soul.

"I've thought I heard her voice a hundred times since that night," he said. "I keep expecting her to poke her head in the library and say, 'Good night, Daddy.'" Nick shook his head. "I want to hear it so bad, my mind plays tricks on me."

"No. It's different. She's calling me, and I have to listen."

"Serena, this is crazy." He took me by both shoulders. "You have to promise me that you will stop. Now."

The rules that had shaped my marriage shouted their orders:

Wife, defer to your husband's wisdom.
He is the spiritual head of the household.
He has the last word, this man who loves you.
Do anything for him.

They were the words I'd lived by for twenty years. They were the things I taught my daughters. So well.

Serve the coffee. Calm the girls.
Bite your tongue and keep his world
Bob your head. Don't rock the boat.
Say his words you've learned by rote.

I stepped back, out of his grasp.

"No, Nicky," I said, "I can't make that promise."

I called Ed Malone the next morning and told him what I'd gleaned from the motel manager. If Nick had already given him the information, Ed didn't say, and I didn't ask.

"I'll get a list of the businesses that are still operating around the hospital," Ed said. "Let me get back to you."

"Can you hurry? It's already been so long since she was there."

"The trail's pretty cold, that's true. But it's still a trail."

I tried to fix an image in my mind of Tristan forging a path for us to follow. It was at once encouraging and chilling. The beginning of that path didn't bode well for the rest of it.

Ed cleared his throat. "I don't want to sound like a father," he said, "but it really isn't the best idea to go into rough neighborhoods like that by yourself."

You don't sound like my father, I thought. *You sound like my husband.*

"If I have someone to go with me next time, I won't go alone," I said.

"Call me."

"You?"

Ed gave a soft laugh. "Yeah. I'm a detective."

"I know that! But you're busy."

"Just let me worry about that."

After we ended the conversation, I sat on the chaise longue in the bedroom with the phone in my lap while my thoughts caught up to me. It was hard to imagine leaving Bethany Beach in a police car, next to a man who wasn't Nick. Hard to imagine, but not impossible. Not if it led me to Tristan.

But for an agonizing five weeks there was no reason to go anywhere. There were no more phone calls or messages from Tristan. No leads from the fliers, which were curling up and fading on bulletin boards all over town. No additions to the tale from Ricky, who, according to Ed, hightailed it back to Georgetown as soon as we were convinced there was no real cause for pressing charges.

"Yet," Nick said.

Ed confided in me that he was glad Ricky hadn't had Nick charged with assault.

Nick stopped suggesting to me that Aunt Pete should go home, especially after he announced that he was going to Dallas.

"Why?" I said.

"It's business," he said.

I watched him carefully as he dealt his folded shirts into a suitcase, eyes avoiding me.

"Tristan business?" I said.

"Look, I have no place else to investigate, okay?"

"I'm not accusing you of anything," I said.

"I guess I could let my entire corporation go down the tubes, but we've already lost enough." He yanked at the zipper on the bag. "If I don't go down there, a whole plant could fold. If I didn't have to leave you and Max alone right now, I wouldn't."

"We'll be fine," I said. "Please don't worry."

In spite of my best effort not to sound defensive, he shot me a look.

"You *will* be fine if you do what I ask you to do and stay put," he said. "But since I can't count on that, yes, Serena, I will worry."

Lissa called every other day or so, trying to encourage me, assuring me that no one at church thought I was a nut bar. I debated over whether to tell her exactly what was going on. I knew if I did, Nick would shrivel in her mind. I would dissolve into the milieu of bad parents. Tristan herself would seem—

What? Real? Normal? Like a girl who could speak without being afraid someone would hear her?

So I filled Lissa in one day in October when she dragged me out for coffee. The longer I talked, the more she looked at me as if I had gone off into a land that didn't exist.

"That just doesn't sound like our Tristan," she said.

"I don't think she was really our Tristan," I said. "I think she was her own Tristan, and she just burst out one day and ran because she thought we'd never let her be who she was." I watched the gentle vertical lines between Lissa's eyebrows deepen. "That's the Tristan I have to find. I have to find her and tell her she can be whoever she wants."

"I just don't understand," she said.

It wasn't much of a stretch to figure out that if Lissa didn't get it, Peg and Rebecca definitely wouldn't. I didn't make any attempt to contact them, and Hazel was like a fullback running interference for me at church. Still, I thought about them.

"So I guess you aren't going to the moms' group anymore," I said to Hazel the day she came with ten pots of chrysanthemums for my porches.

She snorted as she hoisted the flowers from the back of her ancient Suburban into the wheelbarrow I hadn't used since August. "I don't think Rebecca Godfried can teach me a single thing about being a mother. Looks like I'm not the only one, either."

"I heard Christine dropped out."

Hazel cocked an eyebrow over a pot of daisy mums. "Dropped out? When she found out Rebecca was taking over, she ran like a spooked cat. The only other person who still goes, far as I know, is Lissa. It's probably in her contract or something."

I felt a vague pang. "I hope Rebecca's feelings aren't hurt," I said.

Hazel peered at me over green half glasses with black polka dots on them. "See, that's what blows me away. The chick judges you like she's Sandra Day O'Connor, and you still worry about her feelings. Trust me, as long as she can hear herself talk, she's fine."

She rolled the wheelbarrow toward the house, and I looked at her curiously as I walked beside her. "How do you know all this stuff?" I said.

She shrugged her hamlike shoulders, bare even in the October chill. "Just from hanging out at the church. When I'm not working or over here, I do things for Gary—put up bulletins boards, design the newsletter, print the bulletins."

"Are you serous?" I said.

"Sure." She stuck a pot on a step and rocked back to survey it.

"That's really wonderful, Hazel. I'm so glad for you." I leaned my cheek against her arm. "Praise God, huh?"

"Dude," she said.

"What?" I said.

"That's the first time I ever heard you say that 'praise God' thing." She grunted as she picked up a pot of flowers with each hand.

"I haven't had that much to praise about since you've known me."

"Yeah, well, when you bring your kid home, I want to hear it twenty-four/seven." She looked at me sideways. "It actually sounds authentic coming out of *your* mouth."

Autumn had arrived, but except for the mums Hazel set out and watered and fertilized, there was little to show that it was my favorite season. Max and Aunt Pete carved some pumpkins, which led to an entire pumpkin-carving marathon with Hazel and her tribe, including the Irish setters, who scarfed up the seeds. Gary brought over a bushel of apples, and Aunt Pete burned only about a quarter of them in the process of making applesauce and apple crisp and several apple pies that puckered our lips because she'd left out the sugar.

A few days before Halloween, Max reminded me that I *always* made her a costume for the party at church. She looked so crestfallen when I said, "Oh, honey, I don't know about this year," that I went up to the third floor while she was at school the next day to see if I could find something in the dress-up trunk that I could modify. It wasn't what I usually did, but everything I usually did only made me cruelly aware that nothing was at all usual.

The dress-up trunk, once the source of days of endless delight, had been pushed into the back corner of the old sleeping room. It looked rather forlorn with its wicker lid slightly ajar, as if it were waiting, open mouthed, for its little girlfriends to come back and finish the game they were playing when they had to stuff their costumes inside and run off to dinner.

As I knelt in front of it, I couldn't remember seeing it in such a jumbled state the last time I'd been up there. When was that? The end of July when I'd cleaned up after Max's birthday sleepover?

I lifted the lid warily, though I wasn't sure why. Did I think something was going to jump out at me?

Two of Tristan's old tutus did spring loose, and I jumped at least a foot and a half. They'd been stuffed on top of a bunch of garments heaped like the sale table at Old Navy.

I pulled out a purple rayon nightgown Tristan had called her

Princess Leia dress when she was four or five, and I folded it. I did the same with Max's vinyl cowgirl vest and the poodle skirt everybody fought over. The neat pile I made on the floor beside me was somehow comforting. Maybe I could still create some kind of order.

I was reaching for the mime costume I'd made for Max the year before when my fingers touched paper. What I pulled out was folded precisely at the corners. From the outside I could see the round letters of Tristan's handwriting etched into the paper with a gel pen.

"Tristan!" I said.

There was no racing anxiety this time, no fear that I was going to discover what I didn't want to know. I unfolded the poem and dug hungrily into the words.

"Lost, from Self"
by Tristan Soltani

Praying
Smiling
Dancing
Doing
I knew who I ought to be

Sobbing
Sighing
Gritting
Screaming
Ashamed that I could not be

Yearning
Writing
Loving
Risking
I found who I might be

Sinking
Shrinking
Losing
Dying
Afraid I would never be

Hoping
Planning
Dreaming
Fleeing
Till I find refuge to be

Me.

I read it again, out loud, and then again, until I could hear it in Tristan's voice. In the very corner where she might have written it and then stuffed the paper frantically into the dress-up trunk, perhaps at the sound of intruding footsteps, the words rose and fell with her hope of finding herself.

How many times had I scoffed silently when I heard people on talk shows discuss how a woman could "find herself"?

"What do I need to do that for?" I'd said to the TV screen more than once. "I'm not even lost."

But now, following the words that tumbled down the page, I had never felt so separate from the self I had always been content to be. Tristan, it was clear, had known her own lostness. She'd fled to meet herself somewhere.

I listened to her poem over and over, but she wouldn't tell me where that somewhere was. She must have known where she was headed. She'd asked for directions.

I traced my finger down through the *ing* words again, hoping to feel a clue in the ink. She wrote nothing about a specific place. The only place she seemed to seek, in this poem and in "Sanctuary," was a refuge.

I hugged the poem to myself and, crazily, snatched up a tutu and hugged it too.

"I'm so sorry you couldn't find it here, Tristan," I whispered. "But I promise you, I swear to you, it will be here when you come home."

Sinking, shrinking, losing—I cried.

I wasn't sure how long I'd been there when Aunt Pete's voice pierced the silence.

"Serena! Maxine's school is on the phone. She's been hurt."

Chapter Sixteen

I ignored the Please Check In at the Office sign and careened around a corner to the nurse's office. It had occurred to me halfway to Ocean View that if they weren't taking Max to the emergency room, it couldn't be too serious. But I knew now how brittle their little lives were, and I floored the Blazer right through the school zone.

Max was propped up on a cot with a bandage on each knee and a bag of ice on the side of her face. Although I ran straight to her and examined her, face to fingertips, it was obvious nothing was more bruised than her pride. She could barely look at me.

"What happened, honey?" I said.

"I got in a fight on the playground."

"A fight?"

She nodded miserably. "Ashley and them were all talking trash about Tristan, and me and Sun made a pact not to let anybody do that."

"So you punched somebody out?"

She shook her head. "No, we made a pact not to do anything violent."

"Then how—"

"When I told Ashley if she wanted to see a tramp, she oughta look in the mirror, she pushed me down." Max pointed to her bandaged knees.

"And what about your face?"

"I crashed into the wall when I was running away." She blinked hard against the inevitable tears. "I guess I'm not that good at standing up for Tristan. I guess I'm not that good at anything."

I let her cry. When I went into the outer office to get her some Kleenex, Mrs. Abbott was waiting.

"Mrs. Soltani," she said. She clasped my hands. She'd been Tristan's fifth-grade teacher too, and I'd always had the image that her skin was made of cream.

"I've been trying to contact you for some time now," she said. "I know this must be a horrible time for you. I can't even imagine—"

"Contact me how?" I said.

"I've left messages on your answering machine a few times. I've e-mailed you as well. I'm sure there must be so much going on at your house…"

I looked back at Max. She was curled on the cot, as still as a rabbit trying to make herself invisible.

"I'm sorry," I said to Mrs. Abbott. "I don't know what's happened to your messages. Did you want to speak to me about Max?"

Mrs. Abbott motioned me out into the hall, where I stood before her like a truant student.

"I'm sure we can attribute it to her sister's disappearance," she said. "But Max has been acting out for the past—well, ever since she gave her report on runaways. According to some of my little tattlers, a few of the girls make rude remarks about Tristan on the playground, saying she must be on drugs now and she must be a prostitute. Naturally, Max has struck back."

"Meaning?"

"Nasty notes in their cubbyholes. Bursting out with insults during class. I've given her lunch detention twice for launching projectiles at them when she gets mad—Chap Stick, erasers, whatever's at her fingertips."

Stone coasters? I thought.

"I'm trying not to be too hard on her," Mrs. Abbott said. "I'd like to suggest that maybe she see a counselor."

The words "I'll discuss it with her father" came automatically to mind. But I said, "Thank you so much. I'll talk to Max. We'll get this straightened out."

"I'm sure when you do, her grades will take care of themselves." She patted my hand. "They aren't stellar right now."

"Please let me know if there's any more trouble," I said.

"Absolutely," she said. "We'll work on this together."

Max shoved the pillow up to her face when I returned to her. I sat on the edge of the cot and pulled it away. I wasn't going to let another daughter hide from me.

"You want to tell me what happened to the e-mails?" I said.

"I deleted them."

"And the phone messages?"

"I erased them."

"Because you knew you'd get in trouble?"

"No," she said. "Because I knew *you'd* get in trouble."

"*I* would?"

"With Dad. He thinks I'm messing up because you're upset about Sissy. But it's not you, Mom." Her eyes filled up again. "I'm just scared I'll never see her again."

I tried to concentrate on Max as Nick's stay in Dallas dragged on. I was able to get her back on track with her schoolwork, get her signed up for basketball, and take her to a movie, which I sobbed through. The tears had nothing to do with the film.

I couldn't have done any of it without Aunt Pete and Hazel. It was Aunt Pete who packed Max's lunches and made sure the Tristan-shirt Max had to sleep in every night was clean and pointed me toward my car on those afternoons when I didn't think I could make it to Lord Baltimore Elementary to pick Max up.

And it was Hazel who took Max out for pizza and painted her fingernails purple and taught her how to do fancy basketball dribbling on the patio.

They both talked me down out of the crazy tree when I what-iffed myself up to its highest branch. Neither of them would let me sink into the quicksand when I realized how many days it had been since I'd heard Tristan laugh. They took turns telling me I was a good mother, no matter what anybody else said.

The Monday of Nick's fourth week away, Ed came by when Hazel, Aunt Pete, and I were having lunch at the kitchen table. Aunt Pete put a bowl of chili in front of him and ordered him to eat it.

"You're looking awful puny," she said.

Actually he did. He seemed thinner than he had the night we saw Ricky, and his face was drawn. His usually broad shoulders had an apologetic hunch to them.

"Serena," he said, "the Baltimore cops have canvassed every business that's still open within five blocks of Maryland General. Nobody's seen Tristan." He looked at me sadly. "I'm so sorry I don't have more to tell you."

"I know you're trying," I said.

"You need to try harder." Aunt Pete pushed the breadbasket toward him. "Have a roll."

Ed's lips twitched. "You ever think about joining the police force?" He fished a roll out of the basket and turned to me. "If I could just see more of the big picture, ya know?"

"Then you could be Supercop," Hazel said. She sat back in her chair, revealing an inch of solid midriff below her tequila green sweater. A sequined frog on one shoulder rose and fell with her breathing.

Ed grinned at her and ran the back of his hand across his forehead. Aunt Pete's chili was just a little spicy.

"The only one who has the big picture is God," Aunt Pete said. " 'Course, I've been asking Him to give it to me ever since Tristan disappeared, but so far…" She shrugged inside the ratty sweater she'd traded the chenille robe for when the weather had turned cold.

Ed took another spoonful of chili and dabbed at his shaved head with his napkin.

"God's not telling me anything, either," Hazel said. "I'm new at this praying thing, though." She tugged at the bottom of her sweater as she looked at me. "If He's gonna tell anybody, He's gonna tell you."

"You overestimate me, Hazel," I said.

"Baloney. If I didn't see God pulling you through all this, I wouldn't be giving my cigarette money to the church."

I blinked. "You quit smoking?"

"Where you been?" Aunt Pete said, and then she waved me off with a "Never mind."

Ed chewed a mouthful of chili and looked hopelessly at the soaked napkin in his hand.

"Oh, for heaven's sake," Hazel said. She went to the sink and tossed him a sponge. He dragged it across his oozing forehead without taking his eyes off of me.

"No matter what you hear, whether it's from God or anybody else, please tell me. Even if you don't think it's important, if it has to do with Tristan, I need to know." He set the sponge on the table and put his hand on it, gentle as any mother. "Call me anytime, day or night. Deal?"

When I came back from walking him to the door, Hazel was moving restlessly in the kitchen, picking up forks and salt shakers and putting them back down again.

"You're worse than a long-tailed cat in a room full of rocking chairs," Aunt Pete said. "What's the matter with you?"

"I just feel like we should be doing something."

"Don't you ever go to work?" Aunt Pete said.

"I work nights at home after the kids are in bed. I got a couple of good contracts that keep me going—logos, newsletters, stuff like that."

"I've never even asked you where you worked," I said.

"Yeah, well, don't go off on a guilt trip about it. You've had a few other things on your mind."

"So if you work all night," Aunt Pete said, "and you're here all day helping us, when do you sleep?"

Hazel grunted. "I don't think I've slept more than four hours at a stretch since Reagan was in the White House. You need me here, so I'm here."

The phone rang, and I answered, still gazing at her.

"This is Mrs. Soltani?" The female voice was heavily accented in Spanish.

"Yes?" I said. "How can I help you?"

"Maybe I can help you."

"You know, I really don't—"

"Your daughter, she is Tris-tan Sol-tan-i?" She sounded as if she was reading from something.

I squeezed the phone. "Yes."

"There is a paper. I see it just today. I saw her. Here."

The room spun. "Where is 'here'?"

"North Avenue Motel," she said. "Is where I work—as maid. This paper, it was under other things on the wall, but today I see it. I talked to this Tristan."

"Okay," I said. "Okay…"

I lurched toward the counter for paper and pencil, scattering a stack of Aunt Pete's coupons and knocking over the jar of chili powder. Hazel put a pad and pen in front of me and sat me on a stool.

"Okay," I said again. "What is your name?"

"Anita," she said. "Anita Juarez."

"Anita Juarez," I repeated.

Hazel took the pen from me and wrote it down.

"When did you talk to her?" I said.

"This night it say here. August three."

"August third. What did she say?"

I heard a male voice in the background, followed by a muffled rustle, as if Anita had stuck the phone in a bag.

"Anita?" I whispered.

"I hurry," Anita whispered back. "I am not suppose to use the phones in the rooms."

"Please tell me what she said!"

"She was very sad. I find her crying on the steps."

"What else?"

The male voice grew louder and more familiar. I could almost smell the approaching cigarette smoke.

"She said she was going to WCC. I feel so bad for her."

"WCC?" I said. "What's that?"

"I have to go," she said. There was a click.

"Give me that," Hazel said and took the phone from me.

"You calling Malone?" Aunt Pete said.

Hazel nodded, punched in the number, and handed it back to

me. Ed was on the line in an instant, listening and assuring me that he would find out about this WCC and get back to me. Twenty minutes later I was still clinging to the phone as if it might wriggle out of my hands when Ed's Jeep pulled into the driveway. I met him on the front porch.

"What?" I said. "It's not good, is it?"

"It's cold out here. Why don't we go inside?"

"Just tell me."

Ed pulled his leather jacket tighter around him. "WCC," he said, "stands for Women's Care Center."

I mouthed the words, still not comprehending.

"Serena, it's an abortion clinic."

I searched his face for any crack in his statement, anything that would render it untrue. The sadness in his eyes told me I wasn't going to find it.

"Why would she go to an abortion clinic?" I said stupidly.

I could see him swallowing hard. "They wouldn't tell me anything, of course. Confidentiality laws."

"They *have* to tell me! I'm her mother!"

"At sixteen she's a consenting adult in Maryland, remember?"

"But, Ed, an abortion?"

Though none of it was registering yet, I could feel my face collapsing. Before the rest of me could go down with it, Ed opened the front door and pushed me gently into Aunt Pete's arms. She and Hazel were, of course, right there in the foyer. From someplace faraway I heard him explain to them.

"That Mexican woman was full of soup," Aunt Pete said. "Our Tristan was no more pregnant than I am."

Pregnant.

I hadn't been able to form the word in my mind. Now that I'd heard it, I could hear everything else that went with it.

Spider saying he took her to his trailer when we thought she was at work.

Anita Juarez telling me Tristan was very sad—crying on the steps.

That dank, miserable street where she looked for the building.

I pulled away from Aunt Pete and turned to Ed.

"Do you have the address?" I said.

"Yeah," he said, "and I'm off-duty."

Chapter Seventeen

Even with Ed driving me, in a Jeep that felt like it could plow right through the boarded-up windows on North Howard Street, I was almost paralyzed when we pulled to the curb. I stared across the road at a crumbling brick building I'd passed myself, right before the cab driver screamed at me. The entire front was covered by a larger-than-life garage door that told us under no uncertain terms that we weren't welcome.

"That's it?" I said.

"I think so." Ed put his hand on my arm. "Why don't you stay here while I check it out?"

I had no problem with him being the one to step out into the street—until I was in the car alone. I huddled and watched frosty air puff from Ed as he rounded the corner of the building into the alley. It had still been steamy summer when Tristan had taken the same walk.

In that frozen moment, somehow I knew that she had. It was as deep a thing as I had ever known.

Ed jogged back across the street and slid into the Jeep beside me. His face was stiff, whether from cold or concern, I couldn't tell.

"This is it," he said. "The entrance is in the alley."

I shivered. "They do abortions in that place?"

"I'm sure it's not as bad on the inside. These clinics are pretty closely monitored."

"I want to see."

Ed rubbed his hands together, ruddy from the November raw air. "You realize they aren't going to tell you anything about Tristan."

"I know. I just want to be where she was." My voice shuddered. "Maybe I'll be able to feel something. I guess that's not very... detective-ish."

Ed's face softened. "I've solved a lot of cases by following a hunch." He bent his head toward me. "If I go in with you, I might as well hold up my badge. In this neighborhood they can smell a cop a mile away."

"Will you be right outside?"

"You bet. I doubt very seriously anything's going to happen to you in there. In fact, I'm going to make a suggestion."

"Please."

"If you just want to get a feel for the place, don't tell them you're Tristan's mom. Tell them you have a niece or something, some sixteen-year-old girl who wants an abortion and doesn't want her parents to know."

"You mean, pretend I'm going to bring someone here?"

"Just ask what's involved. Who knows? You might see a clue."

"Is this like undercover?" I said weakly.

Ed gave me a small grin. "Sure. Don't even try to hide the fact that you're upset."

"About my 'niece.'"

"Play on their sympathies."

I hoped they had some.

In spite of what I imagined as I crossed to the alley, nothing forbade me to go in. When I followed the directions on the heavy metal door and rang the bell, a stocky Hispanic girl wearing teal scrubs opened it, looked me over, and in a soft voice I didn't expect asked me if I needed help.

For an uncanny moment, I was Tristan, looking into eyes accustomed to terrified young girls. It was a feeling that didn't leave me as I nodded and followed her into a narrow room. She pointed to a row of blue plastic chairs along one wall and said she'd get someone.

No one else was in the waiting area, and I couldn't see anybody behind the thick glass that separated me from the reception section at the far end. There was no opening in the window to speak through anyway. It was like a fortress. Even the walls on either side of the glass were covered in thick Plexiglas.

I perched on the edge of a dingy white faux leather couch along the opposite wall from the chairs and took in what I could through Tristan's eyes. The Plexiglas was plastered with signs, each printed in felt-tip marker:

Rides Must Show Driver's License

Your Appointment Will Take 5 to 7 Hours

Payment May Be Made by Cash, Check, Money Order,
　　　　Debit or Credit Card

I thought of Tristan's empty savings account, imagined her pulling a stack of bills from the pink wallet I'd bought her for Valentine's Day. The first real money she'd ever earned, recorded meticulously in her bankbook.

On the wall above the row of chairs, someone had made an attempt at cheer with butterflies cut from construction paper. They were so faded and dusty Tristan had probably seen them too, three months before. I was sure they hadn't improved her mood any more than they did mine.

I craned my neck to see into the reception area. There was still no one there. Another sign said "Please Be Seated. Someone Will Be Right with You."

If Ricky had been telling the truth, there was no one with Tristan when she sat here, waiting. According to him, she was gone when he woke up the morning of August 4.

But he had also told us Tristan just wanted to get away from home, that he didn't know where they were headed when they left Bethany Beach. Did he know she was carrying his child?

My grandchild?

I closed my eyes. This was another life we were talking about. I couldn't put the idea in any reasonable place, and yet I could put my arms around it and cradle it.

Please God, I prayed.

That was as far as I got. The Hispanic girl came in carrying a can of Sprite and, without a word to me, tried unsuccessfully to reach someone on an intercom beside the interior door. As she left again, I had the eerie sensation that there never had been anyone here. That I had walked into a nightmare everyone else had abandoned.

But she returned with a large African American woman in mismatched sweats and boots. The fur-lined denim jacket on her arm and a canvas bag on her shoulder suggested she'd been on her way out. She took one look at me and pulled a chair up to the couch.

"We're just about to close for the day," she said. "But how can I help you?"

Her voice, like the other girl's, was quiet and unhurried. I wondered if she was the one Tristan had talked to. I wished she'd told her to go home to her parents.

The woman watched me with visible patience. It was hard to lie to her, but I looked down at my lap and told her I had a niece who wanted an abortion. My voice fell over the word and cracked. The woman just waited.

"Anyway," I said, "she's scared, and I told her I would come in and ask some questions for her."

"Sure," she said.

I clenched my hands together. "She's only sixteen."

"Not a problem," she said.

"She doesn't want her parents to know."

"Everything here is strictly confidential. She's protected by law."

I squeezed my hands so hard I was certain my fingertips were purple. My eyes were now riveted on her.

"How much will it cost?" I said.

"How far along is she?"

Another piece of my heart chipped off. "She's not showing yet."

"Up to twelve weeks it's $360. Twelve to thirteen it's $550, thirteen to fourteen $600—"

"Okay," I said.

"We don't do the procedure after eighteen weeks."

The procedure. I could no longer feel my hands.

"Does she just walk in and…have it done?" I said.

"She'll need to schedule an appointment." The woman pulled a pink sheet out of the bag. "These are the days she can choose from."

I took the paper, but I didn't look at it. "So she'd have to call in advance."

Would Tristan have known that? Did she do that, or just walk in as I had, into a world we had no reason to know anything about?

"It won't be necessary for us to do an exam or a pregnancy test if she brings her own results," the woman said. "It's actually five dollars off if she does that. You're sure she's pregnant?"

I nodded. Tristan must have spent agonizing weeks knowing that she was. The question was, how could I not have seen it? I couldn't even begin to sort out what the days before August 3 were like for her.

"Now, if she's sixteen weeks or more, we suggest she have a sonogram. We don't do them here, but if there's anything wrong with the pregnancy, she might choose to wait and abort spontaneously rather than go through the procedure."

The pregnancy. Not a baby. Just *the pregnancy.*

"Like I said," the woman went on, "we don't take them over eighteen weeks. The further along they are, the more risk."

"Risk of what?" I said.

For the first time, she shifted slightly in the chair. "Of rupturing the uterus," she said. "We never had that happen here, but if it did, the hospital is right down the block."

"Isn't there a doctor *here?*"

"A doctor does the procedures in the morning, but he doesn't stay all day. All our staff are certified health care professionals—"

"Did your 'professionals' tell her about the risks? Did they even ask her if she *wanted* to have her baby taken out of her?" I stood up, looking down at her startled face.

Her eyes narrowed. "You're not here to ask questions about your niece, are you, ma'am?"

"I just want to know if my daughter was here," I said. I was breathing like a freight train, and if there had been anything to throw, I'd have grabbed it and started hurling. "Tristan Soltani. August 4. Did you let her have an abortion?"

The woman didn't stir from the chair. She just shook her head as she watched me clutch mine with both hands. "I can't tell you anything about any of the women we see."

"She's not a woman. She's a baby!"

"Then she's a baby with rights. I'm sorry."

I gazed now in horror at the useless butterflies and the list of payment methods that made it easy for any child to make a decision even an adult should never have to make.

"I can't believe she ever came here," I said. But as I made my way blindly to the door, I knew she had.

Ed caught me as I stumbled into the alley and kept his hands on my shoulders.

"They won't tell me," I said at least five times.

Ed didn't remind me that he'd warned me about that. When we were in the Jeep with the heater blasting, he said, "We could get a subpoena to try to get them to turn over the records. They'd probably say, 'Fine, get one,' but if they have a good lawyer, we'd never see them."

His words were not encouraging, but the gentle, even way he said them stopped me from shaking. He let me collect the scattered pieces of Tristan and me until we were almost to Ocean View.

"You okay?" he said.

"I'm not going off the deep end, if that's what you mean," I said.

"Hey, Serena?"

"Yeah?"

"Don't try for a career as an undercover agent."

I just looked at him. "Okay," I said. "But what do we do next?"

Ed offered to call Nick, but as tempting as the idea was, I knew Tristan's father needed to hear it from me.

Max, on the other hand, didn't need to hear it from anybody. After swearing Aunt Pete and Hazel to secrecy, I waited until I was sure she was sound asleep before I went up to the third floor with the phone.

"I was just about to call you," Nick said. He sounded exhausted.

"Things going okay there?" I said.

The weariness disappeared. "What's going on? Come on, Serena. I can hear it in your voice. What's happened?"

Stepping carefully from word to word, I told him. And then I let him grope in silence down the alleys my mind had been up and down all evening. As dark and brooding as that silence was, I wished I were with him. It was too much even for Nick Soltani to navigate alone.

"All right," he said. "In the first place, we don't know if this Juanita Juarez is telling the truth."

"Anita," I said. "And why would she lie?"

"Maybe she thinks there's a reward."

"Nicky—"

"The clinic wouldn't say one way or the other whether Tristan was even there."

"They can't."

"Yeah, well, that's a law that's got to be changed. Don't any of these people have kids? I'd like to see some senator when his daughter goes off to a clinic…"

I was almost relieved. It was at least a sign that he was starting to believe it.

"Ed had the Baltimore police check all the hospitals," I said.

"No record of 'Mrs. Smith,' huh?" Nick's voice hardened against the panic I could hear in it. "So if she had an abortion, why didn't she just come home afterward?"

"I've asked myself that a thousand times today."

"Why did she feel like she had to do it in the first place? Why didn't she just come to us when she found out she was pregnant? What are we, ogres? I've never been mean to her, have I?"

I'd asked myself those same questions. But as Nick ranted on, I had the glimmer of an answer.

"I don't think she could stand the way we would look at her when she told us," I said.

"What does that mean?"

"It was something Virginia Hatch told me—something about craving approval, having to prove her worth. She tried to be everything we told her to be, Nicky," I said. "Can you imagine the horrific looks on our faces if we'd found out she'd made a mistake like that? How could she handle it?"

"I'm getting sick of this being our fault. She made a pretty stupid decision, if you ask me. I know we taught her better than that."

I could feel my eyes opening to the revelation that was right in front of me.

"We never taught her how to make a decision," I said. "We made all of them for her."

"Beautiful." I could hear Nick thrashing around his hotel room, probably with his hand to the back of his head. "Did I decide she should go sleep with some idiot and end up pregnant?"

"No. You decided not to let her have anything to do with boys. You decided she was too young for sex education. You decided to keep her so naive she didn't know what to do the first time a boy flirted with her."

"I did all this," Nick said. His tone turned nasty. "You had nothing to do with it."

"I did it too."

I stopped. With my next words I could change my life into something I didn't yet know how to live out. I struggled, because I didn't know how to make decisions, either.

But for Tristan, and for Max, I had to.

"I went along with it because that was the way you said it should be," I told him. "I didn't even question it, and I take responsibility for that."

"Lord, have mercy," he said.

"I hope so," I said.

Chapter Eighteen

Before we hung up, Nick told me he would be home for Thursday, but he'd have to leave again the next day. I had to think a minute before I realized Thursday was Thanksgiving.

Somehow we got through it. Aunt Pete more or less charbroiled a turkey, and I bought pies at the Food Lion. All day I was able to keep from thinking about Tristan's setting the table for me every year since I could trust her with the china and taking three times longer than anyone else when we went around the table saying what we were thankful for.

But I couldn't keep myself from imagining where she might be this Thanksgiving Day. In a soup kitchen eating instant mashed potatoes and watery gravy? In a lonely room aching for her family—but aching more at what we might say if she crawled back home?

Those thoughts refused to leave me. They made me pray, hard

and bold, for God to bridge that gap. I was doing that, hands in the dishwater, when the doorbell rang.

"It's probably Ed Malone," Nick said. "I invited him over for pie."

"Well, he's gonna get store-bought," Aunt Pete said with a scowl. "Who knew you were suddenly going to entertain, Nicky?"

She and Max went into the family room for the traditional Thanksgiving-night watching of *Miracle on 34th Street.* I took coffee and dessert into the library, where Nick and Ed were already in deep discussion. When I walked in, Nick stopped talking and sat back. Ed didn't miss a beat.

"I think the next step is to go into the runaway shelters in the Baltimore area," he said. "I have a list."

"What makes you think they're going to be any more forthcoming with information than the clinic?" Nick said.

"The staff probably won't be. But if we could just talk to some kids—"

"Aren't the police doing that?"

Ed grimaced, fork poised over a piece of dry-looking mincemeat. "They may; they may not. Thing is, the kids aren't going to tell the cops anything. Street kids can have a pretty fierce loyalty to each other."

"You said they'd know you were a cop," I said.

Ed nodded and chewed.

Nick was looking at me, which he hadn't done much in the twenty-four hours he'd been home. "So I suppose you want to go into these places and see if they'll talk to you."

"If that's what it takes," I said.

He blew a disgusted sigh.

"I'm not going to let her do it alone," Ed said.

"You're not going to 'let her'?" Nick rolled his eyes. "There was a time when I would have thought you could actually pull that off." He rested his elbows on his knees, head in his hands, as if it were too heavy to hold up anymore. When he looked back at Ed, he said, "Look, I'm sure you think I'm being a real jerk about this. I just don't want Serena getting hurt. I guess I could let my entire company go while I look for my daughter. Maybe I should." I saw him swallow. "I have a factory about to go under down in Dallas…"

I stared as he explained the possible demise of part of Soltani Casters to Ed. He hadn't told me how serious it was, how the dilemma was ripping him apart. As I watched him talk, his eyes went glassy.

"Nothing means more to me than Tristan coming home," he said. "But I just can't let this go."

"I'll look out for Serena, Nick," Ed said.

Nick kept his eyes on me. "Don't let her get lost too."

Ed and I agreed to go to Baltimore on Saturday. That day, by tradition, was the day the girls and I got out the Christmas decorations, but Aunt Pete said she'd teach Max how to string cranberries, and it would be fine. I winced at the thought and promised myself I was going to make it up to Max as soon as I found her sister.

Nick left for the airport even before Aunt Pete got up. I made myself hot cocoa in an insulated mug and put on Nick's hooded down coat and a fuzzy scarf of Tristan's. Looking like an overdressed pen-guin, I went down to the boardwalk. If I was going to follow Tristan on her journey, I needed to start where she had. Maybe she'd left some of her thoughts behind.

It was a magnificent late fall day. The temperature was in the twenties, but the sun in an endlessly blue sky made me wish I'd worn my sunglasses. I shaded my eyes with a gloved hand and climbed the steps to the north end of the boardwalk.

From the wooden rail where I leaned, the ocean looked freer than it did in the summer. Undotted by swimmers, undisturbed by the squeals of children and the calls of mothers, it sparkled in a way I didn't notice when it was swarming with people. Only one stark white boat cut through the water, its bow high in the air.

Trailing my hand along the railing, pushing away the frost, I moved southward. The water-darkened rocks of jetties were still furry with green algae, like shiny cushions on the sea. A cluster of pigeons scavenged the shore for the popcorn and bits of chips available to them in warmer times. Their fruitless pecking stabbed me with thoughts of Tristan.

A surprising number of human footprints dotted the sand, from the souls brave enough to enjoy both the sun and the cold. As I got closer to the shops on the boardwalk, senior citizens came into view, bundled up like children in snowsuits, taking their morning walks. There was a lone jogger in Gore-Tex with only her eyes showing. I didn't blame her.

But even in the presence of other people, the loneliness was overwhelming as I passed the boarded-up shops that promised lemonade and Dippin' Dots, the Ice Cream of the Future. As the old people passed me with their chipper good-mornings, I could only wonder. *Did their children run away from them? Were they failures as parents? As people?*

I stopped in front of Boardwalk Fries and stared at its closed eyes.

Did Tristan cry in your back room because she was so scared about her baby? I asked it. *Was she standing over your vat of grease when she decided what to do? Did she fold your apron before she left for the last time?*

It told me nothing. I felt as shut down as it was. All the warmth was gone. I was an empty boardwalk. My teeth ached, and my heart ached, and all I could do was pull Tristan's scarf over my nose and run away.

Just as she had.

But I couldn't go back to the house yet. I couldn't bring my agony into the scene of Aunt Pete soaking cranberries and Max gleefully pulling out the Christmas CDs. I didn't know where else to go, and yet I found myself on the beach, sinking into the sand at the base of a dune.

Even through Nick's behemoth of a coat I felt something hard on my sitting bones. I found the wherewithal to look to see that I'd landed on a clump of beach grass. It was browned and shriveled, and I grunted at it. "You look like I feel," I said out loud.

But in its almost frozen state it seemed to have a better hold on the sand than it did in the summer, especially now that people were no longer tromping thoughtlessly across it in their vacation bliss. Maybe in its wintry state, less of the dune would wash away.

I wished I could say the same for myself. I felt as if I were sliding right into the sea.

"No!" I said. "I can't let that happen. God, please, help me hang on!"

I huddled there, rubbing my gloved hands on the tops of the clumps, and I prayed—begged—pleaded—until I stopped eroding.

I'm in a winter place in my life, I thought. I looked down at the beach grass and up at the endless, almighty sky and saw what could only be seen in such a place. The one true thing that would hold me together.

Come after me, said the whisper.

By three in the afternoon, I deemed our long day fruitless. As Ed and I had moved from one shelter to another, I felt like the pigeons on the cold beach. I could hear their mournful cries in my head.

Just as we expected, none of the staff at any of the places that protected runaways from the streets would tell us if Tristan had been there. The kids themselves were hidden somewhere beyond the for-tressed entranceways where we were stopped. Several staffers said they had come on board long after August 4, and kids were allowed to stay for only seventy-two hours.

"Mostly we try to get them back home," one enormous man with chest hair billowing from his collar told us. I couldn't imagine Tristan arguing with him. If she'd been there, surely she would have slipped away immediately.

Weary at three o'clock, we went into a diner for lunch. I ignored the duct-taped scar on the booth I slipped into and asked for a grilled cheese sandwich.

"That's probably going to taste like rubber," Ed said when the waitress had gone away to yell our order into the kitchen.

"I don't think I can eat anyway," I said. The smells in the shelters had been enough to turn me off food for the rest of my life.

Ed spread out our now dog-eared list. One corner soaked up a grease smear from the table.

"We've hit Teen Challenge, Teen Haven, that Salvation Army place, Foundation 2." He looked up at me, his eyes and mouth drooping at the corners. "That's it for the city of Baltimore, Serena. We could try some of the suburbs. She might have caught a ride out to one of those."

I nodded toward the paper. "What about the one you didn't mark off?"

"The Sanctuary." Ed shook his head. "I asked that one guy about it. He said it's closed down. Some kids still hang out in the empty building, but there aren't any services for them. He's surprised the cops haven't run them out of there."

I took the list from him and ran my finger across the words. The Sanctuary.

My safe place, my God space.
Could love be my sanctuary?

"I want to go there," I said.

Ed winced. "These are going to be kids on the streets, Serena," he said. "We're talking drug addicts, junior con artists—"

"Prostitutes," I finished for him.

The waitress unceremoniously dropped a plate on the table in front of me. I pushed it away. "If Tristan heard that name—the Sanctuary—I know she would have been drawn to it. And if there are just kids—no adults—who's to stop them from talking to us?"

"If *adults* can spot a cop—"

"Then I'll go in alone," I said.

"I can't let you do that." He closed his eyes for a second. "I sound like Nick, don't I?"

"You made him a promise. I get that," I said. I was already slinging my purse over my shoulder. "If you hadn't, I probably wouldn't have gotten this far. Can't you put on some kind of disguise or something?"

Ed laughed, a deep, soft sound I'd heard only once or twice. It kept me from clawing my fingers at the tabletop.

"*I* might be able to pull off a disguise," he said, "but we already know you have no future in undercover work."

"Okay," I said. "Okay, so I'll take them some food. They've got to be hungry, right?"

A slow smile spread across Ed's face until it reached his eyes. "That might do it, only—" He cocked an eyebrow at the grease-soaked sandwich going cold on my plate. "Let's not offer them grilled cheese."

We bought a dozen cheeseburgers at McDonald's before we ventured into a section of town ten blocks from the WCC. I clung to the bag for warmth as Ed pulled the Jeep up next to a chain-link fence topped by sagging barbed wire. Beyond it was a cement basketball court with netless rusty hoops and a cinder-block building minus any glass in its windows.

It looked less like a sanctuary than anything I could conjure up, and yet there was a cracked, weather-beaten sign over the door proclaiming it to be just that in too-blue letters. The only attempt at anything resembling refuge were two curly wrought-iron railings, each of which now hung by a single bolt.

"Seriously, Serena," Ed said, "I don't see any signs of life."

But even as he spoke, a head covered in a black wool cap down to its eyelids popped out of a window and popped back in. I was sure I heard Ed swear under his breath.

"These hamburgers are getting cold," I said.

Ed sighed and opened the Jeep door.

It was surreal, walking across the hard dirt up to that building. I felt like I had no body at all until Ed pushed the door open, and the putrid odor of stale smoke and soured humanity assaulted me. I had to force myself not to gag.

"Anybody home?" Ed called out.

"No!" someone yelled back.

Whoever it was told the truth. This couldn't be home for any living being.

Ed motioned for me to wait while he went inside. I stood shivering, clutching my meager bag of fast food, and listened to the murmur of voices. I strained to hear Tristan's, but they all sounded alike. Low and lifeless.

Ed finally reappeared and nodded me in. "Prepare yourself," he whispered.

There was no way I could have. The stench was worse on the other side of the door, and the air it arose from was thick with what I assumed was cigarette smoke until I saw flames licking the rim of a fifty-gallon drum.

Piles of what appeared to be rags littered the gaping hole of a room. Next to each was a battered paperback book or a piece of candle or a shopping bag that had seen better days. The people who, I decided, owned them were standing around the container of fire, looking at us out of faces as empty as the room.

The boy in the ski cap narrowed Asian American eyes in our direction. Next to him, a girl with hair that might have been red once, when it was washed, lifted her lip.

Ed put both hands up. "I'm telling you, we're not with the Baltimore PD. We're not with social services. We just want to give you some food."

Feeling as if I had "I Am Someone's Mother" printed on my forehead, I held up the bag.

"Mickey D's," said a bony African American kid who couldn't have been more than twelve.

He started for me. The bleached-blond African American girl next to him grabbed for his arm, but she couldn't compete with the smell of cheeseburgers that barely permeated the odors they were living in.

Neither of us said a word as we passed out the burgers and watched the kids retreat to the fire and devour them. They all had the same empty look in their eyes, the same hardness around their mouths that turned them to road-weary adults. But the slightness of their shoulders, the unformed tenderness of their jaws made me painfully aware that none of them was a day over sixteen.

I counted six. Everyone but the redhead inhaled two hamburgers. She put her second one under a pile of rags, while the boy with the baby face watched and all but drooled.

"That better be there when I come back for it," she said to him. Her tone was harsh, but the voice itself could have belonged to any friend of Tristan's. It was a voice that should have been giggling in the locker room or whispering on the school bus.

"Anybody still hungry?" Ed said.

The young kid did some kind of homeboy swagger. "I could use an order of fries," he said.

The blonde poked him, but he waved his hand at Ed, the lines on his palm embedded with dirt.

"We'll get you fries, pizza, whatever you want," Ed said, "if you'll just answer a couple of questions."

Suspicion came down over most pairs of eyes like window shades. The redhead narrowed hers into hyphens and propped herself against the wall.

"I'm not sayin' nothing," the Asian American boy said.

The blonde looked at me. "I know she ain't no cop."

"Man, we're not even from around here," Ed said. "We don't care that you got a squat that hasn't been busted yet."

They all looked at the Asian American kid. He didn't move.

"You want to see my driver's license?" Ed said to him.

"Yeah. Bring it on."

"All we want you to do is just look at this picture," I said. "Maybe I'll take you all out for a steak dinner."

Before I could get the photo out of my pocket, they retreated to the fire, backs to us, casting visceral resentment over their shoulders. Ed had his eyes closed.

"Please," I said to their backs. I knew I had lost all semblance of cool, but I couldn't stop begging. "Her name is Tristan. She has a good home. We're not going to punish her. We just want to know if she's safe."

"Let's go," Ed murmured to me. "I think we're done."

"They wouldn't even look at the picture," I said as he pulled me with both hands to the door. My voice had disintegrated into a whimper. "If they'd just look at it, I could tell if they'd seen her."

Ed stopped us at the end of the pointless railing outside. "It's not gonna happen, Serena. They're all they have. Somebody betrays another one, and there goes the only security they know right now."

As Ed half dragged me toward the Jeep, I looked back at the building full of smoke and stench and baby children who couldn't trust a soccer mom bearing cheeseburgers. A cry came out of me, and not just for Tristan.

I was still looking back as Ed attempted to stuff me into the Jeep. A figure with dulled red hair appeared in the doorway and waved at me as if she didn't want anyone to see her do it. I pulled away from Ed and watched her. She jerked her head toward the basketball court and loped toward the fence. Her legs were thin as dowels and adolescent lanky.

"I have to go," I said to Ed.

"Serena—"

I ignored him as I jogged to the fence where the red-haired girl had already climbed to the other side. She met me at a far corner, me out, her in, our frosty breath meeting in the middle. We both curled our fingers into the chain link.

"Tell anybody I told you this, and I'll deny it," she said.

I was close enough to see that her teeth were yellow, bordering on green.

"You said her name was Tristan?"

"Yes," I said, "Tristan Soltani. Do you know her?"

"We got a Tristan here. Dark hair. Big eyes." Redhead pulled her head back. "Looks kinda like you."

I was almost too stunned to pull Tristan's picture out of my pocket. When I did, the girl studied it and handed it back to me.

"Is that her?" I said. "The Tristan who lives here?"

"We don't none of us look like we used to," she said. "But, yeah, that looks like her."

I recurled my fingers in the fence to get them closer to hers. "Where is she? Is she inside someplace?"

"She's working. She does the day shift."

"Where?"

"Downtown, but you don't wanna go down there."

I shook the fence. "Please tell me where she is."

The girl glanced back toward the building. "Just come back here right after dark. Everybody else'll be gone then except me. She always comes back here when she gets off."

"Are you sure?" I said. "Do you swear to me she'll be here?"

"Unless she doesn't do what she's done every night, like, ever since she got here practically. I gotta go." She took a step backward.

"Wait," I said. "How long has she been here?"

She shrugged. "She got here right before me, so I guess that was like August or something."

I plastered both hands over my mouth as she took a few more steps backward.

"Thank you," I said. I fumbled in my purse and drew out two twenties. "Here—I know you're taking a big chance talking to me."

She stopped and stared at the money peeking out of my glove.

"And please don't tell her I'm coming. She might take off, because she doesn't know what I'm going to say to her."

The girl hissed through her teeth and took the bills I poked through a diamond in the fence. "If I had a mom like you," she said, "I never woulda left in the first place."

Chapter Nineteen

I babbled to Ed until nightfall, just to keep myself from imagining Tristan walking a downtown street on the "day shift." As we went up and down the aisles of a musty grocery store a few streets over from the Sanctuary, loading food for the kids into a rickety cart, I brought up every other option there might be.

"She doesn't necessarily have to be a prostitute, even though it sounded that way," I said. "Maybe she's working in a restaurant. Maybe she's making french fries; she knows how to do that!"

Never once as I tried to talk myself out of a corner too hideous to visit did Ed remind me that without an address or clean clothes, Tristan wasn't likely to have gotten a job. Or that if she didn't want to be found, she wouldn't have shown anyone her ID. He just listened as if I were actually making sense.

Only when we were parked in the shadows a block down from

the Sanctuary, counting the kids as they left, did I get quiet and pray again.

Just bridge the gap, I said over and over. *Please, God, hold us together.*

"That's everybody," Ed said. "I'll help you carry the groceries in, and then I'll wait out here. I think you should be inside when she gets here."

I couldn't think about Tristan arriving, seeing me there, and bolting in fear or even hatred. I only thought of what it would be like to hold her in my arms.

The redhead's eyes widened from their slits when she saw the bags of food I hauled through the door. She was in the process of dividing it up among the rag piles when she stood up straight and said, "She's coming."

I stood still in the middle of the floor, facing the door, my hands drawn up into the sleeves of my coat. Tristan was coming, and I might have only a few seconds, a few words to keep her from running away from me again. When the door opened, I could only blurt out, "Tristan!"

An emaciated girl with dark hair and a mask of makeup blinked at me. Skirt up to her upper thighs, stilettos bowing her shins—she looked every bit the prostitute. But she wasn't my Tristan.

My chest heaved as both disappointment and relief flooded in.

"Who's she?" the girl said.

The redhead looked from one of us to the other. "I thought she was your mother."

"Like my mother's really gonna come lookin' for me."

The girl went to the nearest pile as if it were her private dressing room and kicked off her heels, reducing her to a brittle five foot one at the most. She thrust her fingers into the front of her pink plastic jacket and withdrew a few wadded-up bills.

"I need my purse, Allie," she said to the red-haired girl.

The redhead—Allie—disappeared through a doorway in the back. The girl went to the fire, which had all but burned out, and spread her hands over it. They were raw and twisted into claws.

"Don't you have gloves?" I said.

She gave me a sour look. "Who are you anyway?"

"I'm Tristan's mom," I said. "Another Tristan. I thought you might be her."

Her eyes, brown like Tristan's, widened at the flames. "Forget the purse, Allie," she called. She moved toward the doorway just as Allie appeared and tossed a lime green pocketbook at her. The girl missed it, and it landed at my feet. A faded, once-happy blue *T* stared up from it.

It was Tristan's purse.

Our heads banged together as we both reached for it. I got there first and held it to my chest. She froze, still bent at the waist, and looked up at me. I could see the fear flicker through her eyes, even under the cover of shimmering silver eye shadow.

"Where did you get this?" I said.

The girl straightened slowly. Her face seemed to be trying to find its careless expression, but it was gone.

"It was a gift," she said.

"From who?" I said.

"A girl I met."

She made a feeble attempt to grab the purse from me, but I backed up and pulled it open. The zipper was broken, and the contents smelled of sweet smoke. But the pink Valentine wallet was in there. So was a grimy wad of dollar bills.

"You can't take my money," the girl said.

"I don't want your money." I tore into the wallet and let the plastic cardholder cascade down. Max's fourth-grade face grinned out of it. So did Jessica's and all the other girls Tristan giggled with. The last one to unfold was my Tristan's own face, wispy beneath the Indian River High School logo on her ID.

I stared at the girl now trembling in front of me. A thousand accusations jockeyed for position in my head.

"I didn't steal it from her," the girl said. "We traded. She's got mine."

"Why?" I said. "Why would you do that?"

"So nobody would find us," she said.

I held the unfolded array of pictures in front of her. "I *have* to find her. Look at this. She has a family who loves her. We just want her to come home."

The girl jutted out her hand. "Give me back my money," she said, "and I'll tell you what I know."

"Take it." I thrust it at her and dug once more into my own purse. But I stopped with a fifty-dollar bill between my fingers. "Just use it to buy some decent clothes and get a real job," I said. "Better yet, buy a bus ticket, and go home to your mom."

"Oh, and my stepfather," she said. "Won't that be fun? They don't want me back in Huntington, trust me."

The sarcasm was so fragile, I gave her the fifty and a hand squeeze. "Please," I said. "If your family would welcome you back with open arms, wouldn't you go?"

She pulled her hand away, stuffed the money into her jacket, and glared over her shoulder at Allie.

"Don't look at me," Allie said. "I thought your name really was Tristan Soltani."

"What *is* your name?" I said.

"Who cares?"

"If Tristan is using it, it'll help me find her. Come on. Please."

"It's Brandi," she said. "Brandi Wines. My mother has a warped sense of humor." She glared again at Allie. "You never heard me say any of this."

"Okay," Allie said, "Tristan."

"Tristan has your ID?" I said.

"Driver's license." Brandi managed to get some of the apathy back into her face. "It's not like I have a BMW here or anything."

"When did she leave?"

"She was only here a few days. It was still hot then, so"—she lifted one eyebrow, studded three times with foggy rhinestones—"I'd have to check with my secretary."

"Did she say where she was going?"

Brandi shrugged. "I don't know. She said she was gonna go find some aunt with a guy's name. Joe. Harry. Something like that."

"Pete?" I said.

"I don't know. I guess so. Look, that's all I know. We weren't that close, okay?"

I knew nothing else was coming out of her. I pulled another fifty from my purse.

"Buy yourself some gloves," I said. I looked at the lime green bag I was still cradling under my arm. "And a new purse."

"Don't tell her I busted her," Brandi said.

"I'll tell her I didn't give you a choice," I said.

"Yeah." She gave me the first hint of a smile with her eyes. "Right."

Ed was by the front door when I came out. I headed straight for the Jeep, talking over my shoulder.

"I have to go to Philadelphia," I said. "I know you can't go with me, so just take me to the train station."

Ed stopped me. "What? That wasn't Tristan who walked in there?"

I poured out the story while I walked the rest of the way to the car, ransacking my purse for my cell phone as I went. When we'd climbed inside, Ed put his hand on Tristan's bag that peeked out from mine and said, "May I?"

"Brandi said she was going to look for Aunt Pete," I said as he peered into it. "Nick is going to have a fit, but I have to go to Philly."

"Why would she go there? Aunt Pete was at your place when she left."

I flipped open the phone. "As far as Tristan knew, Aunt Pete was leaving the next week. Tristan only stayed here until she thought Pete would be back home."

"But, Serena," Ed said. His voice went gentle. "That was at least three months ago. When she didn't find Aunt Pete at her house—"

"Then I don't know," I said. "I don't know, Ed, but it's all I have."

I started to cry. It was a wonder to me that I had any tears left.

"She just traded herself in on somebody else," I said.

"But now we know who that somebody is. We actually have something to go on."

"Do we?"

"We'll do the same thing there that we did here."

"What if she's… What if she couldn't make it till now living like this?"

"She's stronger than you think."

"How do you know?"

"Because I'm looking at her mother," he said, "the strongest woman I've ever known."

I leaned my head against the seat and closed my eyes.

"What do you want to do, Serena?"

"Is that what you ask a strong woman?" I said.

"It is."

"Then I want you to take me to the train station."

"You're sure."

"Ed, I'm scared to death. But I have to do this. It's the only thing I *can* do."

He nodded. "That's what a strong woman does."

It was midnight when I got to Philadelphia. I got into a cab alone for the first time in my life and picked a hotel chain out of my vacation memories. I checked into the Wyndham with only my purse and Tristan's and sat on the edge of the bed in frightening solitude until I remembered to call Aunt Pete.

"What are you doing up there?" she said when I told her where I was.

"Tristan was headed for your place," I said. "Just tell me how to get there from downtown, and I'll explain everything later."

"What are you driving?" she said.

"I'll get a rental car in the morning."

"Don't get anything too fancy. They'll strip it down while you're sittin' in it. Matter of fact, if anybody makes a move toward it, I don't care if you're at a red light, you get out of there—"

"Aunt Pete," I said, "I just need directions. And do it slow."

She mapped it all out for me as I wrote it down, street by street, landmark by landmark, and even warned me about the places where I could easily make a wrong turn.

"Now," she said after we'd repeated them back and forth twice, "when you get to my place, go next door to Old Man Clarence's. He's a bigger busybody than any woman could hope to be. If Tristan was there, you can bet he saw her. You're gonna have to yell when you talk to him. He's deaf as a post."

"Okay," I said.

"Call me if you get lost."

"Okay."

"Serena, you be careful up there." Her voice filled with the static I had come to cherish. "Your problem is not their problem. They'd just as soon run you over as look at you—"

"Take care of Max for me," I said.

"Don't worry about Maxine. You find Tristan."

When we hung up, I continued to cling to the cell phone, longing for a voice other than my own.

I dialed Nick's cell number and got his voice mail. His message, pleasantly crisp and leaving no doubt who was in charge, was at once comforting and jarring. Ed had told me I was capable of doing an impossible thing. Merely hearing Nick's voice made me wonder.

I closed the phone and fell back across the bed. Without Ed there, who was going to keep saying I could do this thing? How was I going to get through the night so I could rent a car tomorrow and find Aunt Pete's place and face another disappointment that probably waited there to take me down?

Come after me, she whispered.

And then she added, *The bridge is there. Cross it.*

"What?" I said to her.

That was all she would give me. I fell into a fitful sleep and dreamed of giant clumps of American beach grass.

Something woke me up at dawn. I reached in a fog for the bedside phone and saw that my cell was lit up. "Text Message," the screen told me.

I had the guilty thought that it would be easier to read a message from Nick than hear his voice. But it was from Ed.

"Thought this might help," it said. I scrolled down a list of shelters with phone numbers.

"Bless you," I said. If I found nothing at Aunt Pete's place, I would call them.

Wide awake, I made coffee in the pot at the sink and took a shower. My clothes smelled like nervous sweat, but I ironed them and put them back on. I tried to focus on every move and not get too far ahead of where I was.

The girl at the front desk gave me the name of the nearest rental-car agency, and the good-looking kid outside got me a cab. They were so normal. It helped, but it also made me want to weep.

Please, God, I prayed silently in the backseat of the taxi, *let us find some kind of normal again.*

Then I prayed that I would arrive at Hertz alive. The cab driver went up on curbs and made left turns in front of buses and never took his hand off the horn. When I stepped up to the rental counter, I was once more oozing sweat inside my coat.

On trips I'd always entertained the girls while Nick rented the cars, and he always had them reserved ahead of time. The only thing Hertz had available for me was a silver Lincoln Town Car. When the guy pulled it up to the door, I saw what might as well have been a limousine.

"Where you going?" he said.

"Italian Market," I said.

"Dude," he said.

I didn't take that as a good sign.

I felt like a patient in traction groping to adjust a hospital bed as I tried to figure out how to move the seat so I could reach the pedals. By the time I finished going up and down and backward, I was queasy and had to peel off my coat.

The sides of the Lincoln seemed to hang over the lines on the pavement on both sides, and I couldn't force myself to go more than fifteen miles an hour as I pulled onto the street. The drivers behind me leaned on their horns and shook their fists out their windows. One man let loose a string of expletives.

"Everybody just stop being mad at me!" I said. Suddenly I was the object of hatred simply because I didn't know what I was doing.

Somehow I managed to follow Aunt Pete's directions and find the right neighborhood. Her brick row house was squeezed between two others just like it. The screen on the storm door was torn, and a gutter hung at a rakish angle, weighted down by icicles. But if Tristan had somehow managed to get in and camp out, it was as good as a five-star hotel as far as I was concerned.

Just as Aunt Pete had predicted, the door on the house next to hers creaked open when I went up the front walk, and an old man shuffled out and gaped at me.

Clarence's nose hooked down to meet his chin, a feat made possible by an absence of dentures. He was conveniently dressed for the out-doors, complete with a fifties vintage fedora.

"Good morning," I called to him.

"Heh?" he answered. His voice had all the finesse of an air horn.

I crossed a patch of winter-browned grass and met him as he continued to shuffle toward me. The closer he got, the more wizened he looked, until I was afraid he would shrivel up and blow away before he got close enough to hear me. But his eyes were sharp as a hawk's. Aunt Pete was probably right. He looked as though he saw everybody's business.

"I'm Serena Soltani," I said.

He cupped a hand around one ear under the brim of his hat and shouted, "Who?"

"Mrs. Bernardi's niece."

"Whose?"

I pointed at Aunt Pete's house.

"Oh. Old Pete. Yeah." He pulled a pair of overgrown white eye-brows together. "Worst busybody you ever saw. She didn't die down there in Delaware, did she?"

"No, she's fine."

"Heh?"

I took Tristan's picture out of my pocket and pressed it into his hand. "I'm looking for my daughter," I shouted. "Has she been here?"

He studied the photo for so long I thought I would go mad. I chewed at my lip and prayed myself back from screaming, *How long does it take to figure out whether you've seen her or not?*

"Yep," he said so abruptly I wondered if I actually *had* shrieked at him. "Three or four times."

"Really?" I said. "Are you sure?"

He shifted his piercing gaze to me. "I might be old, lady," he said, "but I'm not blind." He thumped Tristan's picture with his knuckles. "First time was, oh, say, August, first of September maybe. Caught her peekin' in Pete's windows. When I asked her what she thought she was doing, she run like a rabbit."

My heart was pounding so hard I could feel it in my throat. "But she came back?" I said. "When?"

"Heh?" he said and then plowed on with, "She showed up again around Halloween. First I thought she was one of them punks going around smashin' punkins, 'cept I seen her sittin' here on the steps, cryin' like a baby. I figured she was harmless."

"When was she here last?" I shouted at him.

He wheezed and put his hand to his mouth to collect a cough. For an awful moment I thought he was going to keel over before he got to Tristan's last visit.

He fished a stiff-looking handkerchief out of his pants pocket and found an unused spot on it to blow his nose. I didn't wait for him to stuff it back in.

"When was the last time you saw her?" I shouted.

He scowled. "No need to yell. I'm about to tell you." The eyebrows drew together again, threatening to tangle hopelessly.

"Musta been last week sometime," he said. "Just happened to look out the window, and there she was, standin' out on the sidewalk, starin' at old Pete's place like she lost her best friend."

"Was she okay?" I said.

"How should I know?" he said. "I stuck my head out the door and told her the old bag wasn't home, and she run again."

"Where?" I said. "Which direction?"

"Thatta way." He pointed down the street. "I don't guess she got too far runnin', though. Not in her condition."

I stopped breathing. "What? Was she hurt?"

"Nah," he said. "Just pregnant."

Chapter Twenty

She was still pregnant. Tristan had been pregnant, and she was still pregnant, and she was somewhere in Philadelphia.

It was a simple concept, and yet I couldn't grasp it. I could only move where it took me.

I wrote down my cell phone number for Old Man Clarence and made him promise to call me the instant he saw Tristan again—even if it was in the middle of the night. As he shuffled away, he muttered something about me thinking he must spend all his time peeking out the window. I did think that, and I thanked God for it.

I found a deli where I could sit down and ignore a bagel and call every shelter on Ed's list. Of course, no one would tell me whether they'd ever heard of Brandi Wines or Tristan Soltani. It struck me about halfway through the list that my precious, perfect, pregnant daughter had an alias.

My pregnant daughter, who needed prenatal care. I borrowed a phone book from the woman behind the counter and called every hospital in Greater Philadelphia. No Brandi or Tristan currently listed as a patient.

I paid for the bagel and wandered back to the Lincoln. The sun had heated the inside in spite of the below-freezing temperature, and I tried to draw some calm from its warmth, but my hands and my mind wouldn't rest.

I called Ed and got his voice mail, but I didn't leave a message. The reassuring voice was enough. I hung up and dialed 411 for the number of the Philadelphia police.

A woman answered at the police station, but she hadn't said five words before I knew she could have learned a thing or two about phone manners from Ed.

"Officer Slater. How can I help you?" she said. Her voice indicated she was too busy to help me at all.

I told her my story anyway. I could hear her clicking keys, and I was about to ask if she was listening to me when she interrupted with, "She's already on the NCIC as a runaway."

"But now I *know* she's in Philadelphia," I said. "Can't your people do something?"

"Sure," said Officer Slater without enthusiasm. "I'll put out the word. Where can we reach you if she turns up?"

I dug my fingers into the leather seat. "If she 'turns up'? Are you just going to wait until somebody trips over her in a gutter?"

"Look, ma'am—"

"Don't tell me how many runaway kids you have on the streets in this city," I said. "You know what, just tell me where their squats are, and I'll go there myself and look for her."

There was a small silence. The voice that broke it was a fraction softer. "We don't want you to do that. The squats we know of are in places you shouldn't go by yourself."

"That's exactly what I'm worried about," I said. My voice teetered. "If my pregnant daughter is in one of those places, I want her out of there."

Officer Slater cleared her throat. "Have you tried one of the private investigation agencies that specialize in finding runaways?"

"I read about them on the Internet," I said. Or at least on the information Max had printed out for me. "They want the parents to back off and let them do the work. I don't really want my daughter and my grandchild to have a bounty on their heads."

"Okay, okay." The officer coughed again. "Here's what we can do. I have a kid who does some work for me in Kensington now and again—"

"What's Kensington?"

"It's one of those neighborhoods you should stay out of. Lot of white girls who end up on the streets live there. I'll get in touch with my—"

"When?" I said.

"As soon as I hang up with you," she said, less than patiently. "Give me your number, and then just stay cool until I call you back— or she calls you. Her name's Cricket."

"Can you trust her?" I said. "What about that code of loyalty they all seem to have with each other?"

"I'm keeping Cricket out of jail. She owes me."

"And if I don't hear from you or her—"

"You will. Just try not to freak out in the meantime." She let out one more cough. "Actually you don't strike me as the freaking-out type."

If she only knew.

My cell phone was beeping, so I somehow found a Radio Shack and bought a car charger. I kept the phone in my hand throughout the purchase. When the multi-earringed kid who rang me up handed me the bag, I asked him where Kensington was.

"What do you want to go there for?" he said.

"I just need to know where it is." I pulled out a piece of paper and the map I'd found in the glove box. While he talked, I wrote, asking for landmarks and possible wrong turns.

"I don't know what you got goin' there," the kid said, "but, man, I wouldn't go near some of the streets in that neighborhood. A kid got shot over there night before last."

"Thanks," I said.

There was no reason for me to drive into Kensington. I didn't even know if Tristan was there. And the stricken look on the face of the boy with the earrings was enough to back up Officer Slater's warning. Still, as long as I didn't get out of the car...

Besides, I couldn't sit for another second just waiting for the phone to ring. I studied the directions, memorized the first few streets, and ventured back out.

I made only two wrong turns finding Front Street, which, I calculated, was just twelve blocks from my hotel. That was reassuring. I could practically run that far if I had to.

But when I crossed Kensington Avenue and headed toward the Delaware River, I knew I wouldn't be going anywhere on foot.

The bubble-lettered graffiti on the brick walls burned my eyes. A Dumpster on the sidewalk had belched its contents into the road, and a woman wearing at least four sweaters was picking through it. I had a flash of my daughter scavenging through garbage, and I missed seeing the man on the other side of the car until he had spit on my windshield. I couldn't read the bumper stickers on his hat through the trail of yellow mucus, but I heard him wail something about the end of the world.

I was pretty sure it had already happened.

I'd seen it before, on North Howard Street in Baltimore. Yet I couldn't be numb to it. Not with tiny children sitting alone on front steps in ragged, too-big sweatshirts, staring vacantly as I passed. Or with pairs and trios of adolescent boys slouching on corners and in doorways with various items pressed between their teeth—cigarettes, drinking straws, objects I couldn't even identify.

There were girls, too, loitering on the sidewalks and sagging porches of row houses that made Aunt Pete's place look like Buckingham Palace. Each wore some variation on a theme—multiple piercings; tattoos on ankles, thighs, and bellies; ghoulish makeup. Clouds of icy breath hung about their slickered lips, but they all bared their skin to the blistering cold as if they were made of steel.

But they weren't. I drove slowly, grazing the curb with my tires, searching their faces. There was fresh child-skin under those masks. Eyes yearning for tenderness. Mouths aching to smile without a price. I stopped expecting any of their flat-tummied selves to be Tristan. They were all my daughters.

One of them yelled, "Why don't you just take a picture?"

I winced at what she called me, but could I blame her? I was staring at her and her friends as if they were specimens under glass. If I wanted any strength left for Tristan, I had to get out of there.

I gunned the motor and tried to remember which way I needed to turn to escape. I definitely didn't want to go any deeper into the angry maze of walls that screamed obscenities at me.

I stopped at the corner, still debating right or left and watching the harlot-waifs in the rearview mirror. There was movement on my side of the car. It bounded across the hood and quadrupled before my eyes. Four boys took positions at the front of the Lincoln and attached themselves to it. Working like a rowing crew, they bounced it, cruelly, up and down.

I clung to the steering wheel for my life.

One who had a blue bandanna around his head looked straight at me and laughed like an insane hyena. I could hear Aunt Pete telling me they were going to strip the car while I sat in it.

I put my foot on the gas pedal and then on the brake, shaking two of the boys loose to stumble backward. When I mashed the accelerator again, a third one let go, and I missed nicking his backside by an inch. I didn't see what happened to the last one, but as I squealed around the corner, I felt a hard thump on the passenger-side fender.

The air went blue with livid profanity. I slammed on the brakes only long enough to see all four of them running for me at full tilt.

"I didn't kill anyone, I didn't kill anyone..."

Saying that over and over was the only thing that kept me from becoming completely hysterical as I careened the Lincoln over curbs and around blocks until I couldn't see the boys in the mirror anymore. Ahead of me a garbage truck was pulled up next to a line of trash cans. I pulled in behind it and leaned my forehead on the steering wheel, heaving in air that reeked of spoiled milk and rancid meat. At least adults were there, men with jobs, who could throw galvanized metal. Maybe I could count on them in the minutes it would take me to get my mind back into my body, in case the thugs reappeared.

A horn blasted beside me, bigger and more intimidating than the average sedan driver who wanted me to go back to Delaware. A bus driver hissed his door open and informed me that I couldn't park there.

Then *he* proceeded to park there, blocking me in. He left the bus and sauntered to a hole of a store across the street. The garbage collectors now had their backs to me, lighting each other's cigarettes beside a Dumpster. I jerked the Lincoln into reverse and gasped out loud as I plowed toward a van that had just appeared. I jammed on the brakes in time to keep from smashing into it—and to see four figures round the corner, led by a kid in a blue bandanna.

Every pulse point throbbed in alarm. Poking furiously at the seat belt release button, I shoved open the door and screamed for help. The only response was from the growling jaws of the sanitation truck. I could feel the foursome gaining on me.

I snatched up my bag, yanked the cell phone out, charger and all, and stumbled away from the car. I tried to turn and run at the same time, but my feet tangled, and I sprawled chest first into the street. Pounding feet vibrated through the pavement and into the palms of my hands.

"Someone help me!" I screamed.

But there was no time to wait for anyone to bother. I couldn't have come this close to Tristan only to be beaten in the street by a bunch of kids who saw a fancy car.

I scrambled up and dug into my purse for the bills and change I'd been dumping into it for the last day and a half. "Here!" I shouted— and flung it, handful after handful, into the faces that were now so close to me. "Take it! Take it all!"

As the four boys watched money fall at their feet, I shoved my purse under my coat and ran. Only twelve blocks to the hotel. Only twelve blocks.

I didn't know how many I actually covered before I collapsed onto a park bench in a place where no one threatened to relieve me of the rest of my belongings. The few people braving the cold just looked at me curiously and hurried on.

I pulled my hood around my face and doubled over, head between my knees on the bench. It was harder to breathe that way, but it was the closest thing to a fetal position I could achieve. All I could do was say God's name and Tristan's. Surely I must have fit right in with every other poor demented soul I'd come across in Philadelphia.

When my phone rang somewhere in the depths of my coat, I leaped from the bench and fumbled until I could get the thing to my ear.

"Are you Mrs. Soltani?" a female voice said.

"Yes." I said. "Is this...are you Cricket?"

"Look, I want to help you out, but I don't want it advertised—no names."

The voice was young and hard and a bit contemptuous, but there was something confident about it that slowed me down enough to say, "Okay. Sorry. I'm not good at this."

"Are you good at getting to the Chinatown Station?"

"Where is it?" I pawed in my bag for the map and had a flash of it still lying on the front seat of the rental car I'd just abandoned to a street gang.

"Where are you now?" she said.

"I don't know."

"You really aren't good at this, are you? Look around."

I did. "There's a statue of Benjamin Franklin."

"Just go to it and stand there. Can you do that?"

I ignored the bite and said yes.

"I'll be there in five."

"How will I know you?"

Cricket gave me a harsh laugh. "Trust me, I think I'll know you. Oh, and bring cash."

I was halfway to the statue when I remembered I'd just thrown all my cash in the road like pigeon feed. I assured myself that I still had credit cards, that I would buy her anything she wanted if she would just take me to Tristan. I was so close. I had to be.

"God, please, just a little further," I whispered. "I'll do anything. I'll even let Tristan go live with Aunt Pete if that's what she wants—"

"Somehow I knew you'd be the one talking to yourself."

I whipped around and looked into a pair of blue, almost violet eyes. They glittered cold and hard under eyebrows so studded with gold rings they looked like tiny Slinkies.

"Cricket?" I said.

"Either you have a really short memory," she said in a low growl, "or you don't want my help."

"No! Sorry. Yes."

"Whatever." She tossed her head back, though I wasn't sure why. All her hair was covered tightly by a piece of camouflage cloth. The austerity of it matched the sharp angles of her jaw and cheekbones. In another time, another place, she might have looked exotic. Right now, she just looked frightening.

"Cash?" she said.

"I can get cash," I said, "if there's an ATM. I had a little problem on my way here."

I told her about my confrontation with the four boys in Kensington. "It was the only way I could think of to get them away from me," I said.

"Did one of them have a big red birthmark on his neck?" she said.

"I didn't see that. All I remember is one was wearing a blue bandanna thing, and he laughed like some kind of—"

"Okay, I know them." She nodded. "You actually did the right thing. I can probably get your car back for you—"

"What I want is my daughter. Please, Cri— Do you know her? Do you know...Brandi?"

"You mean Tristan?"

My hands froze before I could get them to my mouth, and my fingers curved as if to hold the sound, the sound of someone saying her name.

"I knew the first time I saw her ID that Brandi wasn't her real name. The picture doesn't even look like her." The violet eyes scanned me. "She looks like you."

"I'm her mom," I said lamely. "Can you take me to her?"

She nodded toward my purse. "I'm a little hungry. Why don't we discuss it over lunch?"

I closed my eyes, forced myself not to smack her and say, "Look, kid, where's my daughter?"

But this could be Tristan, anywhere in this city, conning some other girl's mother into buying her a meal because she was close to starving.

She and her baby.

Cricket led me to a smoky sandwich shop where she devoured a Philly cheesesteak and talked at the same time.

"See, the thing is, I don't know if *she* wants to see *you,*" she said. "She's not like she was before. Actually"—she licked a finger thoughtfully—"I don't know what she was like when she was living with you. First time I saw her, she came in the club where I dance, looking for a job. She could move—like, we could tell she had training but not in the, uh, *genre* we typically look for."

"Like, a stripper?" I said.

Cricket gave me a look over the top of her Coke. "Exotic dancer.

Anyway, she seemed like a smart kid. I thought I could teach her, but then she put on the costume and…" She swore. "She had to be five months pregnant."

I could only nod for her to go on.

"There was something else about her too. I mean, kids on the street have a look. You know what I'm saying? I used to have it. They're scared, on their own with nothing, but you can see this thing in their eyes, like what's back where they came from is worse than this. So they get tough, and they don't let anybody see they're scared." She shoved the remainder of her sandwich into her mouth and said, "Tristan didn't have that look."

I pressed both hands to my lips and held back everything. I wanted her to tell it all without stopping.

"So, like, I'm basically the mother figure with the kids in Kensington," Cricket said. "I got myself a job, got off the street, but I can't forget the younger ones are still down there."

"Was she living there?" I said through my fingers.

"Yeah, she found a squat, and some of the girls told her about the club. Up to that point she hadn't done any alcohol or anything as far as I could see, but I knew she wouldn't make it down there unless she started getting some relief."

"Drugs," I said.

"Yeah, whatever. So I told her, 'Look, there's a place you can go where they'll take you in, especially if you're pregnant.' I told her she'd kill that baby if she didn't start taking care of it." For the first time Cricket smiled, a smug grin that briefly lit up her eyes. "I got her with that—she freaked. When she finally stopped crying, I took her to my place, because there was no way anyone would believe she's eighteen, and that shelter wouldn't take her if she wasn't. I put some makeup on her, gave her some clothes, *tried* to teach her some attitude—total loss…"

I closed my eyes. This was the moment; these were the words I'd left my entire self behind for. But I didn't know what to do with it all, which of the barrage of questions to ask first.

"And about a month ago," Cricket went on, "when I thought she might be able to pull it off, I took her to Covenant House. It's up in Germantown. When I get your car back, you can drive there." She sat sideways in the booth, legs stretched out, and concentrated on her Coke. "When she was with me, she cried every night. I said, 'Look, if you miss your family that much, go home.'" Cricket pumped the straw up and down in the plastic cover. "Something about the whole deal was always weird to me. I mean, I went through the checklist: Was she abused? Molested? Neglected? Did the house burn down and kill everybody but her? She said it was none of that, and I believed her. I mean, here's a kid who won't be a hooker, won't run drugs, won't even steal a candy bar. Someone actually raised this kid." She took a long pull on the straw and gave one of the Slinkies a flick. "I pried it out of her. She said she couldn't go back because her father would probably throw her out."

"What?" I said.

She put both hands up, one of them waving the Coke cup. "Lady, I'm just telling you what she said. I said to her, 'What about your mother?'" She stopped. She seemed to measure me with her eyes.

"And?" I said.

"You sure you want to hear this?"

"If you don't tell me exactly what she said in the next seven seconds…" I stopped there, because, of course, I had nothing to threaten
her with. But Cricket actually seemed impressed.

"All right. She said, literally, 'I want my mom,' and she sobbed
for, like, an hour. But she said her mom would do whatever her dad
told her to, because that's what she always did." Cricket leveled her
eyes at me. "I don't see that. You're a little out of your league, but seriously"—she plunked the cup down with authority—"I can't picture
anybody pushing you around."

Chapter Twenty-One

Cricket used my cell phone to make a few calls and then walked with me to the Wyndham, instructing me en route to stay at the hotel and wait to hear from her.

"Maybe I should just take a bus up to Germantown," I said.

"And then you'd have to walk three blocks in the dark." We stopped in front of the hotel door. "You got lucky today. Don't push it."

It was hard to let her walk away, taking her memories of Tristan with her. As I watched, she turned and came back.

"I forgot to give you this," she said. She pried a folded piece of paper out of her jeans pocket. "Tristan gave it to me when I dropped her off at Covenant. I thought you might want it."

As the clicking of her teetering-tall boot heels faded down the sidewalk, I stared through the paper at Tristan's round handwriting.

I managed to wait until I was in my room, huddled on the bed with a pillow to cling to, before I unfolded it.

"*Saving Me for Her*"
by Tristan Soltani

Dribbling down a corner
From a ceiling cracked and torn
A thin dark trickling mourner
A refugee forlorn

Trailing down the plaster
To an ending nil and small
Some long ago disaster
Stained it on the wall

I know its fatal season
As those looking on it see
A blot that has no reason
In this place to be

But can I stop in that same way
A puddle without meaning
Waiting to be washed away
Or painted out of being?

Once this trickle lost its place
It died there bleak and dry
It had no other tiny face
Growing down inside

Stirring deep inside me
Little heartbeat, little soul
Another life besides me
Wants to become whole

I am not a drop of rain
Once leaked in through a crack
I'm a mother bound for pain
Needing her life back

So I can feed my baby
With more than dirty scars
In hopes that someday maybe
We will see the stars.

I smoothed my hands across the page, half expecting to feel a pulse beating in the words. Her other poems had screamed from her head. This one thrummed from a well of desperation. Only a tiny face and a little heartbeat were keeping her from trickling away.

It was a feeling I knew well.

I pulled the phone out of my bag and set it on the night table. Then on the bed. Then in my lap. Its silence was a torment.

I couldn't tie up the hotel phone. I still had no way to charge the cell phone, so I didn't want to run the battery down. But I wanted to call Aunt Pete. Hazel. Even Nick. Maybe Nick most of all. But what was I going to tell him? That his daughter had risked unspeakable horrors because she thought he would throw her out of the house if she came home pregnant?

I looked again at the poem. In all her other verses Tristan had agonized about Nick's—and my—narrow limits and towering expectations. But even from her dizzyingly slanted point of view, it was an impossible stretch from there to being kicked into the street. Cricket herself had said there was more to it than that. Whatever it was crept along in the secret places between the lines of the poem, but it wouldn't show itself to me.

The phone jangled me right off the bed. I snatched up the cell even as I realized it was the room phone.

"Mrs. Soltani," said the first pleasant voice I'd heard all day, "this is Jackie at Hertz. We understand you ran into some difficulty today."

Oh, lady, I thought, *you don't know the half of it.*

She explained that a police report had been filed and that Hertz would be happy to deliver a replacement car to the Wyndham first thing in the morning. When she offered me another Lincoln Town Car, I fell over myself telling her to bring me the smallest vehicle in the lot.

Then I thanked God for Cricket and whatever arrangement she had with Officer Slater.

It was tempting to call Hertz back and ask if they could bring the car right then. Why couldn't I just drive to Germantown tonight? Tristan and I could be back at Bethany Beach before morning.

But a deep weariness descended, and so did the knowledge that I couldn't face the labyrinth of insulting streets again without at least trying to get some rest first. At the end of that twisted path, I wouldn't be able to convince my daughter to come home if I felt as if I'd been hit by a crosstown bus.

I looked that way too I discovered when I dragged myself into the bathroom and caught my reflection in the mirror. The woman who stared back at me had raked her fingers through her hair so many times that it stood up in dark spikes all over her head. Raccoon rings hung in the skin around her eyes, and her lips were raw from the cold and from nervous teeth. If she'd had on makeup, it was gone now, except for the trails of mascara that had formed with her tears. She bore little resemblance to the woman who'd stepped up to the counter at Boardwalk Fries almost four months ago and asked for her daughter. Especially in her eyes. There was something in the eyes of my mirrored self that I had never seen there before. I was just too exhausted to figure out what it was.

The phone rang—the cell this time. It was Cricket, sounding smug and maternal.

"Did I take care of you, or did I take care of you?"

"You did," I said. "I don't know how I can repay you."

"Just make her go home with you," Cricket said, "no matter what your old man says."

When we hung up, it was my "old man" I wanted to talk to. Despite what I had to tell him, I wanted him. I wanted him with me when I went to Covenant House so he could tell Tristan himself that she was wrong about him. Whatever else was holding her back, at least we could bridge that gap.

But Nick didn't answer, and I couldn't think how to leave a message.

"You can't reach him," Aunt Pete said when I called her, "because he's on an airplane on his way home."

"Thank You, God," I said.

Aunt Pete grunted. "You might not say that when you hear how mad he is."

"I don't care," I said. "Aunt Pete...I think I've found her."

She was strangely quiet as I told her what I'd learned, leaving out my run-in with the thugs in Kensington. The only thing I heard was a low raspy sound. My flinty Aunt Pete was crying.

"This is almost over," I told her. "I know I'm going to see her tomorrow."

"I'm just a crybaby," she said.

"That makes two of us."

"Serena—" Her voice cracked. "I hate that I'm probably not gonna be around to watch this baby grow all the way up."

While she went to get Max, I slid to the floor, my back against the bed. Until then it hadn't hit me that I would be taking two children home, one of them yet to be born. Life as we'd known it seeped out under the door. Nothing was ever going to be the same, on any level.

"Mom?" a tiny voice said.

It sounded so fragile and young that I said, "Maxie?"

"Did you find Sissy?" she said.

This could not be the all-knowing ten-year-old I'd left two days before. I could almost hold her apprehension in the palm of my hand.

"I think so," I said. "Maxie, are you okay?"

"Yes," she said.

The *no* whispered through her breath.

"So…tell me about you," I said.

"We're having a Christmas play at church. They picked me and Sun for angels."

"Of course they did."

"Hazel says it's casting against type, but I don't know what that means. Mom?"

"Yeah, honey?"

"Are you ever coming home?"

I didn't remind her that I'd only been gone for two days. It seemed to me, too, that I'd left Bethany Beach a lifetime ago.

"Just as soon as I find Tristan—maybe even tomorrow. It's going to happen, and then…"

I didn't finish, because I could envision nothing beyond walking up the steps of yet another shelter that had no more obligation to tell me whether Tristan was there than any of the rest of them had. I longed for the days when I could cheerfully chirp my girls or myself out of any dark place.

"I love you," I said. "You and Aunt Pete make some Christmas cookies. Tristan's going to want lots when she comes home."

"She's gonna want Aunt Pete's cookies?" Max said.

That was a big enough piece of her outrageous self for me to cradle until I could get home. I had no idea how I was going to make the last four months up to her.

When Aunt Pete got back on the phone, I asked her not to tell Nick anything. I wanted to do that myself.

"He'll be here five o'clock in the morning," she said, the flint restored. "Be prepared for a phone call."

I tried to wash the day off in the shower and rinsed out my underwear and called the front desk for a toothbrush and toothpaste. When I'd done everything I could to distract myself, I turned out the light.

I lay down long enough to know I'd lose my mind if I stayed that way any longer. I propped myself up against the pillows. Knees drawn up to my chin, I prayed for morning to come.

I could almost see God shaking His head. In fact, the picture was so clear in my mind, I was struck by how different He looked to me now. The comforting image of Jesus with a lap full of children had snapped out almost the moment I knew Tristan was gone. But when had this new, more rugged God developed?

This was a God who had borne the hard words I'd thrown at Him and never flinched. Who'd refused to allow me to slosh around in fear until I drowned. Who'd stood me up against the truth and wouldn't let me deny it.

Now it wasn't enough to simply stay safe in His lap. He wasn't going to rock me in His arms tonight and let me sleep. There was no reassurance that this was all going to turn out the way I wanted it to.

But His strength was in the room, so present and so solid that I spoke out loud to it: "You're here."

You came after me. Now stay close.

The catch in my heart, the gasp from my lips were fleeting. It really wasn't surprising that the voice I'd thought was Tristan's was His. It had been all along.

"I'll stay close," I whispered. "There's nowhere else I can be."

I slid down on my side, facing the window, and waited for dawn.

At seven I woke up, startled and confused. I searched under the covers for my cell, but there were no missed calls. The phone, in fact, was dead.

I'd have to charge it in the car. What car? When would that be here? Where was Covenant House? Where was Germantown, for that matter?

Stay close.

Hard to do when I was running around the room, plucking at things. Stay close. Take another shower. Put on the same clothes for the third day in a row. Order some breakfast and choke it down.

Playing each moment close to my chest like a hand of cards, I got directions from the concierge, signed for the Chevrolet Cobalt, and bought an overpriced sweatshirt from the gift shop that said "City of Brotherly Love" on the front. I changed in the lobby rest room and headed north for Germantown, charging the phone on the way.

The Philly streets were clogged with Monday morning traffic, but wide, tree-lined Lincoln Drive that led me through RittenhouseTown and into Germantown was uncluttered with cars and actually had a nostalgic feel. Germantown had once been largely a Quaker area, the concierge had told me, and some of their quiet patience seemed to remain.

The end of School House Road dumped me into a ghostly part of town where prosperity had obviously packed up and left years ago. Still, on the corner was the Christian Center whose banner proclaimed that "God created people who cannot be destroyed." Even the crooked back streets that finally took me to Covenant House, though potholed and lined with incongruous flower shops and long-suffering pizza joints, weren't as threatening as the dead ends I'd reached in my search for Tristan so far.

Still, when I parked in the fenced-in parking lot and sat looking at the bleak building, I was afraid to go in. I was afraid that in spite of all my hopes she wouldn't be there.

Stay close. That pulled me out of the car and across the parking lot where an empty-eyed African American girl sat on a picnic table smoking a cigarette. I smiled at her. She might be a friend of Tristan's. She waved the smoky hand at me.

It was the first shelter I'd been to where I wasn't met at the door by someone resembling a bouncer. Signs pointed me to a long room with a counter where an upbeat young woman in a neon pink sweater set asked if she could help me. I didn't give her my usual spiel. I just said, "I think my daughter may be here. Tristan Soltani. She might also be going by Brandi Wines."

She gave me a long look and asked me to please have a seat. She didn't say, "We don't give out that information," so I banked that in my hope vault. I made another deposit when she disappeared into a cubicle and returned with an airy "Someone will be right with you."

I wanted to leap over the counter and find "someone" myself. But I didn't think that qualified as "staying close," so I sat in one of the expected green faux leather chairs lined up on a curling floor mat and tried to imagine Tristan coming here for the first time.

Had they taken her through the door marked Intake Room with

its round, wired-glass window? Had she been buoyed up from the depths by this woman's hopeful voice? Had she clung to every spot of color that broke up the yellowed walls with announcements about "Choices" classes for parents and scholarships available at St. Joe's?

I was surprised to see people I assumed were residents wander through the office, right where I could see them. One droopy-eyed kid about nineteen complained that he couldn't sleep at night because other people snored. Miss Cheerful handed him a pair of earplugs. Another one slid a portable CD player onto the counter and asked if she'd hold it for him.

"Be happy to," she told him, "but if somebody steals it, I'm not responsible." She delivered that in the same chipper way she said everything else. The kid opted to take it with him.

From somewhere behind the office cubicles, I heard young female laughter. I was straining for a hint of Tristan in it when someone said, "Why don't you come with me?"

I looked up at a gaunt African American woman who smelled like lavender and wore a weary expression so deep it looked like a permanent part of her face. I sprang up, knocking the chair against the wall.

"I'm sorry!" I said. "I'm just a little bit—"

"I understand you're looking for your daughter," she said. And then she smiled, and it changed everything. There was humor in her eyes and optimism in the lift of her eyebrows. "Why don't we go upstairs? It's quieter up there."

Upstairs. Where the kids they sheltered lived and moved and had their being. I clutched the banister as I followed her and tried to suck in every voice, every shadow of a person on the walls of the hall above us. She ushered me deftly into the first room on the left and shut the door.

The room was narrow and lit only by a yellow-bulbed floor lamp in the corner. The chair she offered looked as if it had once belonged to a dining room set. Other mismatched chairs were gathered around a low coffee table with a candle on it.

"This is our meditation room," she said. "It's a nice place to chat." She extended her hand as she sat across from me. "I'm Demetria Hall."

"Serena Soltani," I said. I watched for a flicker of recognition in her eyes. The only thing I saw was expectation.

But I couldn't start over again. I knew Tristan was there, and the thought of pouring out my story for the hundredth time was suddenly ludicrous.

"My sixteen-year-old daughter," I said, "Tristan Soltani. She was brought here; someone rescued her from the streets when she ran away from home." I leaned forward. "I'd like to see her, please."

Demetria folded her hands in her lap and appeared to be studying me carefully. I couldn't read anything in her eyes, and I frankly didn't care what she saw in mine.

"You say she's sixteen?" she said finally.

"Yes."

"We usually don't allow anyone under eighteen to stay for more than a night before we send them to the Department of Human Services. They're much better equipped to help minors there."

My very soul began to sink. I couldn't let it go there, down where one more disappointment might wipe me out completely.

"She was prepared to pretend she was eighteen," I said. "And maybe you knew her as Brandi Wines. That's what her ID said."

Demetria smiled faintly. "Lying about her age might last a week, maybe a week and a half. She would have been assigned to a primary counselor, who can usually figure out from mental health assessments and just from listening to their stories how old kids are."

"Usually," I said.

"The shelter is at risk if we help minors without parental or DHS permission."

"And they might give it to you?"

"That would be rare." Demetria sat up straighter. "Now, if you want the number for DHS—"

"Just tell me…" I put my fingers to my temples and closed my eyes for a moment. "Just tell me what you said to her when she came here."

"What we would have said if she did come here?"

I nodded. She watched me again before she said, "We would have asked her no questions except whether she was hungry or wanted to take a shower or to make a safety call."

"What's a safety call?"

"To let someone know she was alive and unhurt and in a protected place. Then we'd ask her if there was anything she wanted to share with us. During that initial contact we'd try to ferret out whether she was suicidal or homicidal."

I herded my thoughts away from that trail. "Then what?" I said.

"We'd give her a bed, and then as I said, over the next several days we'd get to know her better, let her know what we have to offer."

"Which is what?"

"That's probably a moot point, Mrs. Soltani."

"I just need to hear it."

She put her hands in the pockets of the long scarlet sweater she wore over her jeans. "Okay. Not knowing she was only sixteen, we'd tell her she could stay up to nine months as long as she worked our program. That would involve us getting to know each other, helping her establish some goals, providing her with tools for getting employment, giving her an outfit appropriate for a job interview."

I sank against the back of the chair and realized I'd been holding my breath as she talked.

"Are you all right?" Demetria said.

"I'm so grateful that she came here. Even if it was only until you found out she wasn't eighteen, at least you were kind to her. She's so sensitive—"

My voice snagged. Demetria said nothing. At least she wasn't denying that she'd ever seen Tristan.

"Most of the people who come here are between eighteen and twenty-one," she said finally. "Too old for youth social services and too young for the adult programs. They're desperate to make lives for themselves, but they don't have the tools or the resources." Her face grew grim. "Even the tough ones realize they need a safe place. Kids on the street, girls especially, are exploited every way you can think of. If they're lucky, they find us before they get into prostitution or get addicted to heroin."

"Even if she did, we want her home. We don't want her to have her baby with strangers. I don't know what we did wrong, but we love her—"

I couldn't reel myself back in this time. I leaned my head against the chair and cried. I had been so sure this was the place, that I would leave here with my arms around Tristan.

"Let me just say this." Demetria spoke as if her words were on tiptoes. "If she came here and we sent her on to DHS, we would have asked her who in her family she trusted. We would tell her that if that family member ever inquired about her, we would take that person's contact information and pass it on to her. That's if Tristan told us where she could be reached." She pressed her fingers to her lips before she said, "That's the best I can do for you."

"Then let's do that," I said.

She left to get a form. I closed my eyes and let the hope resurface. The way she had said Tristan's name—she knew her. And she cared about her.

I got up and went to the door, listening for Tristan's light, dancing walk in the hallway. As I leaned against the wall, I saw that I'd been sitting with my back to a high window. A framed piece of stained glass hung in front of it. "I will say of the LORD, 'He is my refuge and my fortress,'" the dusty green letters said, "'my God, in whom I trust.'"

"You found your sanctuary, Tristan," I whispered. "Stay close, and we'll find you."

My confidence wilted, however, after I filled in the form giving my cell phone as the primary number and said good-bye to Demetria. I was leaving without Tristan. My arms still ached. Fear for her still filled my veins like barbed wire. I was still waiting for her to reach out for me.

And I didn't know if I could do it anymore.

I didn't go straight to the car. I crossed the street to a flower shop and pretended to gaze at the display of silk poinsettias trying valiantly to be Christmas. Covenant House was reflected in the glass, and I searched each window for a glimpse of her face, a peek to make sure she could still smile, a breath of a chance to say something that would bring her back.

When I saw the front door open in the reflection, I dug my hands in my pockets and turned toward the parking lot, head down. They probably thought I was looking for a way to break in and steal her.

I was halfway across the street when someone, a woman, called out, "Mrs. Soltani!"

I turned and walked backward. "I'm not going to try anything," I said to the tall figure approaching me. "Really."

She broke into a jog. "No wait, please. I have a message for you from Tristan."

Tires squealed behind me. I dove for the curb, and the woman reached it at the same time. She cupped my elbow in one hand and waved off the cursing driver with the other.

"Are you okay?" she said to me.

I grabbed her arm, clad in tweed, with both hands. "Tristan?" I said.

She put her free hand on my shoulder. "She asked me to talk to you. Shall we get a coffee?"

Chapter Twenty-Two

She was Kate George. The Reverend Kate George. With her mouse-brown choppy hair flattened by her knit cap, her skin blotchy and umpampered, and her bone structure reminiscent of Abraham Lincoln, she was the most beautiful woman I had ever seen. She knew Tristan.

She sat across from me at a tiny table in a corner grocery store, pushed a steaming paper cup at me, and said, "Tristan wants me to tell you some things."

"Is she okay? Is the baby?" I stopped myself and spread my hands on the tabletop. "I'm sorry. You talk."

"Come on, you're her mother. Of course you want to know her vitals." Kate gave her coffee a brisk stir with a plastic spoon. "Physically, she's fine. She hasn't gained as much weight as they want her to at the clinic, but she still has a few more months to go. So far so good."

"You said physically. What about emotionally? Is she afraid?"

"Terrified at times." She took a sip and grimaced. "That's awful." She peeled open a container of cream. "Let me explain my relationship with Tristan. I'm a chaplain at Covenant. One of the first things Tristan told them in her intake was that she was a Christian. Well, she said she used to be a Christian until she 'totally messed up her entire life.' She was sure God didn't want anything to do with her now."

I clenched my hands together.

"Anyway, needless to say, I was called in. That was a God thing." She looked briefly at the ceiling. "I spent a couple of hours with her, saw into her heart a little bit, and I went straight to the director and said, 'We can*not* let this young woman get lost in the system. I don't care how young she is, she needs to be here.' We pulled a few strings with DHS, and she's been with us for a month."

She added another cream to her cup, eyes focused on the process.

"God bless you," I said. My voice was barely audible.

"I've spent time with her every day." Kate smiled wryly. "I don't exactly have a line outside my office door. We usually go into the meditation room, light a candle. That seems to calm her."

The back of my neck crawled. There was something very wrong with this. I had to ask another woman things my daughter couldn't tell me herself. I had to find out from this stranger about her health and her emotional state and her spiritual crisis. This lady was telling me, the mother who raised Tristan, what it took to calm her down.

I balled up my hands and had a sudden Nick moment. He would be threatening the Reverend Kate George with a lawsuit right now, veins bulging everywhere. Another reason *I* was here talking to her, not him. I took a deep breath. "Did she tell you why she wouldn't come home?"

"I have a feeling," Kate said, "that Tristan was very good at concealing her feelings from everyone, including herself, until she came up against some that were bigger than she was. They were so foreign and scary, she tried to run away from them."

"Not to mention the fact that she thought her father would kick her out of the house if he found out she was pregnant. I had to hear that from an 'exotic dancer.'" I squeezed the cup. "It's just not true."

"I've gotten her to admit that to a certain extent. She's still convinced that he won't love her anymore if he finds out, which I'm sure by now he has."

"He's upset. He's confused."

"Of course."

"But he loves her. How can she not know that?"

"Here's where it gets complicated." Kate rubbed her heavy hands together. The knuckles were chapped to a painful-looking red that she seemed heedless of. "Tristan's feelings about her father are all tied up in her misconceptions about God the Father. In her mind, as long as you do everything perfectly, the Father—either one—loves you and is proud of you and showers you with all life's goodies. But if you disappoint Him by being the slightest bit imperfect, you're done. The Father might say He forgives you, but you have a big black mark next to your name, and you are no longer who you and everybody else thought you were. And that's something your Tristan just can't handle." Kate put an empty cream container on the tip of her index finger and tapped it on the table. "She has a deep sense of shame over all this, and I don't think it all came from her father."

She left the rest unsaid. My name was written in the silence.

The nettling in my neck went down my back. If I'd had hackles, they would have been standing up. Since my meeting with Virginia Hatch, I'd been willing to accept my share of the blame for Tristan's choices, even if Nick wouldn't. There hadn't even been any pride to swallow. I'd been wrong, and all that mattered was finding her. But this—

"I came here—" My teeth tightened down on my words. "I came here to take *away* Tristan's shame. I want to tell her that we are *all* to blame." I shoved my untouched cup aside, sloshing cold coffee over Kate's pile of empty creamers. "I have to talk to her. How many mediators do I have to go through before I can speak to my own daughter?"

Kate looked at me as if I had just pulled a veil from my face.

"This is interesting," she said.

"It isn't 'interesting.' It's frustrating. All I want to do is put my arms around my daughter and her baby. You can't do that for me."

"I'm sorry. I didn't mean to minimize it. It's just that what I'm seeing here doesn't match what Tristan has told me about you. I'd have bet the farm she was telling the truth."

"She was."

Kate lifted an eyebrow.

"I'm sure she told you I let her father make the decisions, and I carried them out."

"That's pretty much it."

"That was the way it worked. Nick is wise and loving and strong, and I never saw any reason for it to be any other way. But this—this was a reason. I'm standing by her, no matter what. I have to be the one to tell her that."

"Can you promise her that her father won't make her give the baby up?"

My mouth fell open.

"That's what's terrifying her right now. She's very protective of that baby."

"And she thinks Nick is going to take it away from her?"

Kate rubbed her fingertips across her forehead. "I have come so close to getting her to call you. Serena, she misses you so much I don't know how she copes with the pain." She let out a long breath. "Every time I think she's ready, she looks down at her belly and almost becomes hysterical."

"She's that convinced he's going to make her give the baby away?"

Kate leveled her gaze at me. "She's that convinced you're going to let him."

I shook my head, but inside, the words stayed intact. *Stay close. Go after her. Tell her.*

"You've given me what I need," Kate said. "I can't promise anything, but I think with this and the fact that you're here, so close, I can get her to meet with you."

I put my hand to the back of my neck, just in case I did have quills. They were ready to fire.

"Can I just say I hate having to do it this way?" I said.

"I don't blame you. But as I keep telling Tristan, God's at work in all this. Look how He's strengthened you. Now you can pass that on to her."

I sagged against the table. "I hope so."

"I know so. It's obviously who you are. That's what parents really give their kids."

I closed my eyes and said, "Please, God, bridge the gap between what I am and what she needs."

"Amen," Kate said.

She promised to call me the minute Tristan agreed to see me. Not if, but when.

She said she would talk to her as soon as she came in from school. School. There was so much I didn't know.

Although it could be hours before Kate called me, I couldn't go back to the city and put that much space between us. I'd left nothing at the Wyndham, so there was no reason I shouldn't relocate here. It would give me something to do to keep me from splitting out of my skin.

I was just about to sign the register at the Rittenhouse Inn when my cell phone rang.

"Serena?" Kate said.

"She said yes?" I said.

"She's gone into labor. They're taking her to University of Pennsylvania Hospital in an ambulance. I'll come to you and you can follow me." I could hear her smiling through her concern. "She wants *you*."

A woman at the nurses' station called to me before Kate and I were all the way out of the elevator.

"You Mrs. Soltani?"

"Yes! My daughter—"

"Follow me."

It was as easy as that. After all the closed doors and the privacy policies and the people who claimed to know nothing, I simply stepped into a room and there she was.

I heard her before I saw her face. She was crying as if her soul were dying, sobbing, "Please! Please don't!"

I shoved someone in green out of the way and stepped between two more at her bedside.

"Tristan," I said, "honey, it's Mom."

In the first moment that she turned her face to me, the thought that it wasn't her seized me. This girl's skin was the color of a dove, and her long dark hair had been chopped off at the chin. The tendons in her neck hardened like wires just beneath the surface as she clenched her jaw.

Only her eyes were the same—two soulful, fathomless brown eyes that found their focus in me and pulled me deep inside her.

"Mama!" she said. "Please don't let them!"

I took her head in my hands. "Don't let them what, baby?"

"Don't let them take her! They said they were going to take her!"

I looked helplessly at the green-clad woman at the end of the bed who was trying to pry Tristan's knees apart.

"I said as soon as your baby's born, we have to take her straight to ICU," the woman said in a tone usually reserved for the hard-of-hearing. To me, she said, in a lower tone, "You her mom?"

"I am."

"Then maybe you can convince her that we're not going to give her baby to somebody else."

"Don't let them, Mom!" Tristan screamed.

I hitched one hip onto the bed and made my hands firm around her face. "Tristan, honey, listen to me."

She bit down on her lip, face writhing.

"They're just trying to help you have your baby," I said. "*Your* baby. Nobody is going to take her away from you. Not the doctors. Not the nurses. Not me." I pressed her cheeks with my palms. "Not even Daddy."

Her hands came out from under the sheet and grabbed my wrists.

"Do you mean that?" she said. "I know I've been terrible. I know I don't deserve her—"

Her face contorted again. I thought she would burst the blood vessels in my wrists.

"Breathe, Tristan!" someone called to her. "Breathe through it."

"Mom, I don't know how to have a baby!" Tristan cried. "It's too soon. I didn't get to go to classes yet!"

"We're trying to help you—"

"Okay, Tristan, listen." I hiked myself all the way onto the bed so I could put my face close to hers. "This is your baby, and you know how to bring her into the world. I'm just going to give you a little crash course, okay, so it won't hurt so much. Stay with me, now. Stay close."

Her eyes devoured my face. "You won't leave me?"

"Not for a second. Now, before the next contraction comes, just try to relax. Let the baby rest."

"She wants to come out, and she's not ready."

"She thinks she's ready," said the woman at the end of the bed. Her voice had softened.

"Will she die?" Tristan said.

The frail tremor in her voice shook through me.

"We're going to do everything we can to make sure she doesn't," said the woman, who I assumed was the doctor. "Let's get her born first."

"Oh!" Tristan cried.

I slid my arm around her back and helped her sit up. "Nice big breaths, little mommy. Come on, breathe…breathe…breathe… This one's almost over."

When it was, she sank against me, her eyes wild.

I looked at the doctor, who was now examining Tristan. "Can't you give her something?"

"Too late," she said. "Tristan, it's time to push."

"I don't know how!"

"Of course you do," I said into her ear. "Just press down from your hips, and she'll be right out to see you—"

"I see a head," the doctor said. "What's the little one's name, Tristan?"

"Serena!" Tristan said. "Serena Grace. Oh—push now?"

"You're the mom," I said. "If you want to push now, push now."

☙

Serena Grace Soltani was born at 1:06 p.m., weighing in at one pound, seven ounces. At 1:11 her mommy hemorrhaged. Both girls were crying as bevies of people in green swept them away from me in opposite directions—Baby Grace in a thin, exquisite wail; Tristan calling, "Mama, please don't let her be alone."

"We'll let you know as soon as Tristan's out of surgery," a nurse told me. Double doors sighed closed behind her.

I ran the other way behind the tiny gurney that held my granddaughter. But the closest I could get to her was a couch in the hallway outside the Neonatal Intensive Care Unit. Kate joined me with some sandwiches and a cup of tea.

"One lump or two?" she said.

"Give it to me straight," I said. I cradled my hands around its warmth and sank against the sofa. It was white and clean, and the lighting above was soft. The gentleness was too much.

"God, please don't let them die," I said. I looked at Kate. "You don't think He will, do you?"

"I don't know," she said.

I took a scalding sip of tea. It was the best thing I'd tasted in days.

"Thank you for not telling me that God is good all the time; all the time God is good."

"I think I saw that on a bumper sticker once." Kate unwrapped a sandwich and broke off a piece.

"Maybe it should be more like 'God is in it all the time; all the time God is in it,'" I said.

"I like that," Kate said. "Toughing it out right alongside us."

"I never got that before."

Kate chewed thoughtfully. "You probably never had to. I got the impression from Tristan that you've never had a real crisis in your family."

"Not really. My parents are both gone, but it didn't affect me the way this has. I feel like I've been groping around in a strange place." I picked up a sandwich and then put it down. "I guess that's exactly what I've been doing."

"On a number of levels, I'm sure," Kate said. "Your parents dying in your adult years—those are the normal sorrows of human life. They don't usually plunge you into a dark night of the soul."

"Is that where I've been?"

"You tell me."

It was automatic to say *I don't know.* But I did know. It was new, and it was tentative, but it was knowledge.

"I've felt like God was far away. But really, He just got so big I couldn't see all of Him," I said. "You know, like when you're so focused on one thing that you can't see the big picture."

"I have a feeling you could say the same thing about yourself right now."

I shook my head. "I'm not sure I can get my mind around all that."

"Why try? Just embrace who God is—and who you are."

I nodded with her. "And who Tristan is."

"I like the way you think," she said.

She left me alone with the egg salad on rye and went to make phone calls. I sat sorting my fears between the two children suffering at different ends of the hall, one I'd come so far to know again, one I wanted desperately to know at all.

When rubber soles finally squeaked down the hall, it was Tristan's obstetrician. She looked younger and less severe without her headgear. I liked the fresh-air-and-granola-bars look of her smile.

"She's going to be fine," she said. "We've stopped the bleeding, and I don't think there's any permanent damage to her uterus. I'm Dr. Kelly, by the way."

"Serena Soltani."

"Ah, so your granddaughter's named after you."

I smiled a little. I hadn't even had time to absorb that.

Dr. Kelly nodded toward the NICU door. "How's our little girl doing?"

We didn't find out for another hour, when a tall man with less hair on his head than he had on his arms stepped out of the unit. He had to sit by degrees to fold his lanky body into place on the table beside me.

"Dr. Branaugh," he said. "I'm a neonatologist. I understand you're the grandma."

"I am," I said. "My daughter's still in the recovery room."

"She's young, isn't she?" His eyes were as blue and wholesome as blueberries.

"Sixteen," I said.

"It might be the best thing if I tell you what we're dealing with, and then you can break the news to her. I'll be there in case you need me to clarify anything."

Something gave way inside me. "It isn't good, is it?"

"I'm afraid not."

Using most of his fingers, Dr. Branaugh counted off the problems Baby Grace was struggling with.

Respiratory distress syndrome.

Possible IVH, bleeding in her brain that could cause pressure and possibly brain damage.

Immature digestive system.

Anemia.

The first signs of jaundice.

The danger of heart failure.

She had already had two episodes of apnea, where she stopped breathing completely.

"She's medically fragile," he said. His fingers were still fanned out in a display of her vulnerability. "We're doing absolutely everything possible to keep her alive, but at twenty-eight weeks gestation, 510 grams birth weight, she is at extremely high risk."

"How high?" I said.

Two sad dimples appeared as he pressed his lips together. "She has a 40 to 50 percent chance of surviving, given all that we're doing for her. If she does make it, it'll probably be two to three months before she can leave the hospital, and after that she's very likely to experience developmental problems—speech, behavior…"

I folded my arms, which were almost too heavy to hold against me, and my head dropped forward.

"We're giving her a transfusion right now," the doctor said. "As soon as your daughter comes to, they'll get her to pump her breasts, and we'll get that good nutrition going through the feeding tube. After that, you can see her if you want to."

"Just through the window?"

"No. You can come in and sit by her Isolette and talk to her. You won't be able to touch her yet, but we've found preemies do a lot better when their families spend time with them." He unfolded to a stand and smiled down at me. "It'll be at least another hour. You can get some rest, make phone calls—whatever."

Phone calls. Nick.

I'd turned my cell off as the signs had directed when I'd entered the hospital. I powered it up as I went downstairs.

Dusk had set the city's dark silhouette on fire, and lights winked on along the front walkway as I stepped outside and found a place on a bench out of the wind.

The phone screen informed me with alarm that I had nine new messages. I ignored them and called my home number.

When Nick answered, I scarcely recognized his voice. The word "Serena?" broke like hot glass, as if it had been waiting for the final fracturing touch.

"It's okay; I'm okay," I said.

"Where *are* you? Serena, what is going on?"

"Nicky, just listen, okay? I'll explain everything, but just listen. Please."

Stay close, I wanted to say to him. I leaned my head against the brick wall behind the bench.

"I've found Tristan, here in Philadelphia. She's all right...she *will* be...and, Nicky..." My voice thickened. "She just gave birth to our granddaughter."

I let him absorb that in silence before I said, "But the baby is very sick. None of her organs are ready to function outside her mommy's womb yet. She may die, Nicky."

"Dear Lord," he said.

"Yeah," I said. "That's what I keep saying."

Chapter Twenty-Three

Nick said he was leaving immediately for Philadelphia. He still sounded numb when we got off the phone, and I prayed he'd have enough presence of mind for the drive. *Ironic,* I thought. *My doubting* Nick's *competence.*

When I got back upstairs, they had moved Tristan to a private room with tender pink walls and a rose chair and bedspread. It somehow softened the intrusion of the needle in her arm and the beeping of the machine that flashed her blood pressure. I slid the chair closer to the bed so I could brush my fingers against her cheek. She didn't stir.

There had been so little time to really look at her in the emergency delivery suite. A woman probably never looked much like herself when she was giving birth, anyway.

A woman.

The face I stroked was warm and smooth with sleep, just as it had been when she was three years old. Her lashes feathered the fine skin below her eyes, and her eyelids moved with dreams. When I'd watched her sleeping as a toddler, I'd always liked to imagine that she was dreaming of angels dancing on clouds.

But two delicate lines deepened between her brows, and she moaned, softly and yet from a deep place. She wasn't dreaming of anything so diaphanous as angels or clouds. She had the hard, solid worries of a woman now—a tiny baby fighting for life, a troubled journey to recover from, a future changed from anything she had ever imagined. Or been prepared for.

I kissed her forehead and kept my lips close to her as I whispered, "God will bridge the gap, little mother. That's what we can pray for."

Her eyes fluttered open and searched my face as if she were emerging from a mist.

"Mama," she said.

"I'm here, Tristan."

"I'm so sorry."

Her lids fell again, and her breathing returned to its sleepy richness.

"I am too, baby girl," I said. "I am too."

Tristan was still asleep when a round, maple-skinned nurse with a wonderfully ample bosom peeked in and told me I could see the baby.

"My name's Debbie," she said as she walked me toward NICU. "You need anything at all, you just let us know. This is a tough time for the whole family, and we're here for all of you."

I touched her arm, felt the supple flesh give under my hand. Philadelphia was quickly redeeming itself.

Dressed in a full regalia of paper gown, cap, face mask, and shoe covers, I pulled on pale pink latex gloves and turned to take my first look at my granddaughter.

Baby Grace lay in her little Isolette world, bathed in warm light and swaddled in white blankets. Only her tiny balled-up fists and parts of her face were visible amid the bunting and the tape that secured her tangle of wires and tubes. Still, I gazed at her in awe.

Her head—though it was no bigger than an apple even with its snuggie cap—seemed too big for her spindly body. I could have cupped all of her eight and a half inches in the palm of my hand.

Yet the places I could see were perfectly formed—fingers, a foot that freed itself from the blanket, even an indignant little chin that made me think of Max. Her skin, tinged a pale yellow, was so thin I could see her veins running like silk threads beneath it. I watched in wonder as her chest, the size of a deck of cards, lifted and fell with life.

"It's always a little disconcerting when you first see them," a voice murmured behind me. "But there's a real live baby in there."

Baby Grace poked her minuscule arm from her cover. Fingers small as matchsticks groped the air and found a wire draped across her blanket. For an instant, she tried to curl them around it.

"Just like any child," the nurse whispered. "Into everything."

I smiled. But the baby before me wasn't just like any child. Maybe none of them were. Maybe our job as parents was to let each of our unique offspring tell us who they were and how they needed to be raised.

"What about you, Baby Grace?" I whispered. "Who are you?"

She kicked her foot, half the size of my thumb, farther out of her bunting. The nurse, who until now had stayed out of sight, put her hands through two openings in the Isolette and checked the device attached to the miniature heel.

"You don't want to lose that, sweet baby girlfriend," she said. "We need to make sure you're oxygenating your blood."

Oxygenating her blood. Raising the surfactant level in her lungs so she could breathe on her own. Lowering her bilirubin to prevent brain damage. Those were things no brand-new life should have to fight to do. If she lost that battle, I would never know who she was. There would be no time for her to know any of us, her mommy or her grandparents or her Aunt Max. And there was so much I wanted her to know.

I pressed my hand on the end of the Isolette near her head. "I'm just going to tell you this one thing, Serena Grace," I whispered to her. "Whoever you are, whatever you feel or think or do, God loves you. What you need might be a long way from what any of us can give you, but God will bridge the gap."

Grace poked her foot out of the blanket again, as if her teeny toes yearned to be free. I decided she'd heard me.

Hours later Debbie and I rolled Tristan to NICU in a wheelchair so she could see Baby Grace for the first time. I watched through the window as she stroked the Isolette with hands I knew were aching to hold her baby daughter. Her lips moved in a soundless monologue I didn't have to hear to understand. She was every woman who's given birth. She was a mother.

After Dr. Branaugh and I explained the baby's condition to her, Tristan was so white and brittle, she seemed transparent. When I got her back into bed, I pulled the covers up to her chin and said, "Try to get some rest."

"I can't," she said. "How can I sleep when I don't know what's going to happen to my baby?"

I heard myself in her voice, in the anxiety that no one could soothe away.

"You're right," I said. "You probably can't sleep."

"You haven't slept in a while either, have you?" She reached up and ran a finger under my eyes. "Mom, I'm so sorry I did this to you."

"No, Tristan, don't," I said. "Don't go there."

She let her hand fall back to the sheet. "You have to let me."

I searched her face for reasons not to—for the innocence and the fragility we'd shielded for so long. All I saw was the tender young woman we'd never let out.

"Yeah," I said, "I do."

Tristan closed her eyes. "It wasn't supposed to turn out like this. Ricky was just going to take me to Baltimore to get an abortion and bring me right back the next day. He said he would fix it with Daddy so you two would never know about it." She opened her eyes and gazed out the window, as if she were now seeing the scene from the other side. "It was stupid, but I believed him. I thought he could make everything perfect."

"So he thought you were both coming back to Bethany Beach?" I said.

"That night at the awful motel he said once we got rid of the baby, we could go back to the way we were before. He'd never said it that way till then. 'Get rid of the baby.' It was like I all of a sudden knew who he really was, just from those five words." Tristan clawed the sheets into her fists. "I couldn't have the abortion. I got the directions to the clinic and everything, and then I just couldn't do it. But then I thought how it would be if I came home and told you and Daddy that I was pregnant, and I couldn't do that either. I couldn't do anything. So I ran. I just…I ran."

She forced her gaze back to me. "I knew you would all hate me—"

"Hate you? Honey, no—"

"And it was like if you hated me and I couldn't go home, you just weren't even there. There was just me, and you know something?"

I shook my head.

"I figured out I'd never been alone before. Not in my whole life. I had to keep feeling my face to make sure I was still there. It was like I was going crazy."

"No, Tristan," I said. "That's the beginning of sane."

She seemed to drink that in before she said, "There was this one day when I was thinking I was, like, invisible, and I felt this flutter—here." She spread her hands across her belly. "I knew it was the baby, and then I knew I wasn't alone."

Tristan struggled to sit up. When I moved to help her, she wound her fingers in my sleeve.

"Did you mean what you said, Mom?"

"About—"

"About not letting Daddy take her away from me? Because if you can't stop him, then I can't come home. There are people here who can help us."

I took her hand from my sleeve and held it between my palms. "Do you want to come back, Tristan?"

Her eyes filled. "I miss you. I miss Max. But…"

"Go ahead."

"I'm not the person you think I was."

She spoke it like a confession, as if penance would now have to be paid.

"I know that," I said.

"No, you don't, Mom—"

"Oh, but I do."

I reached into my pocket and pulled out the folded squares that had lived there for days. Tristan put her hands to her mouth, just the way I had so many times in the shock upon shock of the last four months.

"Mom, I'm sorry. Please—"

"Stop," I said. "You told me who you were in these. You led me straight to you. How else would I have ever found you?" I pulled her hands from her mouth and pressed her poems between her palms. "Now, tell me, do you want to come home?"

She looked from me to the little folded maps to herself. "I need you to help me raise my little girl."

"Then I'll be there."

Her eyes came back to me. "What about Daddy?"

What about Daddy? The question she'd asked me her whole life. The question I'd always scurried back to him to find an answer for— an answer I would coat and pad until I made it okay. It was the last question she'd asked me before she'd walked out of our lives. *What about Daddy?* If I had answered differently then, would she be in this pain right now?

I kissed her hand and let it go. "I don't know about Daddy," I said. "I only know about me—me and God."

"Not God in a box," she said.

"What?"

"Kate says I've had God in a box. I always imagined Him in this little box that I could open up and pray into. It seemed like everybody had Him all figured out so He'd fit right into a neat little package." I saw a wisp of a smile. "I told her I knew it was weird, but she said a lot of people kind of think of God that way. Anyway, she said if I stopped imagining Him at all, He would just be, and then I'd stop imagining who I was, and I could just be." She lifted her graceful chin. "I'm not getting there very fast."

I put my forehead against hers. "You know something, Tristan?" I said. "I'm going to have to start running if I want to keep up."

I sat up and looked at her. "God doesn't have us in a box, either,"

I said. "If He did, He'd be like your father and me, forcing you to remain a little girl long after we should have been letting you grow up."

"I shouldn't have run away, Mom," Tristan said.

"You're right," I said. "But now I understand why you did."

When Debbie poked her head in, Tristan was asleep.

"I think you should do the same thing," she said to me. She pointed to the rose chair. "This reclines. It isn't a Sealy Posturepedic, but I bet you could sleep just about anywhere right now."

"I don't know if I'll ever sleep again," I said as I let her slip a pillow under my head.

"Uh-huh," she said.

The noise woke me up to cold morning light filtering through the blinds. It was a low, mournful sound, and it gathered me up from sleep with its utter helplessness.

Tristan?

As I parted my lips to say her name, I heard her whisper, "I love you too, Daddy."

It wasn't Tristan I heard crying in reply. The person sobbing as if his spirit was crushed was Nick. My heart broke—once again—just listening to him.

"I'm okay, really," Tristan said.

Her voice was guarded, maybe a little too high. My chest drew in. I sat up and stirred them from their hug. In the half shadows, Nick smiled and cleared one cheek with the heel of his hand.

"We have our little girl back," he said.

I couldn't answer him. I watched Tristan sink against the pillows and pull the bedspread over her shoulders. I half expected her to pull them over her head.

Don't, Tristan. I wanted to say to her. *Don't ever hide yourself again.*

There was a light tap on the door, and a curly head poked in, announcing that it was time for Tristan to give up some breakfast for Baby Grace.

"You can come back as soon as we're done, Grandpa," she said to Nick with a wink.

I led him to my couch in the hall, where a pearly gray light was just reaching the walls. Nick sat beside me, buried his face in my neck, and shuddered a sigh. I held on and kissed his head.

When he sat up, he massaged my shoulder. I was sure it was an effort to comfort himself as well as me. "She does seem okay," he said. "She's pretty thin, but I'm sure once we get her home, you can fatten her up."

"That may be awhile," I said. I nodded toward the unit door. "If the baby lives, she could be here for several months. Tristan isn't going to want to leave her."

Nick opened his mouth and then closed it, as if he was giving himself a chance to get it right. I'd never seen that kind of hesitation in him before.

"Look, Serena." Once again he paused, then squeezed the bridge of his nose between his fingers. "I've been thinking about this and praying about it, and I know I've been too heavy handed with you."

I didn't say anything.

"It's not that I don't still believe in my role as husband, but I've never really discussed things with you. I've never asked for your input. I just always thought I knew what was the best thing to do."

Somewhere inside me a placating voice flipped on automatically, like a recording when someone pressed One for *No, honey! You* should *make the decisions. Whatever you say is fine.*

"Just let me finish," Nick said. "From now on, I'm going to consult you. I think I must have been treating you like all you can do is make lasagna, you know?" He moved his hand from my shoulder to my cheek. "I need your wisdom. Your instincts."

Another voice bubbled up from within. Press Two to lighten the moment with *All right. Where is the real Nick?*

But I couldn't say it. I couldn't say any of it. He *had* been wrong to discount my instincts, as wrong as I'd been to put on a happy face and let him.

Nick ran his thumb across my cheekbone. "I hate that you had to find Tristan by yourself. I should have come with you."

He was pressing Three for *You're absolutely right. I needed you, Nicky.* I erased it. I erased the whole menu.

"No," I said. "This was a journey I had to make alone."

I expected to see hurt in his eyes. Or anger. I saw only confusion.

"I do want us to discuss things. I do want to be consulted about decisions." I took the hand that began to slide from my cheek and squeezed it. "But I couldn't have done it before. I didn't even know I had any wisdom, not until I came here on my own."

Nick sat back from me, scrubbed his face with his hand, searched mine with his eyes. He didn't seem to land on anything certain. Finally he pulled his mouth back into its firm line and said, "Okay, then let's talk about this baby."

"She's right in there," I said. I nodded toward the door. "Do you want to see her?"

"Let's wait." I watched him swallow. "I don't think any of us should get attached to her yet."

"I think it's a little late for that. Tristan already talks to her like she's—"

"Tristan's seen her?"

I stared at him. "Of course."

"Do you think that was a good idea?"

"Nick, she's her mother."

The inevitable hand went down the back of Nick's head before he leaned toward me. "See, I think we—you and I—need to discuss the options. If the baby lives, what's going to happen? It's not like the father's in the picture. There's adoption—"

"Nick."

"I'm not saying she *has* to give the baby up—"

"You and I can talk about options until we're hoarse." I kept my face close to his. "But this isn't our decision to make. It's Tristan's."

Nick stood up so abruptly the couch jittered backward. "Sure, since she's done such a fine job of making decisions up to this point—"

"She's made some bad choices, but she's made some good ones too. She didn't have an abortion. She didn't prostitute herself. She didn't turn to drugs—"

"She wouldn't have had to make any of those choices if she hadn't made her *first* decision to sleep with some sleazebag—"

"She did that because—"

"Don't start in that it's our fault because we never taught her how to make her own decisions—"

"Nick," I said, "please don't point at me."

His jaw muscles jerked as he lowered his finger.

"So suddenly we just let her make decisions about another life," he said.

"We can guide her," I said, "but she's already made up her mind."

Nick shifted his gaze to the NICU door. "Does she have any idea what that would involve for us as a family? It would turn us upside down."

I didn't point out that we were already standing on our heads.

I could only focus on an inner pull that drew me to the edge of a gap that seemed to yawn between two parts of myself. I could stay where I was and let go of all the new strength that had brought me to this edge.

Or I could chance a leap over the gap to find that other me—the real me.

I swayed there, knowing that so much of what Nick wanted to say about the toll a sick baby would take was true. But I knew that my instincts about my daughter were just as real. While I tottered, I felt something move—something beyond me, shifting the ground beneath me until the gap closed with quiet finality. I stepped into me.

"You can choose not to stand behind her on this, Nick," I said. "And I'll respect that. But I'm going to support her decision."

"The idea is for us to decide that together. We need to be a united front."

I stood up and stepped toward him. "*We* don't get to decide how *I* feel. Not anymore."

Nick turned away, hands on hips, face toward the floor. I fought back an old urge to go to him and promise the tension out of his back with the words he was used to hearing. I wasn't sure what this was all supposed to look like. And I knew that Nick, for once, didn't either.

"Okay," he said. He turned around, but he didn't really look at me. "I'm going to find a place to get cleaned up, call Aunt Pete, get us something to eat."

"That's a good idea," I said. And then I watched him go off to do things he could still be certain of.

While he was gone, Tristan paid Grace another visit. Watching her whisper to her baby and examine her every tiny part with her eyes, I realized I knew my daughter better as a woman than I ever had as a child.

But everything else was suddenly new, strange, as if I, too, had just been born. When Tristan fell into another exhausted sleep, I reached for something familiar and called home. Hazel answered.

"Aunt Pete finally gave out," she told me. "When I got back from taking the kids to school, I found her asleep in Tristan's room. Poor old broad."

"Tell me about normal things," I said.

"You mean like my dogs got busted, and I had to bail them out of the pound? Let's see, Desi won't go to sleep at night unless Max calls and says prayers with him on the phone. Tri put Herbie in her bed—"

"Herbie?"

"His pet sand crab. I told her it just means he's into her."

"Of course."

"And Sun and Max have decided they want to be *Charlie's* angels in the Christmas play." I could hear the sardonic Hazel-grin in her voice. "That normal enough for you?"

"I don't know how to thank you for doing so much for Max."

"The kid does more for us than we do for her, trust me. And Lissa's been helping. Pastor Gary comes by and prays with us every evening." She grunted. "It's not like I've moved in, but I'm here a lot."

I let the homesick tears fall freely. "I don't know how long I'm going to need to be here. I don't expect you to—"

"Stay as long as you have to. Just let me know when you're coming back so I can schedule my baptism."

"Hazel!" I said.

"Yeah, one of the only two smart decisions I've ever made."

"What was the other one?" I said.

I heard her smile again. "Knocking on your door," she said.

Nick was still gone when I returned to the unit. Tristan was sitting up in bed, her eyes wide with panic.

"Mom, something's wrong," she said.

"What, honey?"

"That curly-headed nurse just came in here looking for you, and she was all in a hurry, like—I don't know—something's just wrong."

I went back down the hall. A cold anxiety crawled through me when I saw the nurse coming my way. She was walking stiffly, grimly.

"Something *is* wrong," I said.

She reached me with both hands ready for my shoulders. "Heart failure. Her lungs have filled up—"

"Is she—"

"She's hanging on by a thread. Shall we get Tristan?"

There was no decision to be made. We lifted Tristan bodily into the wheelchair and ran with her to NICU. Dr. Branaugh met us at the door. His face was almost ghostly.

"There's nothing we can do," he said. "She won't make it through a surgery, I know that."

"Is she still alive?" Tristan's voice was clear and mother-sure.

"Just barely," Dr Branaugh said to her. "I thought you'd want to be with her."

Tristan got out of the wheelchair and pressed her hands to the window. "Please take all that stuff off her," she said. "I want to hold her."

Baby Serena Grace died in her mother's hands ten minutes later. The nurses let Tristan rock her as long as she wanted to, and Nick and I watched from a respectful distance while Tristan whispered to the still, tiny being.

"She's cradled in the arms of a loving God now," Nick murmured to me.

I stared up at him, but I wasn't surprised. Nick Soltani was a good and godly man. He loved me, and he loved his daughters the best he knew how.

Stay close, our Father whispered to me.

What else can I do? I whispered back.

Chapter Twenty-Four

As many times as I'd pondered the sand dunes from our porch, I could never remember them looking the way they did now.

Even without a whisper of their summer glory days, they seemed stout and stalwart. From the side porch I could see their sand shifting; I could almost hear them laughing at the wind. I leaned into the sound and let it weave into the cacophony in the house behind me:

Aunt Pete's high-pitched static, giving the kids their last call for hot chocolate because she was closing down the kitchen.

Hazel's gravel voice, telling Desi he'd better not knock over those poinsettias or his name was going to be Mud.

Max's husky giggle mingling with Sun's.

Irish setters barking. The teakettle whistling. The phone ringing.

It all stirred toward normal, whatever that was going to be now, with the sands shifting the way they were.

"You okay, Mom?"

I held my hand out to Tristan. She closed the door behind her and moved into the circle of my arm.

"I'm just feeling a little bit like a sand dune right now," I said. "Who was on the phone?"

"Detective Malone. He called to welcome me home." She let her eyebrows lift and settle. "I don't know him, but he sounded nice."

"He's part of your story," I said.

A shadow passed through her eyes. I'd seen it drift in and out of her mood during the week we'd just been through. Sometimes it appeared for a fleeting moment, but more often it lingered. This one seemed to settle on both of us.

"You want to walk down to the dunes?" she said.

She linked her arm through mine, and we picked our way between the rows of potted poinsettias Hazel had set out on the steps for our arrival. We clung together in the wind as we walked toward the beach.

"Do you think Serena Grace would have liked her memorial service?" Tristan said.

"Oh, I'm sure of it. All dressed up in her little pink thing. All the people who loved her singing to her. Reverend Kate wrapping her in prayers. I think she would have loved it."

"I loved her," Tristan whispered.

Our boots churned in the sand as we moved to the sunny side of a dune. That was the only sound until Tristan coiled herself gracefully at its base and said, "There's more beach grass than I remember."

"You think so?" I said.

"That's funny, since it's winter." Tristan brushed her fingers across one tufted head. "I used to worry all the time because I was afraid our whole beach was going to wash away."

"You did?" I said. "I know Max would always get all feisty about it and want to run people off."

"I think Serena Grace would have been like Max. I hope so, anyway."

"Not like you?" I said.

She touched the grass with only the tips of her fingers. "Not like the old me."

"Maybe there was never an old you. Maybe there was always just Tristan, waiting to come out."

"Is that the way it is with you? Is that why you're different now?"

I heard myself laugh. Not Marlene Dietrich's laugh, escaping from a hidden imp. A loose, free laugh that I could no longer hold back. "I let something out, all right," I said.

"I like it." Tristan leaned her head against my arm. "I think Serena Grace would have been like you."

"You know what?" I said. "I hope she would have just been whoever she was. That's a lot to be."

"That's a hard thing to be."

I watched another cloud pass through her eyes as she moved her gaze to the top of our steps. I turned to see Nick's tall, smooth form beginning to silhouette in the dusk.

"Do you think he'll let us?" Tristan said. "Be who we are, I mean? He's already pushing me to go right back to school and to start dancing again." She looked away from him. "I don't know about all that yet."

I shielded my eyes with my hand, and I could see Nick's face. It was strained, as it had been for so long. I waved to him. He let himself smile, with a sadness and a longing I could almost hold in my hand.

"Just pray, Tristan," I said. "Pray that God will bridge the gap between what each of us has and what each of us needs to just be."

I kissed her cheek and rose from the sand and walked toward my husband.

The difference between Nick and me, I decided, was granite versus clay. And maybe that difference would never be more apparent than when we were talking about our daughters.

But when we got right down to it, everything always came back to God.

Acknowledgments

An entire network of people helped close Tristan's gap, and mine:

Dale McElhinney, Doctor of Psychology, priceless consultant

Nikki Ivey, Search and Rescue advisor

Mike Redmon, Bethany Beach Police

Candy and Drew Abbott, Fenwick Island, Delaware—perfect hosts

Brenda and Ron Ulman, Gambrills, Maryland—Baltimore research buddies

Pam Palumbo, Bowie Crofton Pregnancy Clinic—invaluable source of information

Cordella Hill, Covenant House, Germantown, Pennsylvania— compassionate guide

Sarah Todd and Keely Cutts, Drexel Hill, Pennsylvania— Philadelphia cohorts

Joyce Moccero, Drexel Hill, Pennsylvania—reader and brainstorming partner

Marijean Rue—research assistant, reader, supportive daughter

Jim Rue—reader, wonderfully non-Nick husband

Don Pape, Dudley Delffs, Lee Hough—tireless confidence builders

Shannon Hill, Elisa Stanford, and Carol Bartley—insightful editors

About the Author

Nancy Rue centers her ministry around our need to be the authentic selves God created us to be. To that end, she has written over eighty books for tweens, teens, and women, and speaks and teaches extensively. She lives in Lebanon, Tennessee, with her husband, Jim.

To learn more about WaterBrook Press and view our catalog of products, log on to our Web site: www.waterbrookpress.com